THE TRIAL

THE TRIAL
LAURA BATES

SIMON & SCHUSTER

First published in Great Britain in 2021 by Simon & Schuster UK Ltd
Text copyright © 2021 Laura Bates

The right of Laura Bates to be identified as the author of this work has been
asserted by them in accordance with sections 77 and 78 of the Copyright,
Design and Patents Act, 1988.

1 3 5 7 9 10 8 6 4 2

Simon & Schuster UK Ltd

1st Floor, 222 Gray's Inn Road

London

WC1X 8HB

www.simonandschuster.co.uk
www.simonandschuster.com.au
www.simonandschuster.co.in

Simon & Schuster Australia, Sydney
Simon & Schuster India, New Delhi

A CIP catalogue record for this book is available from the British Library.

PB ISBN 978-1-4711-8757-5
eBook ISBN 978-1-4711-8758-2
eAudio ISBN 978-1-3985-0016-7

This book is a work of fiction. Names, characters, places and incidents are either the
product of the author's imagination or are used fictitiously. Any resemblance to actual
people living or dead, events or locales is entirely coincidental.

Printed and bound by CPI Group (UK) Ltd, Croydon, CR0 4YY

For Grace

DAY 1

A flaming sock.

It seems like such a ridiculous thing. But that's what Hayley is looking at as she lies flat on her back, staring at the bright, blue sky. A smouldering gym sock, twirling in slow motion, trailing a smudge of smoke as it floats gently down towards her.

Hayley tries hard to swallow but there is something wrong with her throat, with her eyes. She can't move her arms or her legs. She isn't meant to be here – this isn't right. *Concentrate, Hayley. You aren't here, you can't be. You're on a plane. Think back.*

Bing

The seatbelt signs were turned off and Brian was first out of his seat, lumbering down the aisle towards the bathroom next to the cockpit. The back of his neck looked even paler than usual beneath his ruddy curls, freckles standing out like a smattering of fawn paint drops flicked off a brush.

'Actually, Brian, please take your seat for a moment.' Coach

Erickson ushered him back towards the rest of the team. Hayley saw Brian's eyes bulge a little. Was it just the artificial overhead lights or did he look faintly green?

'I really need to get in there, coach,' Brian mumbled, gesturing towards the bathroom door.

'This will just take a moment, son.' Coach Erickson grinned, clapping his weathered hands to attract everyone's attention. Brian collapsed reluctantly into a free seat, cradling his stomach with his hands.

Erickson ran a hand through his thinning hair. Greying now, but the same floppy cut he'd sported since the grainy photos in the school trophy cabinet that showed him lifting the all-state high-school basketball championship cup forty years before. His face had leathered since; decades of working outdoors sending tiny red thread veins criss-crossing his nose so he looked permanently flushed with enthusiasm.

From her seat over the wing, Hayley twisted to look towards the back of the small private plane. May and Jessa were fast asleep, their backs pressed together, knees drawn up. May's glossy black hair spilling forward over a blanket clutched in her arms, Jessa's long, plump twists hanging over May's chest as her head lolled back onto her best friend's shoulder. Across the aisle, Shannon was looking out of the window, her back poker straight, one foot automatically rotating and pointing through a complicated series of flexibility exercises.

The boys looked vaguely disinterested. Jason was lounging back in his seat with his legs stretched out across the aisle, playing a game on his phone. Elliot was sitting a little way apart, as always, bent over a sketchbook, his eyes flicking up and down at the other kids as his hand moved quickly back and forth across the page. Brian looked like he was focusing all his energy on keeping his mouth closed.

'Guys, I need your attention for a second.' Slight irritation flashed across the usually placid face of the coach. He put his fingers in his mouth and let out a shrill whistle so that all eyes swivelled towards him. May and Jessa reluctantly disentangled themselves, yawning.

'Jeez, you lot. Do we need to talk about what happened last night?' There was a sudden silence, the air practically crackling. Jason shot a glance towards Shannon, who continued to look doggedly out of the window. Hayley thought she saw Jessa jerk as she sat up straighter. Elliot's hand froze on the page.

Erickson gave a sly smile. 'Oh ho, you think a coach doesn't know what happens on the last night of tour? You think this was my first rodeo?'

Brian convulsed slightly and started fumbling in the seat pocket in front of him for a sick bag. Hayley watched curiously as May leaned towards Jessa and whispered loudly, 'Where did you go last night? I lost you halfway through the party . . .'

Erickson beamed and waved his hand dismissively. 'Hell, you can all relax. What goes on tour stays on tour and all that. I know about the last night "rave".' He sketched quote marks in the air with his fingers, and Hayley cringed for him as his shirt rode up a little, exposing a hint of late middle-age spread. She'd never seen anyone look less like they knew the details of what happened at a 'rave'.

'I just wanted to tell you all how proud I am of you,'

Erickson went on, smiling at them. 'I know not all of you are here, but I've already said a few words to the players who went back on the other flight. Of course, we're very grateful to the Angel family for extending the use of their company planes.' He nodded towards Jason who grinned and tipped a small bag of salted peanuts into his mouth.

Erickson cleared his throat. 'Now, I know the off-season prep tour isn't the be all and end all of tournaments, but it's an important lead-in to our main season and you all showed up and gave it your all. Ladies—' he tipped an imaginary hat to the back of the plane, 'your enthusiasm and athleticism were outstanding as always. A team is nothing without its cheerleaders. And guys . . . well, what can I say? Not many of you know this, but this is actually my very last tour. I'll be retiring at the end of the next semester.'

Hayley watched Coach Erickson carefully, her chin resting on a cupped hand. Were his eyes getting a little misty? Erickson was a 'drop and gimme twenty' kind of coach; the sort of old-school educator who'd never owned a cell phone and believed there was no problem in life that couldn't be solved by a brisk run and a hot shower. She began to reach for her notebook. That was a good line. There'd be a tribute in the school paper, maybe even a piece in the local press. 'Drop and gimme twenty coach comes to the end of his last lap.' She should get that down before she forg—

It happened so suddenly it was like a light going out. One second, Erickson was talking, his back to the cockpit door, the students staring at him from several rows away. The next, everything moved at once. The chairs dropped out from underneath them as if they'd been snatched away by an invisible hand. The windows that should have been to the left and right were suddenly on the ceiling, then spinning round to appear beneath her. Backpacks, drinks cans, plastic food trays, shoes, paper cups, phones, magazines – everything was whizzing through the air like the inside of a snow globe, flying debris smashing into elbows and scratching faces. Limbs crashed and tangled into each other, spines bowed, heads whipped helplessly from side to side.

The noise was deafening. A crunching, screeching shriek of grinding metal; the roar of machinery; the din of alarms all blaring at once. And over the top of it, screaming and screaming.

There wasn't time to think. No time to wonder what was happening, to process or brace, or react. There was only sensation. The lurching, roiling lightness in the stomach. The clench of panicked eyes scrunched closed and sharp scratches sparking hot and angry against the face and forearms. A strange sort of emptiness in the brain, like air pushing against the inside of your skull. No pain, not yet. Then darkness.

And, presumably some time later, a flaming sock. Floating down towards Hayley as she lies on her back, unable to move.

There isn't any sound. It's like watching a TV screen with the mute button on. The sock drifts in and out of focus. Hayley blinks and it has fallen away somewhere else, the screen all blue again. Then a shadow passes over it and she thinks, ludicrously, that the signal has gone, but then her eyes begin to sting and she realises it is smoke.

When it hits the back of her throat, it's like the world has been turned back on. She chokes and starts to retch, acrid fumes thickening in the roof of her mouth, her eyes streaming. She vomits, her head twisting automatically to the side. She finds that she can move and that her whole body is throbbing with pain.

The shock feels like a heavy blanket, weighing down every limb, clouding the air around her, making it almost impossible to see. Slowly, Hayley raises her head, her neck screaming in protest. She lifts a hand to shield her eyes from the white glare of the sun and registers, distantly, as if she were looking at someone else's fingers, that there is a deep wound across the back of her wrist, that her skin is streaked with something black and sticky, that one of her fingernails is ripped and half hanging off. The hand is shaking.

There is sand everywhere. Grittiness in her eyes, between her teeth. Granules between her fingers, prickling the backs of her knees.

In the years afterwards, when Hayley thinks back to that afternoon, she will only ever be able to see it in snatches, like photographs laid out in a line. Moments and sensations: jumbled and out of order, some so vivid she can taste them, others so alien she doesn't know if they really happened at all.

Black skin a metre away, streaked with red. Jessa. A jam-like sticky goo on the side of her arm, every muscle in Hayley's body straining not to look at it.

A twisted carcass of metal, unrecognisable. Wires hanging like streamers. Little fires crackling with sparks.

Bodies scattered in the sand. Some moving. Some not.

Shannon's narrow, sheet-white face inches from hers, shaking her shoulders lightly, asking Hayley something, the sound distorted like she's underwater.

Relief like a liquid gush when Shannon moves to Jessa, puts two long fingers in the hollow under her chin and says: 'There's a pulse.'

The weirdest sensation of hysterical laughter somewhere deep in her chest, as she watches Shannon bending over Jessa, and a sing-song voice in her head intones 'A head cheerleader never cracks under pressure.'

Stumbling to her feet, a clean, hot pain flashes through Hayley's ankle and she drops to the ground again.

Elliot is sitting up, spitting into the sand. He looks at her, nodding mutely and waves her past with a blood-streaked hand as she crawls from body to body, the sand burning grazes into her knees.

Sobs, shuddering, screaming sobs grind into Hayley's ears like someone scraping the inside of her head with a metal spoon. She wants them to stop so she can think, so she can breathe. She isn't here, she's on a plane. She is meant to be on a plane.

May sits up slowly, the side of her face deeply grazed. Her pupils are like lagoons. Jessa's body shakes and convulses as she screams, her arm sticking out at the wrong angle, black oil running down it and mixing with blood and torn skin.

One day, when she thinks back, Hayley will remember how her girl-scout first-aid training flashed into her mind as she knelt next to Jessa. How strange it felt to remember a smiling first-aider in mint green overalls, a blue plastic dummy on the floor.

Brain numb. Clogged, claggy cotton wool. Something about breathing? And circulation? ABC? Or ACE? But that smooth, clinical blue plastic had looked nothing like this. It wasn't meant to be ugly and dirty, sand and blood and a mess like congealed treacle. It was meant to be clean and pleasant. Time for mistakes and starting over and asking for tips. Do I put my hands here or here? How many breaths again? Comforting, firm hands on top of hers, mint overalls swishing.

Someone says they need to set Jessa's arm and holds Jessa down. Elliot pulls, like ripping at a butcher's carcass. Hayley feels useless, standing there trying to remember her girl scout acronyms. She holds Jessa's other hand instead, letting her grip hard, painfully squeezing sand into open cuts.

Even years later, she will know that the noises Jessa made then caused Hayley to vomit again and again onto her own feet. But her brain won't let her remember them.

Time moves strangely. She knows they are on a beach. She knows that the front of the plane is missing, that there is no sign of Coach Erickson or the pilot. She can't remember how she knows this or who told her. The pain in her ankle throbs and rages and she can't walk very far. Sometimes she looks down and sees, in surprise, that her arms and legs are shaking.

She doesn't know how long it is before Jason staggers out of the line of trees along the top of the beach, dragging Brian's motionless body.

'He's alive,' he says, grimly, pre-empting the unasked question on all of their faces.

Jason lets Brian slump limply to the floor and runs to Shannon, wraps her in his arms, stroking her long, curly dark hair like a child. 'My baby.' he murmurs. Seeing the two of them entwined like that makes Hayley feel terrifyingly alone. But there's a stiffness in Shannon's back. Her arms hang at her sides and she doesn't return the embrace.

Time jumps forward again.

Hayley is sitting at the base of a palm where the beach meets the treeline, rough bark reassuringly solid behind her back. A few metres to her right, in the shade of another tree, Jessa is lying, mercifully asleep, her head in May's lap. May is stroking the baby hairs on Jessa's forehead with the tips of her fingers. Jessa usually gels them flat but they've started to curl wispily at the root in the humid air. It makes her look younger, more vulnerable somehow. Jason puts his hands under Brian's armpits, heaving him over to lie next to Jessa.

Palm trees with shiny, rubbery leaves that Hayley doesn't recognise and thick bushes spread behind them in a dense tangle. The beach stretches out uninterrupted to left and right like a smooth slick of butter. The smouldering wreck of the plane is hunched, gargoyle-esque, 20 feet away, its wing forced deep into the sand. Elliot encouraged them to get away from it, in case there was a fuel explosion, but the flames have died down. It isn't the whole plane, but a torn-off hunk, one wing and the tube of its body, the tail ripped and twisted to one side. There is no sign of the nose or the front third of the plane. The beach is strewn with parts as if the carcass of the plane has been ravaged by scavengers, trailing its innards across the sand. Ripped seat cushions dribbling foam stuffing, metal panels and glass shards littering the beach. A piece of tasteful beige carpet flaps listlessly in the breeze.

In the distance, beyond the wreckage, is a shimmering swipe of pale, golden turquoise that must be sea, though the tide is so far out that Hayley can't make out where the water ends and the cloudless sky begins. The chances of them landing on an island rather than plunging into the sea were infinitesimally small, Hayley realises. Lucky. An odd way to look at it – but they are.

'I shouldn't be here,' Hayley says, to no one in particular, a stream of giggles burbling suddenly and unstoppably out of her. It seems hopelessly, ridiculously funny. Things like this do not happen to Hayley Larkin – everything in her life is perfect, controlled and calculated down to the very last detail. Or at least that's what it looks like from the outside. She wouldn't be here at all if it weren't for the unwelcome revelation from her guidance counsellor that even being on track for valedictorian and maintaining a flawless GPA wasn't enough to guarantee admission to an Ivy League college, without diverse extra curriculars to boost her application.

Her head feels light, somehow, as if there's too much air inside her skull, and she can't keep hold of her thoughts. Suddenly she's back in that drab, airless office, its grey walls closing in on her even as her feet sink gently into the sand.

She expects the appointment be a formality, a check-in on her excellent progress, a pat on the back. She is on track for

Princeton or Harvard, she has ticked every box. A major in English with a stint on the college paper, then internships at the *New York Times* or the *Washington Post* in her junior year and a position as a cub reporter at a local outlet when she graduates. She has it all planned out. So it's a shock when Mr Curtis looks at her file and frowns. 'Right now, on paper, you look like a very ... *solitary* candidate. What you need is something that shouts *team player*!'

She hopefully suggests debate club and reminds Mr Curtis she is already editor of the *Oak Ridge Tribune*, but he frowns and gently suggests something 'a little further from your comfort zone ... less academic.' 'It needn't be long term,' he adds, catching her expression of dismay as she mentally tries to work out how she will cram anything else into her already packed schedule. 'It might even be fun ... what's the worst that could happen?'

And suddenly she is on a windy field one Monday at recess, tugging her cycling shorts out of her crotch and trying to remember to smile while she high-kicks her way awkwardly through her audition routine.

Which (thanks to two drop-outs and a nasty bout of strep throat) lets her scrape into the bottom of the cheerleading tour squad. Which, in turn, leads her here. To this beach. And suddenly she is back on it, this beach covered in vomit and blood and twisted metal.

Hayley Larkin does not belong on this beach.

The strange thing is that she cannot seem to move. Distantly, she is aware of activity around her. Shannon is moving purposefully from Brian to Jessa, gently lifting their wrists to check pulses, bending down low to feel their breath on her cheek. Jason has wrapped a wet basketball jersey around his face as a makeshift smoke mask and is diving in and out of the plane's wreckage, pulling out anything that looks like it might be useful or edible and piling it high on the beach. With the sun shining on his muscular, lightly tanned arms and swept-back blond quiff, he looks like something out of a superhero movie.

I always thought I would be the unlikely superhero, Hayley thinks, vaguely, as she feels the sand prickle the backs of her thighs. Sure, she might be the weakest link in the squad, the last one to be invited to social events, more likely to attend prom as a student reporter than somebody's date. But she's always somehow believed when it came down to it, when 'real life' started, she'd show them all. She'd secretly pictured herself one day becoming the front-page story instead of the person who wrote it. Graciously accepting her Pulitzer for blowing a sex trafficking ring or a corruption scandal wide open, while the cheerleaders, weirdly still in their teens, stood by, mouths open, pom poms hanging limply. She'd daydreamed it, in the long, tedious hours sitting in hotel rooms on the tour, pretending to be glad to have the time to study while she listened to the other girls shrieking with laughter as they watched re-runs of *Married at First Sight* on cable.

Yet still she cannot move. She wants to sit here with the solid tree against her back for as long as it takes until things don't feel like they are spinning out of control any more.

She sees May gently ease Jessa's head onto a folded sweatshirt and walk over to help Jason, sorting through the growing heap of supplies next to the plane. Her willowy frame bends and straightens, bends and straightens as she sorts through the items.

Hayley watches as May stacks a small tower of those foil-covered trays of plane food on top of each other, watches as they slide down in all directions, crashing into the sand. She sees the exasperation on May's face as she wipes beads of sweat from the bridge of her nose, running her hand over her perfectly groomed, arched, black eyebrows. Numbly, Hayley thinks that the food shouldn't be left there in the sun. Someone should move it into the shade. But she can't move. 'It'll spoil so quickly in this heat,' her mom tuts, unexpectedly, in her head.

Mom.

Hayley sees her walking towards the front door, frowning, glancing at her watch. Taking off her glasses, wiping them automatically on her sleeve and tucking them in the collar of her jumper. Swiping her dark blonde hair back over her shoulder with one hand as she reaches for the doorhandle with the other. Sees the panic cross her face as red and blue lights cross her forehead. Sees Dad appear behind her at the open front door, place a hand on her shoulder, start barking urgent questions at the police officer as Mom falls silent. Sees the tension in the tendons of his neck, stiffening beneath the short cut salt-and-pepper hair, jaw clenching, dark brown skin carefully clean shaven.

'A phone,' she croaks, surprised to find how sore her throat is. 'Does anyone still have their phone?' Shannon looks up from where she's kneeling beside Brian, one dark eyebrow raised in the sort of patronising expression Hayley has become far too accustomed to in cheer practice.

'Don't you think we've already tried? No signal,' she replies curtly, tossing her phone into the sand at Hayley's feet with a soft thud. Shannon and Jason grin cheesily in the lockscreen picture, all wide white smiles, his teeth practically sparkling. They look like an advert for All-American high-school sweethearts. Shannon's right. No bars.

Shannon moves practiced hands to Hayley's ankle, rotating it expertly as Hayley winces and draws a sharp breath. 'It's swollen but it's probably just a sprain. You wouldn't be able to put any weight on it if it was broken.' And she's so grateful for someone taking charge, to be touched with firm, confident fingers that show her limbs where to move and when, that she doesn't find Shannon's know-it-all tone as annoying as usual.

'The soreness in your chest is probably from smoke inhalation,' Shannon adds, almost smugly. 'Lucky I took my first-aid extension certificate last month.'

'Or bruising from the crash?' Hayley asks, indicating a nasty bruise blooming below Shannon's collarbone.

'Maybe,' Shannon agrees, handing Hayley an open bottle of water. She takes it and swigs great gulps, then suddenly stops, the bottle still raised to her lips.

'Should we be . . .' It sounds so silly, so melodramatic. 'Should we be saving our water?' she asks uncertainly.

'I don't think it's going to come to starvation rations.' Shannon smirks. 'It's the Gulf of Mexico, not the Bermuda Triangle – I'd be surprised if someone hasn't found us by sunset.'

'Speaking of sunset . . .' Hayley glances at the horizon. The sun pulses egg-yolk orange, lower in the sky now, and the incoming tide, while still distant, has crept closer, so that she can see a faint white line where the frothy edges of the waves meet the shore.

Hayley passes the water bottle to Jason and he swigs thirstily, wiping his lip with the back of his hand, his eyes on Shannon, who is hovering over Jessa again.

'So,' he says, sitting down in the sand with his legs out in front of him, knees bent. Hayley notices little grains of sand hanging onto his sun-bleached blond leg hairs. They all turn towards him instinctively. It's as if, with Erickson gone, he's the natural source of authority. As if being captain on the court has anything at all to do with this. As if a carefully crafted defensive play is going to help them now. Hayley feels giggles fizzing inside her again. It is all so completely absurd.

Jason holds up seven fingers. 'Shannon, Hayley, May, me – all okay or near enough.' He nods at each of them, folding down his fingers one by one as he checks them off.

'Elliot too, though I don't know where he's gone.' He folds down the thumb, leaving a curled fist and two fingers still sticking up on the other hand. 'Jessa – hurt but conscious.' They all turn to look at Jessa, curled in a foetal position, her long, glossy twists splayed on the sand, lips slightly parted to reveal the gap between her front teeth. There's some swelling around her shoulder, but the blood on her upper arm has congealed to a dark paste.

A small fly lands inquisitively at the edge of the dark blood. May brushes it away angrily, glaring at the others as if all this is their fault. Jessa has always been hers, as long as anyone can remember. They've come as a pair since day one of first grade, fingers interlaced in a wordless playground pact before the bell even rang. Jessa's gentle, considered thoroughness and May's spiky, scrappy boldness somehow fitted together and made a whole.

'The mouth on that girl,' Hayley's mom had gasped, half admiring, half disapproving, after she'd stopped by to pick up Hayley after practice one night, just in time to hear May unleash a stream of profanities in the direction of a truck that had blocked her in the parking lot. Hayley has never seen May without a comeback. But she looks shrunken and lost without Jessa awake and alert by her side. Her straight black hair hangs around her shoulders like a silk curtain. Like she's already in mourning. Her delicate features look crumpled, long black eyelashes shining with tears.

They all stare at the seventh unchecked finger. Jason doesn't need to say it. Brian's body lies motionless in the shade, his meaty calves and forearms limp, his thick neck looking strangely delicate and vulnerable.

Only a few hours ago, they'd been ribbing him on the plane for having to wear his basketball jersey because he'd run out of clean laundry two days before the end of the tour. He grinned proudly and started explaining how underwear lasts twice as long if you turn it inside out, at which point Hayley very deliberately stopped listening.

Now Brian's arms and legs glow an angry red, his fair skin burned under the relentless sun before Jason found him. The pale brown freckles that usually dust his round cheeks have been swallowed into the new rose pallor, which clashes with the ginger of his messy curls.

'He's breathing,' Jason says, a little too loudly. 'Maybe he just needs to sleep it off.' Hayley resists the urge to point out that he hasn't regained consciousness yet: that the situation is significantly more serious than an extended nap. She looks at Brian's slack face again and feels a wave of nausea rise in the base of her throat. She swallows it down and looks away.

'OH MY GOD, NAKED TWIN LESBIANS!' Jason shouts suddenly, leaning towards Brian and shaking his leg. Brian's head lolls loosely to one side, his cheek pressing into the sand.

'Yeah, he's genuinely unconscious.' Jason smirks, apparently oblivious to the fact that he's the only one who seems to find this amusing.

'We queer women don't only exist for your amusement, Jason, you might be shocked to hear,' May mutters, without looking up. And Jason at least has the grace to look awkward, though he doesn't apologise.

'Has anybody seen Erickson? Or the pilot?' Hayley asks.

Jason shakes his head. 'I walked pretty deep into the trees looking for Brian. He must have been thrown further from the wreckage because he wasn't wearing his seatbelt. But there was no sign of anyone else, or the front of the plane.'

'It probably broke away much earlier,' Shannon says grimly, looking out to sea. Her pale, angular face is serious, dark circles making her eye sockets look hollow and gaunt where usually she exuded an unusual kind of sharp glamour. 'That grinding, screeching noise started a good minute or two before we crashed. It could be miles away.'

'Or it could be somewhere else on the island,' May snaps. 'They could be injured, or worse – they might need our help.'

'I don't think so, May,' says a quiet voice, and Elliot steps out of the bushes, his curly, chestnut brown hair wild, his arms piled with sticks and twigs. There's a thin diagonal cut across his right cheekbone and his knee-length, khaki shorts are torn. He bends down, carefully piling the wood in the sand.

'There's a pretty steep incline to the north.' He jerks his head back towards the trees and to the right. 'I climbed up far enough to get a sense of the whole island and I didn't see anybody else, or anything that looked like it was from the plane. There's a lot of tree cover across the centre of the island, so I guess it's possible there was something I didn't spot, if part of the plane went down there . . . but I'd still have expected to see some debris; broken branches . . . something. I think Shannon's right. We're on our own.'

There's a surprised silence. Hayley isn't sure she's ever heard Elliot talk uninterrupted for that long. She sees a sudden flash of him skulking into the first joint practice at the start of the semester, head bowed, not meeting anyone's eye.

Then the reality of what he has said hits her like a cold blast. *On our own.* Stranded. Stuck. The enormity of it is so great she almost can't think about it at all. She looks down at her bloodied hand, and notices that her torn fingernail is beginning to throb. Somehow it's easier to focus on that one small thing, the immediate pain, than it is to contemplate what Elliot is telling them. There's a wave of panic hovering, threatening to completely overwhelm her. She picks at the nail and earns herself a sharp stab of pain. The panic recedes a little.

'How do you know that's north?' May blurts it at Elliot like she wants to pick a fight. Hayley looks at May's dark, glinting eyes and knows that she isn't the only one at risk of being swept away by that wave of fear.

Elliot holds out his arm, showing them a worn leather watch whose soft, threadbare strap is the same sandy golden brown as his skin. 'You can work it out by pointing the hour hand at the sun: a line drawn between the hour hand and 12 points south.' The others stare at him. 'My family camps. A lot,' he adds, awkwardly.

'Anyway.' Elliot crouches and starts arranging little twigs and scraps of wood in a pyramid. 'It's going to get dark and cold pretty quickly once the sun goes down. And if anyone comes looking for us, a fire is the best way to get their attention.'

Hayley feels like an idiot. They've been sat here for hours – why didn't any of them think of a fire?

'Nobody has a lighter,' Jason scoffs, shifting his weight forwards like he wants to draw the others back towards him. Heads obediently swivel in his direction. On the court, Elliot might've ducked his head in embarrassment, danced to Jason's tune, but here he ignores him, walking over to the pile of supplies by the plane.

'I said there aren't any lighters or matches, man,' Jason repeats, a tougher note in his voice daring Elliot to contradict him.

Elliot picks up a plastic water bottle, murmurs to himself, and starts walking up and down the beach, picking through the debris. With a grunt of satisfaction, he pulls his sketchbook out from under a pile of clothes and shoes, flicking past a half-finished picture of them sitting in the back of the plane, and carefully rips out a piece of paper covered in dark pencil lines.

Hayley leans forward to watch, wondering how he can manage to stay so calm. Bending close to the tepee of twigs, Elliot folds the paper in two and holds it in his left hand, then gently tilts the water bottle back and forth using his right hand. A bright spot of light appears on the paper, a circle that grows and shrinks, as he experimentally moves the bottle around. When the light is at its brightest, a tiny, concentrated pinprick, he holds it still, and almost immediately the paper begins to smoulder and smoke. A dime-sized circle scorches out from the centre, the edges curling white. Jason raises his eyebrows and puts his arm around Shannon's waist. 'Nice trick, cub scout.'

Elliot's lip twitches with a tiny smile as he gently waves the paper back and forth, feeding it oxygen, patiently encouraging it until an orange flame flickers up. He pokes it between the twigs he's arranged, pulling a handful of dry, dead grass from his pocket and stuffing it into the gaps.

Elliot puts his cheek to the sand and blows gently and a little spiral of bluish smoke rises up again, chased by tiny tongues of flame licking at the twigs.

There's a low whistle. 'Impressive,' croaks a voice. Brian is struggling weakly to raise himself up on one elbow.

Hayley feels the relief thrum warm in her chest.

'Fuck's sake, Brian. Do you have any idea how long you've been out?' Jason's voice is rough, accusing, even. He wipes his hand swiftly across his face and frowns at Brian like he's committed five fouls in a game and been benched.

Brian grins sheepishly. 'Where are we? What happened?' He looks around, taking in his surroundings, and mutters 'Jesus.' He raises his hand to the back of his head and winces.

'The plane crashed,' Shannon says, simply. 'We're on an island.'

'Is everyone okay?'

'Everyone except Jessa ... she's been conscious, but her arm is hurt. We don't know about Erickson and the pilot. We think they went down somewhere else.'

Brian's gaze wanders from the fire to the trees to the plane, then out over the beach towards the sea. The heat of the sun is waning now, a breeze rushing up the beach and into the tree canopy above them as if to whisper that the sea is coming, coming. They can smell it – the wet, fresh scent of salt and seaweed that tethers Hayley to reality, forces her to acknowledge that this is actually happening.

Brian is eyeing Jessa. 'Is it just her arm? Because I saw something like this on *Grey's Anatomy* where they thought the guy was totally fine because he was awake and talking, but then he had a delayed brain bleed and he just died.' Brian snaps his fingers, 'like that.'

'Oh, good.' Shannon rolls her eyes, 'I didn't realise we had a qualified brain consultant with us.'

May's eyes shoot daggers at Brian as he shuffles into a sitting position, wincing and rotating his head from side to side.

'What? They have medical advisers to make it realistic, you know.'

It's quiet around the fire as they peel back the metal foil from the food trays and start picking at the contents with plastic forks. Cold macaroni cheese isn't exactly appealing but at least it fills their stomachs. Hayley peels the plastic wrapper off a small bread roll and is about to take a bite when Elliot walks out of the trees, carrying another large armful of sticks which he dumps in a pile near the fire.

'What are you all doing?' Elliot pants, gaping at them.

They blink at him, this new, different Elliot who isn't sitting on the side lines with his patched backpack guarding the seat next to him, listening silently to post-practice pep talks, emerging from the locker room like a ghost after the other boys have tumbled out in a loud group.

'What do you mean, what are we doing?' Shannon looks at her macaroni and wrinkles her nose 'We're eating dinner, if you can call it that.'

'Guys,' Elliot speaks urgently, angrily. 'You can't just eat everything. We have no idea how long we're going to be stuck here. We need to ration our food and drink.'

'Oh, come on, man,' Jason drawls, taking a bite of a candy bar he has helped himself to from the supply pile.

'No, "man", *you* come on,' Elliot shoots back. 'The plane only had food on board for one meal, plus whatever snacks people had on them. That's it. How long do you think we're going to last if we eat it all at once?'

There's an uncomfortable silence.

'It's only a matter of time till someone finds us,' Jason says, dismissively. 'My parents are going to have people out looking, believe me.'

'I'm sure they will,' Elliot retorts, drily. 'But do you have any idea how big the Gulf of Mexico is? How long it could take? We're talking about more than a million square miles.'

'They know our flight path,' Hayley points out, swallowing a claggy mouthful of macaroni and trying to quell the rising fear Elliot's words are igniting in her stomach. 'Houston to Miami. That'll narrow it down.'

'Sure, if we'd stayed on it. But who knows how far we zigzagged or what went wrong with the plane? We have no idea whether the radio transmitter was still working, whether the pilot was able to issue a mayday call ...' Elliot frowns. 'Even in the act of falling out of the sky the plane could have covered miles and miles! And they might have lost track of us long before we went down.'

'Aren't we on a barrier island?' May asks, uncertainly. 'I assumed we were somewhere close to land, just not close enough to see it.'

Elliot shakes his head. 'I've been fishing off some of the barrier islands with my dad. They're basically just big sandbars. They're flat, grassy.' He waves his hand at the thick trees behind them and the darkening shadow where the land rises to the right. 'Nothing like this.'

'Right.' Jason claps his hands loudly, speaking over Elliot. 'I think we need a plan. Let's assume it could be a few days before we're rescued. We need to do an inventory of our supplies and ration them out.'

There are six untouched, foil-packed plane dinners left in the pile, and a smattering of squashed confectionery.

'Each tray has a carton of macaroni, a salad, a bread roll, crackers and cheese,' Jason announces. 'Let's call that four portions of food.' He pauses, and Hayley physically bites her tongue not to do the sum for him. 'Twenty-four portions in all. There's seven of us, so that's enough for three days if we each eat just one portion per day. Plus, two Snickers, a Slim Jim, three bags of Cheetos and a few sweets. There's no way it'll take them more than three days to find us.'

'They better find us faster,' Brian mutters. 'This puny salad is not a day's worth of calories. Although,' he says, brightening, 'If Jessa doesn't wake up tomorrow, I shotgun her macaroni.'

'What?' he asks defensively, as the others look at him in horror. 'I'm not saying I don't *want* her to wake up ... I'm just saying, there'll be more food to go around if she doesn't. It's a simple fact.'

'What about water,' Hayley interrupts. 'It's more important than food, isn't it?'

They separate the pile of supplies into four sections. Food, drinks, clothing and things like cushions and towels that they can use for bedding. There are twelve unopened bottles of water left. Hayley feels her chest tightening as she does the maths. Four bottles a day if they're rescued in the next three days. Four between seven. Less than a bottle each per day.

'We should keep the water all in one place,' Shannon says, as Jason stuffs the rest of the candy bar in his mouth. 'Make sure it's shared out fairly.'

'Good idea, sweetie.' Jason nod. 'You be in charge of that, okay?'

Shannon doesn't reply. She begins stacking the water bottles methodically. 'And we should stay out of the sun,' Hayley adds, 'then we'll dehydrate less quickly.'

She feels an automatic rush of relief that she's thought of something to contribute, then realises how ridiculous the impulse is. It's not debate club. Nobody here is being graded.

'That's all settled then,' Hayley says. 'Nobody eats or drinks alone. We'll put the food and drink in the bushes to keep it cool.'

'What about animals?' May's voice is uncharacteristically small and uncertain. 'How do we know it won't get eaten by wild animals?' she repeats. 'How do we even know it's safe to sleep out here?' She gestures to the beach, where the tide has crept much closer, little waves running up the sand and stopping about 30 yards away. 'Who's going to keep Jessa safe in the night … what if something smells her blood—' Her voice is rising, there are tears in her throat though her eyes look fierce, and Hayley wants to hug her, to tell her it'll all be okay. Except that she doesn't know whether it will be, and she knows that May would hate a hug, shrugging off the pity as if it burned her skin.

And underneath her sympathy, her urge to comfort, there's a colder, selfish part of her that just wants May to shut up, to stop pointing out problems. She wants Elliot to stop going on about search areas, wants to stop counting bottles of water over and over again in her head. A part of her that doesn't want to accept what has happened or to start thinking about the reality of what it means. And a part of her that really, really doesn't want to think about wild animals.

'It's okay, May.' Jessa has woken and is suddenly next to her, looking shaken but standing, uninjured arm round May's waist where anyone else's would have been scornfully rejected. The very fact that she's standing is the shot of relief they all desperately needed. 'We can sleep in shifts.'

'Here's what we should do.' Jason stands up, and Brian instinctively lumbers to his feet too, leaning towards him, wheezing a little. It almost looks as if they're going into a tactical huddle on the deserted beach.

Jason grabs Elliot's arm, and Hayley realises he's the only one with an old-school wristwatch. Jessa and Jason both have Apple watches and the others just rely on their phones. It won't be long before the batteries die.

'It's just turned seven,' Jason says, 'and sunset probably isn't far off.' Elliot looks as if he's about to say something but doesn't. 'So, Brian and I will stay awake until ten, then wake Elliot. He can take the next shift until one, then wake us. We'll keep watch until four then switch again.' The others nod in agreement.

'And what are we, chopped liver?' Hayley asks, taking herself by surprise. The boys blink at her.

'No offence, but this is a guy's job,' Jason laughs. 'Are you really going to chase off a wild dog or a boar or whatever with no weapon?'

'Are *you*?' Hayley retorts, her confidence growing. 'What are you going to do, flirt it to death?'

'They're offering to protect us,' Shannon mutters. 'There's

no need to start burning our bras, we should just be grateful.'
Jason grins, reaching a hand out to touch her hair.

'We need weapons. We can sharpen some sticks from the
forest,' Brian suggests enthusiastically, as Hayley glowers. He
crashes off into the undergrowth, followed by Jason, leaving
Elliot with the girls.

'The tide won't come up much higher,' he says to May, as
if the last few minutes' conversation had never happened.
'You see the line of debris just there?' He walks down the
beach beyond the plane, a few yards from where the waves are
rushing up the sand. When you look closely, there's a line of
broken shells, little pieces of driftwood and scraps of seaweed,
stretching the length of the beach. 'That shows you where the
tide was at its highest point,' Elliot explains. It won't reach us
if we sleep up near the trees.'

May nods with a nonchalance Hayley suspects might be
fake. 'As for animals, I don't think it's likely there are any large
predators on this island.' Elliot looks back into the forest.
'I've been quite far into the trees and haven't seen any sign
of tracks, and the island isn't very big. You could cover the
whole thing in a few hours. Animals aren't what we need to
be worrying about.'

'What do we need to be worrying about, Elliot?' Hayley
asks in a low voice.

'Thirst,' Elliot replies, simply. 'We can survive weeks
without food, but only a few days without water. And I'm
really glad everyone's so optimistic, I hope they're right, but
honestly, we have no guarantee of when we might be found.
If it looks like we're going to run out of water, we need to

do something about it before that happens – plan ahead – otherwise it'll be too late.'

There's a long silence. Hayley knows he is right. But the others look sceptical. None of them are used to hearing Elliot speak, let alone taking orders from him. She wants to back him up, tell them they have to listen. But that means letting in the fears at the very edges of her mind, the ones tap, tap, tapping to get in and willing her to absolutely lose her shit. Hayley Larkin doesn't lose her shit. She doesn't panic or lose control. So, she stands there, looking at Elliot, and says nothing.

'Fine.' Elliot spits the word out sharp, but it's swallowed in the sand's softness before it can reach any of the others. He turns on his heel and starts rifling through the supplies, heaving at something. It's the plastic drawstring kitbag that holds the practice balls, except the balls are all long gone. For a moment, Hayley pictures them raining from the sky, dropping into the waves like cannonballs. But then she sees other things dropping, like Erickson's body, and feeling sick, she turns away. Elliot disappears again into the trees.

Night comes suddenly, just as Elliot said it would. It's not a slow, lingering beach sunset like the ones in the movies. The night swallows them whole. And it's cold – colder than they could possibly have imagined. Elliot hasn't come back when Hayley curls into herself under a coat, huddling near the fire and waiting for sleep to come. Through her eyelashes, she watches Jason marching up and down, clutching a freshly broken-off branch, his strides long but his knuckles clenched white.

But sleep doesn't come. And the island comes alive at night, becomes a roiling, writhing, terrible thing, outraged at their presence. The sand belches tiny flies that tap dance across Hayley's flesh with heels like tiny needles. They want to claim her body and gnaw away at it until the beach is smooth and untouched once again. She can't say when the noise starts exactly, only that suddenly it's around her and inside her all at once, a rhythmic, vibrating, denseness that she can feel in the back of her jaw, in her teeth.

She shifts uncomfortably, trying to find a position where her shoulder blades and hip bones aren't grinding uncomfortably against the sand. Listening to the steady *thud, thud, thud,* of Jason's footsteps as they recede and approach. The sea seems to be further away again, its cycles governed by a timetable she doesn't recognise, its low, uneven whispering like a conversation just out of earshot, leaving her straining to hear.

And if it feels like the island is closing ranks against her, like the sand and the sea and the invisible chorus of rasping, scuttling creatures are all united in harmony, it isn't exactly the first time.

Suddenly she's back in the school gym, echoing with shoe squeaks and rank with the smell of rubber and slightly damp crash mats. Stood awkwardly in the corner, slow panic rising as she realises she's wearing totally the wrong thing. Tugging down the edges of the purple nylon pleated skirt, wishing the tank top emblazoned with the Oak Ridge crest came below her belly button. Everyone else is in leggings, oversized T-shirts or slouchy sweaters. May in a graceful front split position, back arched forwards, arms extended. Shannon pacing out a new routine, her face lined with concentration. Jessa puts a quiet hand on Hayley's shoulder and hands her a spare T-shirt. 'Sweats are fine for practice. You'll know for next time.'

'Looking good, new girl.' Jason wolf-whistles. 'Didn't know it was dress-up Friday!' Hayley glances instinctively at Shannon, but her back is turned, hunched over some complicated diagrams. Brian and some of the other boys snigger appreciatively, circling Hayley like hyenas.

'Knock it off, pigs,' Jessa shouts, rolling her eyes.

'She might like it, Jessa.' Brian leers, his eyes creeping up Hayley's thighs. 'Not every cheerleader's as uptight as the Virgin Mary.' He gestures to the crucifix hanging on a fine silver chain around Jessa's neck and she stiffens, flipping it under her top.

'The Virgin Mary got knocked up outside marriage, you tool.' Jason takes careful aim and bounces a basketball off the back of Brian's head before catching it and dribbling up the court to shoot. Brian stumbles, cursing behind him.

'Uh, it was an immaculate conception,' Hayley mutters, unable to stop herself.

'Impractical come what now?' Brian mimics her, his voice high and reedy.

'Never mind,' Hayley mumbles, grateful for the interruption as Coach Erickson arrives, gesturing the boys over to the benches, and Coach Robinson walks in behind him to start cheer practice.

'Thanks,' Hayley murmurs, as Jessa stands next to her in the huddle.

'Let us know if you're going to need a babysitter every practice,' Shannon whispers. 'We'll need to know in advance if we've got to bring an extra squad member on tour to hold your hand.' Hayley's stomach curls up at the edges, shrinking in humiliation.

Trying to block out the memory, Hayley squeezes her eyes tighter closed. She can hear a soft, repetitive whisper, almost like a chant. May and Jessa are a couple of yards away, flickering in and out of view as the flames from the campfire rise and fall. They're curled together in a kind of tight nest fashioned from spare pieces of clothing. Behind them, she can just see the curve of Shannon's back, unmoving. May is fast asleep, her face smooth and peaceful, her breathing slow and steady. Hayley watches the smooth, light fawn skin rise and fall beneath her collarbones. But Jessa is staring into the fire, her necklace grasped between her fingers, murmuring the same prayer over and over again.

DAY 2

There's gentle warmth, a soft swishing noise and the rich, savoury smell of woodsmoke. Just for a moment, Hayley is lying in her own bed with her eyes closed, the warm weekend sun streaming through her window, her stomach awakened by the smell of Dad barbecuing bacon outside. In a minute, she'll stretch and open her eyes, pull on a fluffy robe and slouch downstairs to perch on a high stool by the breakfast bar, sipping orange juice while she watches Mom flip perfect, plump pancakes. She'll slide them onto a serving plate in a great warm pile and they'll head outside. Dad'll take the plate and make the same joke he always does: 'Thanks, but what are you two going to eat?'

But she can't stay there, her body won't let her linger. The illusion disperses like smoke as the physical pull of pain drags her back to the here and now. Something hard is sticking into her back. Her ankle throbs and her hands are sore. She itches all over. There are aches in places she didn't even know could ache, and for someone who went from a total non-athlete to a member of a cheer squad (okay the weakest member, but still) in less than two months, that is really saying something.

Screaming.

Hayley's eyes fly open. Scrabbling to sit up, she scrapes her wrist against a stone, and painfully jolts her ribcage against the floor.

The shrieks come again, shredding the air. They suddenly multiply, echoing terrifyingly above her. There's a flash of green. Hayley's racing heartbeat judders and begins to slow. The feathery tips of the palm trees are heavy with birds, acid green and scarlet plumage swirling in the sunshine, sharp cries louder than any birdsong she's ever heard.

Brian is sprawled in the sand, fast asleep. In the centre of the group, a few charred sticks are still gently smoking in a circle of grey ash. The fire has been out for some time. May and Jessa are stirring sleepily, cardigans and jumpers tangled between them. Elliot, Jason and Shannon are nowhere to be seen. With a nasty little surge of panic, Hayley wonders if Elliot ever came back last night.

The sun is already skimming over the sea's mirrored surface, the sky cloudless. It's hot, but not uncomfortable yet, just humid enough to stick the hairs to the back of her neck. The sand is still again, the waves running smoothly up and down the beach.

Hayley runs her hands through her short, rich brown pixie cut, her fingertips discovering a smattering of little bumps on her scalp. Her whole body is dotted with raised bites, screaming to be rubbed and scratched until they bleed.

'Don't scratch it,' her mom would tut, 'You'll only make it worse.'

She staggers to her feet, her muscles protesting sluggishly. Tentatively, she tests her ankle, putting a little weight on it and then a little more, pressing the ball of her foot into the sand. It groans a little, gives a grumpy burst of pain but then subsides into grudging acceptance as she walks a few paces, deeply relieved to be mobile again.

Out in the distance, a solitary figure is standing in the shimmering water, her silhouette outlined against the amber flood of morning light. Hayley, squinting against the glare, thinks that there's something different about Shannon here, on the island. She's more *still*, somehow. Watchful. Another silhouette approaches, Jason's solid frame dwarfing Shannon's, her thin shadow almost rippling at the edges. Shannon seems to flinch, turning her head to the side as Jason approaches. Are his hands flailing in the air, or is it just a reflection? The silhouettes seem to writhe, gesticulating as if they're arguing, but Hayley can't see properly. She can't hear anything but the endless white noise of the waves on the shore and the sun drills into her retinas until she has to blink and look away.

May stirs and stretches like a cat, unfurling her slim frame and baring her neat, small teeth in a yawn. She sees the sleeping guard and grins, jumping lightly across the sand and landing almost on top of him with a loud bellow: 'GOOD MORNING!'

Brian startles to attention, his body snapping rigid in alarm.

'God's sake, May,' he slurs, cradling the back of his head in both hands. 'What are you, a goddamn ninja?'

'Oh nice.' May narrows her eyes and juts out her

strawberry-shaped chin. 'Because I'm Japanese American I must be a ninja, right?'

'Jesus, that's not what I meant, and you know it.' Brian looks uncomfortably at Jessa, who offers him no help. 'My head is pounding, I just—'

May bursts out laughing. 'Chill, man, I'm kidding.' She runs down the beach, past the wreckage of the plane and splashes straight into the sea with an exhilarated whoop. 'Can you believe the others are missing this?' She shrieks and throws herself backwards into the waves. 'Flying back early lost them the chance of the best vacation they'll ever have!'

They all watch her silently as she begins to sing 'Come Alive' at the top of her voice, splashing around. You can almost believe she's having the time of her life, except it feels forced, like she's performing for some inane sunscreen advert. 'Let's go wild . . .' she sings, launching herself into the air and plunging under the water.

None of the others move to join her.

'Oh, come on!' She runs back up the beach, panting, her sodden white cotton skirt and pale pink blouse clinging. 'Everybody's okay, Erickson's probably already been rescued, we'll be picked up in a couple days and in the meantime we're on an all-expenses-paid desert island getaway. This is paradise! We should stay forever! No adults, no rules—'

'No food, no medicine, no way to communicate or let anyone know where we are,' Hayley breaks in.

'Don't be such a buzzkill.' May waves her hand dismissively at their paltry stockpile of food. Her excitement is too deliberate, her voice a little too high, like she's trying to persuade herself as much as the others. It would be a bit more convincing if the deep scratches from the plane crash weren't standing out like a dark red barcode stamped across her cheek.

As her now-transparent blouse rides up, revealing a flash of muscular, tan stomach, Brian puts his fingers in his mouth and whistles. She immediately responds with a middle finger of her own, so he forms his fingers into a 'V' shape and lasciviously begins to lick his tongue between them.

Hayley sees May's face crumple just a little before she wheels around. And she knows she should say something, knows she should call Brian out on his misogyny and homophobia, but she hesitates. There's a fear in her that is so familiar it slips around her shoulders like a well-worn shawl. The fear of confrontation. Of ridicule. Of escalation. Of his anger. And she says nothing.

May stalks away down the beach, but the look she throws Brian over her shoulder is one of mingled distrust and real, cold hate.

Then, as if nothing had happened, she picks up a towel from the pile of improvised bedding, spreads it ostentatiously on the beach and stretches out in the sun, fanning her wet hair out on the sand to dry.

'So much for staying in the shade,' Hayley whispers, but nobody answers her, and she's not surprised. This new May is appealing and joining in with her obvious state of denial is tempting. Last night's vulnerability long forgotten, it would be so comforting to block out the crash, Erickson, the possibility of running out of water ... to stop worrying.

What if this is the Spring Break nobody ever would have invited her on? Her one chance to be part of something – how had Mr Curtis put it? – *outside her comfort zone*. Well, she's definitely out of her comfort zone now.

By midday, Hayley's stomach is clenched tight with hunger and the single bread roll she has been allotted for the whole day is already a distant memory. When her eyes slide towards the remaining food trays for the third time, she decides she needs to distract herself. There is still no sign of Elliot, which makes her feel uneasy. She feels untethered here, insecure. If a plane can fall out of the sky, suddenly there are no guarantees any more. No safety. And as much as Elliot's dire warnings scared her, the idea of not being near him somehow scares her even more. He's the only one who seems to have any idea how to survive.

She sets off in the direction Elliot headed last night, passing Jessa sitting in the shade, examining the crusted wound on her arm and tentatively trying to rotate her shoulder, biting her lip in pain.

Purposefully striding into the trees, Hayley finds herself almost immediately tangled in the matted vines and creepers that cover the floor. She has to pick her way forward, grabbing onto tree trunks for leverage and ripping through patches of thorns that bite at her shins and leave gleaming pearls of blood on her forearms. Once, she freezes as a snake ripples liquidly across the path ahead, paying her no notice. A few minutes later, she thinks she sees a scorpion glinting on a tree trunk, but it scuttles into the shadows before she can be sure. She shudders and spends the next few minutes swiping phantom insects from her arms and back. Each leaf that brushes her bare shoulder might be a two-inch spider, each weed tickling her ankle a millipede's myriad legs.

There's a smell amongst the thickness of the plants, a kind of woody, vegetable wetness like the humid tang of her mom's greenhouse. There seems to be less air here than out on the breezy beach, the trees catching any movement in their net of stillness, bearing quiet, slow witness. Some of them are breath-taking, their ancient bark scarred and gnarled, brittle pieces peeling back to reveal softer flesh. They wear their curling necklaces of creepers lightly, reaching effortlessly up to tangle their branches in the dense canopy. Hayley wonders if another human being has ever been here, feels like she is intruding on something silent and precious. With every footstep she feels she is being somehow weighed, judged by the island.

Which Hayley does it see? The dogged student journalist who chases down leads, holding the school board to account for failing to keep its promises on recycling food waste from the cafeteria? Or the awkward girl on the edge of the crowd, wishing she could find the words to blend in?

She can see herself, picking at her chicken burger in the corner of the red leatherette diner booth after their first tour game, wishing she had Jessa's easy laugh or May's quick wit. Watching while Jason ordered for Shannon without even having to ask her what she wanted to eat, while May reduced everyone to fits of laughter with her impression of Erickson falling asleep on the bench in the last quarter. Jason dropping his AMEX on the table to cover everyone's bill: 'Someone else can get the next one. I'm looking at you, Brian, you freeloader.' Brian grinning and stuffing his triple burger with chilli fries while May pretends to vomit into her milkshake.

'I'm not hungry.' This from Elliot, counting out the change for his Diet Coke and putting it in a neat pile next to Jason's card. 'But we should talk strategy. Am I the only one who's bothered that we lost that game by thirteen points?'

'Don't worry about it,' Brian told him. 'It's tour, it doesn't count for anything. It's about the free ride, loosen up and enjoy it.'

As she thinks of this, wondering how it could only have been six days ago, she hears a raspy, gnawing sound. There's a thud and a muffled curse that comes from her left. She turns away from the incline where the trees start to rise, pushing further through the bushes on the flatter ground instead. Elliot is sitting on the floor, sucking the palm of his hand. It can't be called a clearing exactly – the vegetation is too dense for that. But next to him there's a sort of gap where two saplings have been roughly broken off at shoulder height, a third bent and splintered but still standing.

Elliot looks up and holds out a large stone with a sharp, narrow edge. 'Got myself by mistake,' he grunts. Hayley wordlessly takes the stone and starts to attack the tree trunk. It's a lot harder than she expected. The fibrous trunk is tough and sinewy, and hacking at it makes no headway whatsoever.

'Like a saw,' Elliot offers, and she starts to rub at it with the edge of the stone instead, feeling the fibres give way one by one like cutting through a thick rope. Her hands, already cut and sore, start to chafe against the stone within moments, but she doesn't stop until she's panting and hot in the cheeks. She leans against the trunk for a minute then starts again, painstakingly making a few millimetres progress at a time. She wonders how long Elliot's been at it.

'Here.' He takes the stone from her, his hand wrapped in a bandana from his pocket, and starts sawing away again.

Hayley watches his back, taut with the effort, his narrow shoulder blades lifting his thin, grey T-shirt away from his smooth, light brown skin. He's different here, too. Her eyes are drawn to the damp hair that curls at the base of his neck, the sinews of his hip tautening above the waistband of his scruffy khaki shorts as his T-shirt lifts slightly.

She shakes her head and looks away. 'What are we doing?' she asks.

'Trying to make a water collection point,' he gasps, without looking up. Hayley sees the plastic kitbag lying on the floor and understands the plan, though she can't see how he intends to fix it to the tree stumps.

Experimentally, she picks at one of the thin green vines snaking across the floor. It's wiry, but when she wraps it around each hand and pulls hard it snaps in two quite easily.

'Going to plait them,' Elliot pants, looking up. His eyes are golden brown, a metallic, amber glint there that Hayley has never been close enough to notice before.

As he continues hacking at the sapling, Hayley starts to forage for vines, tracing them across the floor and around tree trunks, gathering the longest ones she can find. When she's collected three, she ties the ends in a firm knot, clamps it between her knees, and starts to plait.

They work in a silence that is broken only by Elliot's heavy breathing, the buzzing of insects and the occasional shriek of a bird.

'So, why'd you wait until eleventh grade to try out for the team?' she asks.

Everyone was kind of surprised when Elliot signed up for the tour squad since he wasn't exactly jock material. But he turned out to be a natural shooting guard, his instinctive ball handling and near-flawless basket record causing something of a sensation at try-outs.

The steady rhythm of his stone grinding against the tree fibres pauses, stutters, resumes.

'Couldn't afford it before.'

Hayley, expecting a different answer, feels stupid and embarrassed. Suddenly the unbranded kit she'd always taken for a snobbish aesthetic choice, the dodging of diner visits, even the out-of-control curls make more sense. She's glad he has his back to her as she composes her face, hiding her surprise.

But then he turns, shrugs like he's letting go of something and looks her straight in the eye.

'I can only play in the off season because in term time I work a part-time job with the groundskeeper after school and weekends. The past few years tour team members have paid for their own flights, which ruled me out. But it was different this year when Jason's parents offered their firm's jets.'

'I didn't know.'

'Yeah, well it's not exactly something you advertise at a school like ours.'

Suddenly Hayley pictures Elliot at the bottom end of the school fields, bent over a lawn mower in a pair of mud-covered boots, watching through his curls as the other kids start their flash cars or jump into their parents' SUVs at the end of the school day. Oak Ridge is one of the most prestigious private high schools in the state, sandwiched between similar upmarket schools in Fort Lauderdale. Close enough to Miami for the wealthy business owners and real estate magnates whose kids attend, near enough to the coast for the students to get a local reputation for lavish beachfront parties with occasionally scandalous outcomes.

'Hope nobody from that firm needs to fly anywhere any time soon,' Hayley jokes, trying to break the tension. 'I wonder if they'll be liable for the crash . . .'

'I doubt it,' says Elliot shortly, turning back to his task. 'People like that tend to protect themselves.'

'It would be pretty ironic,' she concedes. 'Jason's dad founding one of the most successful law firms in the country and then getting sued himself. I wonder how much you have to pay out for a plane crash . . .'

'Depends whether anyone ever finds us alive or not,' Elliot replies, without turning around, and Hayley falls silent, seeing those blue lights again, Dad's hand clenched on Mom's shoulder.

By the time Elliot finally rips through the last stubborn bit of bark and punches the air in satisfaction, Hayley has plaited two long, tough lengths of vine 'rope'. Elliot runs them through his hands and nods his approval. 'We can use the drawstring from the bag for the third one.'

He carefully removes the drawstring, spreads the plastic out flat and then lashes it to the three tree stumps in a rough triangle, leaving enough slack for it to sag in the middle, creating an improvised basin suspended about two feet off the floor.

'Looks great.'

'Sure,' says Elliot. 'If it actually rains.' They both look up at the sky through the canopy of leaves above. There's not a cloud in sight. Hayley can feel the thirst like dry clay cracking in the walls of her throat, sticking her tongue to the roof of her mouth.

Apparently, she's not alone. Before they even get back to the beach, they can hear a cacophony of raised voices. They look at each other and start to move faster, stumbling over rocks and plants.

'—was supposed to be for everybody, you selfish asshole!' It's May's voice, sharp and fierce. She's leaning forward, fists clenched at her sides, screaming furiously into Brian's face.

'—not that big of a deal—' Brian is protesting, his hands raised defensively.

'—point is about knowing we can trust each other—' comes Jessa's voice softly, half drowned out by the others.

'—time of the month?' Brian shoots churlishly at May, who looks like she's inches away from raining a hail of blows down on him.

'What's going on?' Hayley waves her hands above her head to grab their attention and they all fall mutinously silent. Shannon sighs like an embarrassed parent admitting to her child's misbehaviour. 'Brian drank a bottle of water while nobody was looking.'

Hayley almost laughs. It sounds like something a kindergarten teacher might say; the punchline to a joke about a petty argument whipped out of all proportion. Except that it isn't petty here. Here a single bottle of water might be the difference between life or death. She looks at May's contorted face, Jessa's distress, Shannon's scowl.

'You can't just decide things unilaterally,' she shoots at Brian, surprising herself.

'Uni what?' Brian asks sarcastically. 'Sorry, we're not all on the honour roll, Hayley.'

'On your own,' she snaps, feeling heat rising in her neck. 'It's not fair. We're in this together.'

'Jeez, stop being so melodramatic.' Brian tosses the empty water bottle in the sand behind him. 'I'm the one who was unconscious with a head injury, remember,' he adds sulkily. Though he has seemed much more like his usual, bullish self today, Hayley realises with wry relief.

Elliot is looking at Brian like he's never seen him before.

'How long is it going to take?' he asks, and his quiet fury is more alarming than May's explosive anger and Jessa's disappointment put together, 'Before you all stop pretending and realise how serious our situation is? How long is it going to take until you start to listen?'

DAY 3

It takes three days.

By morning on the third day, the food and snacks are long gone. The water has been administered in stricter rations under watchful eyes since the 'incident'. But even the careful single swallows, measured out three times a day, have emptied the bottles. And there isn't any sign of rain.

That morning, the last phone battery dies. They all sit around and watch it as it flicks down from two per cent to one per cent and finally goes black. Their last remaining connection to the outside world. Dead.

It's a thirst like nothing Hayley has ever experienced before. Sometimes it pulses angrily in the back of her throat. Sometimes it blurs into hunger, her stomach gnawing desperately at itself and releasing only the painful warmth of bile. Mostly it makes them weak and irritable, sniping and arguing with each other endlessly. They spend a lot of time asleep, finding brief release in semi-conscious snatches of rest, but Hayley is plagued by fitful dreams and cruel visions of cool lemonade splashing freely into a glass just out of reach.

At first, she swallowed too much. Now her throat is too dry to let her swallow at all.

She begins to get confused. She watches Shannon and Jason enter the gym together at the first tour game. The crowd goes wild, Jason jogging a lap and waving to the crowds, Shannon cartwheeling and backflipping behind him. She ends with a lift, his hand up her skirt, her arms in a triumphant V, both basking in the applause. But that's not right. Hayley isn't in that gym, sitting awkwardly on the bench while the other girls flash megawatt smiles and jump up and down, loving the pageantry and hullaballoo. The roaring in her ears is the rush of water on sand and grit, not the shouts of the home crowd welcoming the touring side.

The island looks soft and gentle, as it slowly squeezes the life out of her. The sand is like fine sugar, the heat radiating from it blurring her vision and throbbing in her head.

Elliot is trying to organise them, and Hayley knows she should listen, but it's so hot and she is so tired. She watches a mosquito crawl slowly up her leg, pausing at the soft fuzz that has begun to regrow in the cleft next to her kneecap. She doesn't have the energy to care if it bites her or not.

'We have to split up,' Elliot is saying, wearily. 'We should have been taking survival measures from the moment we arrived: now we're playing catch-up.'

'All those who vote we survive by killing Elliot in his sleep and drinking his blood, raise your hands,' croaks Jason. 'What? Too soon?' Hayley shudders and wonders if it is really cold or if her body is just starting to shut down.

Elliot hesitates, but ignores Jason, turning to the others instead. Behind him, Hayley thinks Jason looks like a lion lounging in the heat, powerful but prone, lacking the energy to lift a paw and take a swipe at the . . . what kind of animal would Elliot be? Her brain is too frazzled to finish the thought.

'The most urgent thing is finding something to drink. We can't just keep waiting and hoping. We have to act now, before it's too late. The island's covered in palms: there could be coconuts somewhere. I've been looking, but there's too much ground for me to cover on my own. We should search through the denser vegetation for fruit trees or bushes and check for any sources of fresh water.'

He pauses and looks around, frowning, as if he's waiting for the insults to begin. For the first time, nobody contradicts him or sneers. He looks a little surprised, then nods.

'After that,' he says, standing up a little straighter, 'we should focus on ways to signal to rescuers. We need to collect a huge pile of wood for the fire and we should make an SOS sign on the beach that's big enough to be seen from the air. And we should make some kind of shelter for sleeping in. We don't know what the weather's going to do and we should really try to be prepared.'

Brian picks at the peeling skin on his sunburned forehead. 'Maybe Elliot's got a point,' he mumbles, looking down at the sand, his head turned slightly away from Jason. 'I could really use a fruit juice right about now.'

Hayley watches as Jason's face contorts in quick betrayed fury, then flickers through a range of expressions, like he's choosing which one to wear. For the briefest moment, she wonders if he's going to cry.

'Nice idea, Brian, maybe you should visit the juice bar with the girls,' Jason laughs, sweeping his golden hair out of his eyes. 'You stay here and rest, babe,' he says loudly to Shannon, without looking at her. 'I'll get the wood for the fire.' And he turns and crashes noisily into the trees, jolting Hayley out of the heavy daze that had settled on her like a blanket.

'Brian, you and I should head to the opposite coast of the island,' Elliot says, urgently, as Jason retreats. 'The coconut palms are most likely to be along the beach.'

He turns to Hayley. 'Can you guys look for fruit and make the SOS?'

She nods, wearily, dragging herself to her feet.

'Jessa and I will look for fruit,' May volunteers, and Hayley looks at Shannon, who hasn't moved since Jason left. She shrugs. 'Hayley and I will do the SOS then, I guess.'

'Look for any edible fruits or roots, any water source,' Elliot tells Jessa and May. But don't eat anything you don't recognise. Bring it back here first. Start with the trees and bushes to the south.'

May looks at him expectantly.

'That way,' He points, turning to the treeline and waving his hand to the left. 'It's where the trees are thickest, and the part of the island we've explored the least.'

Jessa stands next to May, putting her hands on her best friend's shoulders.

'Look, this beach faces east: that's why we see the sun rise over the sea in the morning.' She rotates 180 degrees, to face the treeline, May swivelling with her. 'Brian and Elliot are going straight across, to see if there are coconuts on the beach the other side of the island, the west side.'

Elliot points to the right. 'The land rises to the north and there are fewer bushes or trees, that's where I climbed up on the first day to get a bird's eye view.'

Jessa turns May 90 degrees left. 'So south is the jungly side, where the trees and bushes are thickest and there's the best chance of finding fruit or water.'

'The SOS needs to be really eye-catching, as big as you can,' Elliot tells Shannon and Hayley.

'Oh really?' Shannon's voice is biting, a shade of her usual sardonic sharpness returning through the exhaustion and thirst. 'Because I was going to write "NOTHING TO SEE HERE PLEASE CARRY ON" in really tiny letters.'

'Right.' Elliot smiles awkwardly, caught somehow between his unexpected leadership role and his usual detached silence. 'Well, good luck.'

Jessa and May haul an empty backpack from the pile of supplies still heaped on the beach and set off into the trees behind Brian and Elliot, soon peeling off to the left and disappearing into the bushes.

'OW!' May yelps loudly, 'If Jason thinks this was the easy option, he did not account for thorns,' she mutters furiously, her voice fading as she moves further away.

Hayley turns awkwardly to Shannon. 'Shall we?'

Time crawls. Hayley and Shannon slowly pile wood and rocks at the edge of the treeline, working in the shade for as long as they can. When they've collected a mound of materials, they drag it down the beach piled on a towel, Hayley tugging at the front corners and Shannon walking behind, holding the pile steady and collecting the sticks that tumble off.

They lug the heavy rocks painstakingly across the sand, then start tracing out the letters 'SOS', two metres tall, carefully keeping the message above the high tideline so their efforts won't be swept away. The heat beats relentlessly against Hayley's shoulders, burning uncomfortably into her hair, finding every unprotected part of her and biting down hard. They only salvaged a single bottle of sunscreen from the plane and she's wearing the faintest smear. And while Brian slathered handfuls of the lotion onto his angry red skin she knew hers could cope better with the sun, but now it feels like her whole body is screaming in protest.

Her tongue feels heavy, like a furred slug too big for her mouth. Her breath comes in short rasps, uncomfortable and hot on her cracked lips.

The sea dances tantalisingly close, its cruel ripples calling to her parched throat. It sparkles innocently, taunting her. Her brain knows that drinking saltwater would be a death sentence, but her body leans magnetically towards the liquid. She forms the letters as quickly as she can, ignoring the splinters driving into her soft palms, exhaustedly kicking the stones into place. As soon as they can, she and Shannon turn their backs on the sea and take refuge in the shade. Closing her eyes, Hayley feels herself come untethered from the beach, like she's slipping out of her parched, dry, cracking body. Pictures float on her eyelids. She drifts backwards and forwards in time.

A huge white yacht, lined with smart sailors in shining uniforms, saluting as they approach the beach. An airplane improbably dangling seven long ropes like jellyfish tentacles, each one miraculously attaching to a castaway before they whoosh into the sky to safety.

The whistle blowing as the first game of the tour kicks off. A whirl of colour and sound, violet pom-pom tassels rustling and spectators chattering and cheering. Erickson barking orders left and right. Hayley zooms in and out as if she's watching it from above.

She marvels at the deftness of the other girls as they leap in formation, muscles taut and quivering, their athleticism easily as impressive as the boys making free throws and streaking down the court. Squatting at the bottom of the pyramid or just high-kicking to one side, Hayley is left out of the more complex routines she hasn't mastered the skills for, left to gasp along with the crowd as Shannon flips dizzyingly from a three-metre height to land on her feet, hands extended to receive the rapturous applause.

The cheer squad comes alive in front of a crowd in a way Hayley had never seen in practice, their individual talents coalescing into an almost liquid, golden thing, a single body that swirls and morphs in front of her as she tries, sluggishly to keep up. A group of people she's always somewhere deep down felt herself superior to, pulling off moves she can't even begin to attempt.

She drifts forward again, suddenly, to arms reaching out to pull her into a fishing boat, the sweet relief of cool, bottled water, splashing over her face and bathing her fiery neck. Her parents, there in the boat, with oars, rowing and rowing but the boat sitting still in the water . . .

Hayley's drifted in and out of sleep so many times before Elliot and Brian return that she doesn't trust her eyes at first. But the familiar grumble of her ankle (the pain muted now but not gone completely) reassures her that she is awake as she scrambles to meet them. Coconuts. Four pale, milky brown, slightly wrinkled, waxy-skinned coconuts, clasped to their chests, and the widest smiles she has seen in days.

They let the coconuts thump heavily, miraculously into the sand, and Hayley reaches out a wondering hand to touch their cool, smooth skin.

'How do we open them?'

'Here.' Jason appears from nowhere, an armful of sticks and wood tumbling into the sand. He holds out a fist-sized rock, grey on the outside and shiny black where it has been split down the middle, leaving a long, sharp edge. 'I've been using it to cut wood.'

Elliot holds out his hand for the rock, but Jason grabs one of the coconuts instead and starts hacking at it.

'Don't cut the sides—' Elliot's voice is drowned out by Jason's grunting. Hayley can see his ears slowly reddening as his broad shoulders tense and release, tense and release.

'You don't want to—' There's a splintering crack as the stone finds the coconut's heart. Little white flecks spray up onto Jason's dimpled cheeks and the milky water gushes quickly away into the sand.

'Jason!' Shannon screeches, flying at him, clawing at his back. 'You idiot. You fucking asshole. We could have drunk that.' She's almost sobbing, dried spit flying from the edges of her mouth, her long dark hair, electrified into frizz by the humid weather, splaying wildly out around her face. Her mouth is like a red slash, her pale face consumed with rage.

'SHANNON!' Brian grabs her delicate shoulders, pulling her easily backwards as Jason gapes in shock, staring at her as if he has never seen her before. 'There are others. It's okay. There are others.'

She turns on her heel and stalks off down the beach without looking back.

'Ooh-kay,' Brian sings quietly. He turns to Jason. 'Dude, you got beat by a girl.' He sniggers, then stops when he sees Jason's thundercloud face.

Hayley can't remember ever seeing Shannon properly lose her temper before. Biting sarcasm, yes. But there's usually a coolness about Shannon, a haughtiness that seems to radiate off her. Has this hot, furious temper always been there, hidden underneath? Or is the maddening thirst transforming them all into people she doesn't recognise?

Elliot is picking through the pile of branches. Choosing a piece of wood about three yards long and as thick as his forearm, he takes the cutting tool from Jason's hand. Jason, still looking dazedly in the direction Shannon disappeared, doesn't protest. Elliot saws off the wood at an angle, then cuts the remaining edge into a sharpish point. He drives the blunt end of the stake as deep into the sand as he can.

Hayley cannot resist. 'Please tell me that's not for a pig's head,' she deadpans. She sees a flicker of recognition in Elliot's eyes, but everybody else looks nonplussed.

'There are pigs?' Brian asks, excitedly.

Hayley rolls her eyes. '*Lord of the Flies*? Sixth Grade English lit?'

'Yeah, we made Arthur Windley do that assignment for us.' Brian grins, punching an unresponsive Jason on the arm.

Elliot selects a coconut and brings it crashing down onto the stake, splitting the brown skin, opening up a long crack down one side.

'Camping,' he says again, with a sheepish smile, as the others look on helplessly. 'None of you guys ever taken a tent to the Keys?'

'I've stayed at the Waldorf Astoria there,' Brian offers, helpfully.

'Yeah, not quite the same thing,' Elliot mutters. He smashes the coconut down on the stake again, then uses his hands to pry off a long strip of the brown outer husk, caramel coloured straw-like fibres ripping slowly away from the nut like Velcro. The others watch as the little round centre emerges, a miraculous orb that calls to Hayley's dry throat like a siren.

When the husk lies in discarded sections at his feet, Elliot rests the coconut gently in the palm of his hand, testing its weight.

He looks at the three dark spots on top of the coconut carefully, turning it so they resemble two eyes and a mouth. He pulls a sharp sketching pencil from his pocket and carefully pierces the soft shell, right through one of the eyes.

'Hayley, can you hand me one of the empty water bottles?' He takes it, and gently upturns the coconut, sending a stream of slightly cloudy water trickling inside, until the bottle is about a quarter full. Hayley feels her tongue twitch involuntarily. Hawkishly, she watches as Elliot prepares the two remaining coconuts, adding their riches to the bottle.

They pass it round the circle like a holy cup, each taking a few precious sips before handing it on.

When it's Hayley's turn, she closes her eyes and lets the warm, almost salty liquid gush into her mouth. Stopping herself from gulping down the whole lot takes more self-control than she knew she had.

When the bottle is drained, Elliot uses the sharp stone to split the coconuts down the middle and they use their fingers to tear out the firm, white flesh, hungrily devouring each piece until only the hollow shells remain. Hayley chews gratefully, enjoying the feel of the firm meat giving way between her teeth, the sensation of actually swallowing something solid at last.

'We should get more,' Elliot says, looking at the smooth, empty bowls. His eyes flick towards the trees, and with a lurch of guilt Hayley realises they haven't saved anything for the other girls. It didn't even cross her mind.

'Let's all go,' Jason says, and Hayley wonders if he's scared of what might happen when Shannon comes back. Elliot pockets the cutting stone, wrenching the stake out of the ground and resting it over his shoulder. Hayley wonders why, then realises they'll be able to eat and drink some of the coconuts before they return, fuelling them for the journey back and freeing their arms to carry more. Elliot has already thought of this.

Fear drives little tendrils into Hayley's brain every time she stops to lets herself think. How long can they really last? The coconuts feel like a goldmine, and the thought of being able to drink her fill makes her feel almost dizzy with relief, but coconuts won't last forever. And what then? How much longer?

It is best, Hayley tells herself, firmly, *not to think too far ahead*. She concentrates on putting one foot in front of the other, weakly picking her way through the trees behind Elliot, trying to avoid scratching her legs as they stumble through dense bushes. She has given up slapping at mosquitos, her skin so used to the constant, gnawing itchiness that she barely registers it any more. She claws at her scalp periodically, sunburn and raw-scratched bites combining in a constant ebb of discomfort. Her usually soft hair is becoming stiff with sweat and sand.

Her hot feet feel swollen and angry in unwashed socks, her sneakers starting to rub red blisters on her sore ankle. 'Try. Something. A. Little. Less. Academic,' she mutters, angrily, as they push through the trees. '"Branch out", Mr Curtis said . . . "It'll be fun", he said. I swear, if anyone else ever asks me "what's the worst that could happen?" . . .'

They head west, cutting a perpendicular line from the beach through the trees. There's no sign of May and Jessa, who must be somewhere further south. To the north, she can see the beginning of the rocky incline Elliot had talked about. But they push forwards, heading straight across the island to the other side. After about half an hour of heavy going, the trees begin to thin and Hayley can see the sparkle of the sea in the distance. Their meagre rations of coconut water are a distant memory, her exertions leaving her desperately thirsty again, light-headed and short of breath. The humid air sits heavy in her lungs. Sweat makes her sleeveless white vest cling uncomfortably to her armpits, her thighs chafing under the cheerleading skirt she pulled out of the salvage pile this morning in a pointless attempt to freshen up. She left off the cycling shorts she'd usually wear underneath, because of the heat. Now she wishes she'd put them on.

To her right, Brian staggers to a stop, steadies himself with one hand against a tree trunk, and vomits weakly. Thin bile and spittle dribbles down his front, and a few small chunks of coconut. There's nothing else left in his stomach. He looks at Jason, eyes wide, all his usual clownish vulgarity stripped away. He looks like a scared little kid. Elliot and Jason support him from either side, wrapping their arms around his waist. 'Nearly there,' Elliot encourages him, with surprising tenderness. 'You can do this.' Jason just grunts and heaves Brian forward.

They emerge onto a rockier, wilder beach than the one Hayley has become used to. The sea is rougher here, crashing onto large rocks which scatter the beach and jut out of the water. To Hayley's immense relief, palms grow thick along the shore, thick clusters of smooth green and yellow coconuts hanging beneath the leaves in large, pendulous bunches. At the base of the trees are dozens of brown coconuts in different stages of decay, some rotting away or split, but many smooth and intact, just starting to wrinkle.

Nobody speaks. For the first time since they arrived on the island it's like they are all on the same team. Elliot helps Brian to the foot of a tree, carefully lowering him down in the shade. He sits with him, rubbing his back, while Brian puts his head between his knees, breathing fast. Jason drives the stake firmly into the sand nearby and Hayley roams the beach, selecting the most promising coconuts she can find, delighting in their weight, and depositing them in a pile at Jason's feet. Together, using the stake, the cutting stone and the pencil, he and Elliot work to open them.

When the first coconut is pierced, Elliot hands it wordlessly to Brian, and they all pause, standing motionless across the beach, and watch as he suckles at it like a baby animal, eyes scrunched shut.

Elliot works quickly, handing the coconuts out until everybody is slurping at the sweet, nutty liquid. When they've drunk, they open more and drink again, then claw at the flesh, or split the shells into pieces and scrape at it with their fingernails. For the first time in three days, Hayley feels sated. Now accustomed to gnawing need, her belly feels uncomfortably swollen, though in reality she's eaten only a little.

'Take it slowly,' she warns the others. 'It's going to take our stomachs a while to adjust.'

They sit there on the beach, quietly feeling their bodies resettle, not saying much but each, Hayley imagines, feeling the same soft flood of relief. Only now the clamour of thirst has abated does she realise how noisy it has been, crowding out other thoughts, her stomach and brain consumed with need and panic. She knows how serious their situation still is, but just for this moment she lets herself lie down and breathe, her shoulders sinking into the softly yielding sand, the breeze stroking her cheeks and the soothing splash and pause, splash and pause of the waves hypnotising in its regularity.

It's late afternoon before they stagger back to the wreckage of the plane, their return journey slowed by the heavy coconuts. They carry nine between them. Brian, still staggering weakly along, is unable to manage any at all. Hayley sort of waddles awkwardly with one tucked under each arm. Jason, shirtless, drags his yellow T-shirt like a makeshift kitbag with four coconuts stuffed inside, his muscular stomach gleaming with sweat. Elliot, whippet-like by comparison, balances three in a pyramid under his chin.

May greets them with an excited shriek, clamouring for coconut milk.

And the girls have their own bounty to share. Shannon is with them, picking over a pile of bright fruit, quiet and focused, not looking at Jason, who hovers, looming behind her, as if he isn't sure how to approach. 'There are bushes and trees with more, further inland, but this was all we could carry,' Jessa gasps, between gulps of coconut water. Hayley notices that she is only using one arm, her injured one hanging heavily by her side.

'Look what we found!' May is chirpy, boastful even, gesturing to the tumbling pile of fruit. Its plump sheen and delicate, sweet scent makes Hayley's stomach clench again, and she reaches out an eager hand to grab a small, bright green sphere like a little apple.

'STOP!'

Elliot leaps towards her, knocking it roughly out of her hand. The fruit rolls across the sand, coming to rest innocently a few feet away.

'Ow!' Hayley looks down at her hand and sees a nasty red rash springing up on one side of her palm, angry red dots straining her skin. It itches and burns as if she had plunged her hand into scalding water. 'What the hell?'

'It's a manchineel,' Elliot gasps, breathing heavily. 'A beach apple,' he adds, looking around at the confusion on their faces. 'Wow, you guys really never have been camping, have you?'

He walks over to the fruit and nudges it with his toe, turning it over. There's a thin cut in the skin, a little whitish juice oozing out. 'The sap is poisonous,' he mutters, nodding to Hayley's hand.

She gasps, feeling panic close her throat and fill her lungs. 'It's okay,' Elliot says, kindly, seeing her fear. 'It's just a surface reaction. You didn't eat any, you'll be fine.'

He turns to the other girls. 'Were there any more of these?'

Shannon looks shocked as she shakes her head. 'No, we just brought one back to try, we thought the others looked more promising.' She points towards the fruits, and Elliot stoops to examine them, sorting through the pile carefully.

Hot tears spring to Hayley's eyes. Tears of shock, fear and relief. The horrible sensation of lurching from good news to deadly danger in a split second. Wondering if she'll ever feel properly safe again. Her hand sears, and she squeezes it angrily into a fist, letting the tears prickle her eyelids but brushing them quickly away before anyone else notices.

'I think they're okay,' Elliot is saying. 'I don't know the names of them all but my dad taught me how to recognise anything poisonous when I was a kid. I don't see anything here to worry about.'

So they fall on the pile of fruit greedily, ravenous hands tearing, lips sucking, tongues eagerly licking.

There are luscious mangoes, their honeyed flesh bursting through reddening skin, sticky juice running down fingers and arms. Round, firm guavas with pinkish hearts, their bitter skin yielding reluctantly to insistent teeth and offering a woolly, subtle sweetness within. There's an earth-brown fruit the size of a small avocado with a thin wrinkled skin like a baked potato, its flesh soft yellows bleeding into crimson like a sunrise, its shining black seeds half the length of a thumb. The supple, pulpy flesh tastes sweet and malty and they quickly learn to eat only the softest of the crop after May bites into a firmer fruit but then sucks at her teeth, her mouth dried out by its sour shock. And, strangest of all, a squat green fruit like an overgrown tomato, its skin dark and bruised, a star-shaped circle of leaves standing up around its stalk. They pierce the skin, expecting a firm orange or green flesh, and recoil at the monstrous reality: a blackened, jellyish fruit with seeds the shape of large, shelled walnuts sticking out in a central circle like a sea-monster's teeth, the flesh making an obscene sucking noise as it pulls apart. 'Ugh, it's bad,' Jessa grunts, discarding it in the sand, but each one they open is the same, so, after Elliot has given it a cautious smell, they taste it and find it to be subtly sweet and silky smooth, like a heavy, slightly pumpkin-flavoured custard.

One of the coconuts has sprouted, its bright green shoot just developing leaves. When they open it, instead of water and flesh, it yields a spherical, spongy ball, wrinkled like a yellowish brain, filling the cavity of the shell. It is light and salty-sweet, the spongy texture giving way with a slight crunch.

They sit in a circle on the sand and eat their fill, scooping flesh from skins with plastic spoons left over from the airline meals, dragging teeth across fruit peel to strip the last scraps of flesh.

Suddenly, with a quiet rustling of leaves, a pair of shining eyes is watching them from the edge of the treeline. Hayley sees the creature first, scrambling to her feet with a sharp intake of breath, her mind whirling with tusks and claws and images of charging boars or pouncing wild cats. But as the others spin around in panic it creeps forwards, its pointed, triangular nose followed by a bushy, bulbous body and a fluffy, striped tail.

'A racoon,' Hayley breathes, collapsing back to the ground with relief. 'Here, little guy. You hungry?' She holds out a husk of fruit, expecting the creature to be wary of her, but it darts eagerly forward and seizes the morsel straight from her fingers, sitting up on its back legs to nibble it, black button nose twitching enthusiastically.

They laugh in delight and continue to feed it, though Shannon tuts that they should save their supplies and if they encourage it now, it'll never leave them alone. But even she yields when the little creature darts over to pick up a piece of coconut flesh that's fallen on her knee, gently putting its handlike claw on her leg first and looking up at her as if to ask permission.

There's something deeply reassuring about it, somehow, a surprise that is pleasant instead of horrifying. It gives Hayley a welcome boost to realise that not every secret the island guards is potentially deadly.

After they've eaten their fill, there's an exuberant mood of excess and celebration, and even Elliot, glancing at the glassy still sea, agrees that shelter construction can wait until tomorrow.

They keep the campfire burning and sit around it late into the evening. There is a camaraderie born of success that balloons almost into hysteria. Shannon and Jason, sitting on opposite sides of the campfire, both seem prepared to set aside what happened earlier, or at least to ignore it for the time being.

May teaches everyone a campfire game that involves spotting their foreheads with charcoal and they shriek with laughter as their graffitied faces become increasingly distorted in the twilight.

That night, Hayley is back on the plane again. Everybody is unbearably relaxed. The boys are joking around, throwing Jason's signet ring back and forth between them, crowing and shouting as he stretches to catch it. May and Shannon are painting each other's toenails, legs extended over the empty seat between theirs. And Hayley is screaming at them, shrieking that the plane is about to fall out of the sky, begging them to listen, to do something, but nobody can hear her.

And they can't seem to see the choking smoke that starts to fill the cabin, or smell the bitter reek of petrol. She forces her face in front of Elliot's, tries to shake him by the shoulders, but he just smiles and carries on sketching, sketching. Only Jessa looks worried, frowning at her arm, and mouthing something, but Hayley can't hear her, as the plane begins to shake and shatter around them, the lights flashing and fizzing and they plummet into darkness.

DAY 4

'*What* are you doing?' May tilts her head to one side and squints at Jason and the uneven mess of branches precariously propped next to him in a vague pyramid shape.

'What does it look like?' He huffs, squatting down and stretching up, as he attempts to heave a thick stick onto the top of the pile.

'Like a constipated chicken in an aerobics class,' May answers, without hesitation.

'Ha ha,' Jason pants, then swears loudly as the whole lot collapses around him with a clatter. 'Stupid piece of—' he kicks out, scattering wood everywhere. 'Get over here, Brian, dammit!'

'Tepees are too complicated,' Elliot says, quietly, from behind him. 'It has to be more of a lean-to.'

He waves the others over to a tree near the campfire, where he's propped a sturdy, long, forked branch up against the trunk so it makes a sloping triangle with its right angle at the base of the tree.

'Then prop thinner sticks against the central pole from

65

both sides,' he explains, demonstrating with a few supple, thin branches, balancing them in a triangle shape.

'We can use palm leaves to make a kind of matting on top,' Jessa suggests, seeing where Elliot's plan is going. 'Nothing fancy, but it'll be big enough to keep one person dry if they lie down, and that's better than nothing, especially if it rains or the wind picks up.'

'And we can upgrade to a longhouse once we've been here a few years and had the chance to really hone our skills,' May jokes, but it falls flat.

Elliot makes it look easy, but the others struggle. At first, the sticks slide repeatedly to the floor, but Jessa deftly starts weaving the palm leaves together with her one good hand, clamping the thick, rubbery stalks between her knees, the tip of her tongue poking out between her teeth in concentration. By weaving the ends of each leaf into the next, they create much longer mats, which they layer on top of each other until no sunlight penetrates into the small space below.

'Ooh, pretty,' Brian says, looking over from the shelter he and Jason have put together. 'Glad you guys are focusing on aesthetics, because it's super important for your island survival base to be properly styled.'

He pats the hulking structure Jason is piling with leaves and vines and it falls apart in a crashing tumble of foliage, leaving the others in fits of laughter.

'Hmm.' Jessa gently takes hold of one end of the palm matting, giving it a firm shake. It bends supply, the structure sturdy beneath the intricate weaving. 'You were saying?' She flashes her wide grin, tongue tip poking beneath the gap between her front teeth.

The inquisitive racoon makes another appearance, scuttling boldly down the beach to sit near them, 'Judging the heck out of the boys' construction attempts,' May says. 'He'd have that thing rigged up in no time, wouldn't you, Rocket?' she says, affectionately, throwing him a strip of coconut.

'You've named the raccoon after the Marvel one?' Elliot asks, and May nods. 'Yup. Thought he might come in handy if we need a violent weapons expert who's good with a machine gun.' He grins and shakes his head, as the stripy creature scampers eagerly at May's heels, hoping for more.

Next they collect thinner sticks, stripped of their leaves, and lie them in parallel rows, trying to create a kind of floor matting to lift them above the sand with its flies and irritants. But the sticks roll in all directions when May clambers awkwardly into the first shelter to test it, and she complains that they dig uncomfortably into her ribs and thighs.

So Elliot shows them how to make strong, thin cord from long strands of dead seagrass, pulled in great crackling handfuls from a patch along the beach, where the bushes peter out into scrubby grass. They soak the dead, sun-bleached grass in seawater, then take three strands, twisting and turning one at a time, over and over, until a fine rope begins to emerge. When they near the end of one strand, they twist another into the pattern, carrying on until the 'rope' is almost three metres long before starting a new piece.

When they've got enough rope, Elliot uses it to tie the floor poles into a flexible, flat mat, managing to only roll his eyes very slightly when Jessa exclaims that it looks exactly like a larger version of the one she uses at home to roll sushi.

'Speaking of sushi.' Brian grins, 'who's up for some spear fishing?'

Elliot looks doubtful, but doesn't say anything; Hayley senses he knows there's only so far the other boys will be willing to accept his authority and he's picking his battles. He shrugs. 'It might work, but you'll need something really sharp.'

'Yeah, *obviously*, dickweed.' Brian rolls his eyes and pulls out a chunky stick from behind his back; one of the amateurishly sharpened branches they'd used for 'protection' that first night. The patrols have not resumed since the snoring failure of the first attempt, though everybody has tactfully avoided mentioning it.

Brian has split the tip of the stick and wedged a jagged piece of broken glass from the plane wreck firmly into the crack, making a kind of brutal-looking, primitive spear. Hayley isn't convinced he'll catch anything; the makeshift weapon looks heavy and she doubts Brian has either the delicacy or the patience for spear fishing, but she hopes she's wrong. Fresh fish would make a welcome change.

After two meals, the novelty of an all-fruit diet is already beginning to wear off, the sweetness of the fruits becoming cloying and having an unwelcome effect on their bowels. ('Step away from those bushes,' Jessa had thundered, when she spotted Brian slinking off towards the treeline the previous night, armed with a few sheets of paper torn out of Elliot's sketchbook. 'New rule. Zero toilet activity within a five-hundred-metre radius of the camp,' she'd ordered, sending a ripple of sniggers from around the campfire. 'AND BURY YOUR BUSINESS AFTERWARDS' she shouted, as they shuffled off down the beach.)

'Want to share one?'

Hayley stops plaiting and looks up, half hidden by a clump of seagrass. Jason and Shannon are alone, standing by the nearest lean-to as Jason jerks his thumb towards it and grins at her. She tuts, turns her head away. Her hair falls over her face in a dark cloud, obscuring her expression.

'What's going on, Shan?' Jason asks, his tone more gentle than Hayley has ever heard it. 'I love you, babe, you know I do, why are you being like this?'

'Like scared and panicked and constantly anxious?' she retorts, still not looking at him. 'Gee, I can't imagine.'

'I'm here. You're my girl. You know I'll take care of you like I always do.' Jason moves closer, his hand circling Shannon's waist and caressing her stomach, lifting the black strappy top she's wearing above a white tennis skirt.

'Jason.' Shannon's voice is careful, softer now, but Hayley can see her hand moving beneath his, gently pushing him away. He flinches, and Shannon quickly interlaces her fingers with his. She turns and leans into him briefly. 'It's just a lot, okay. I'm trying not to break down and freak out, same as everyone else.' She takes a tiny step back, away from him. 'And those shelters are built for one and one only. They're tiny.'

He steps closer. 'We could squeeze in ...' She holds up a hand, a fragile barrier between them. 'C'mon, baby, we nearly died, isn't that worth something?' Hayley squints at Shannon.

She seems to be holding her breath. 'I know, I know you want to wait,' Jason wheedles, 'but there's . . . other stuff we can do. No parents, no curfews . . .'

She looks up at him. 'Not things that can be done in a tiny leaf-covered beach shack without getting sand in some extremely uncomfortable places,' she says lightly, quickly side-stepping him. 'Trust me, the only thing worse than being stuck on a desert island would be being stuck on a desert island with a sand-filled vagina.'

'I deserve better than this, Shan, you know I do,' Jason calls after her, a low warning in his voice, as she walks lightly back down the beach towards the others.

And Hayley watches as Jason frowns and sets off to meet Brian, kicking up sand as he goes.

Elliot and the girls work steadily on through the day, heaving the biggest branches into position, propped as securely as possible against a sturdy tree. They learn as they go along that the branches are most stable if driven into the ground, wet sand and mud swathing the bottom of each in the hope it'll shore them up against the wind. They work their way along the beach, a few metres between each shelter, building up the sides of each one with sticks and then covering them with plaited leaves. There's a strange satisfaction in watching each one look a little straighter and sturdier than the one before, the sleeping mats neater and firmer. Jessa and May soon fall into a rhythm, May placing the leaves Jessa has painstakingly plaited, quietly humming as she works. It's the same smooth cooperation that makes them so effective on the team; Jessa providing a stable base as May catapults into a backflip from her shoulders, knowing exactly where her best friend's palms will be as her pointed feet plummet down to land on them. Their connection is so fluid they give the impression of a single body moving to the music. Not that anybody is going to be climbing on Jessa's shoulders any time soon, Hayley realises, watching the stiffness in her movements, the way she automatically twists her body to protect her damaged arm.

Once the trunks are all in position, Elliot disappears to fetch more firewood and so Hayley finds herself paired once more with Shannon, their awkward silence noticeable in contrast with the others' easy companionship. She glances at Shannon between the palm fronds, dark eyebrows drawn together in a sharp frown of concentration, black curls, greasier now, swept back in a ponytail. Hayley wants to ask her about Jason, check if she's okay, but she doesn't know how. It's not like she and Shannon have ever exactly been friends, even over all the weeks of practice and their time on tour.

In the distance behind her, Hayley can see Brian, still lumbering about in the shallows, stabbing excitably at the surf. He shouts something to Jason, who seems to be bent double, examining something near his foot.

She doesn't know what it is, exactly, that makes her feel sort of on edge around Shannon. Maybe it's that she sees more of a reflection of herself in the cheer captain than she'd like to admit. When she first joined the squad, Hayley had a pretty clear idea of what it would be like, or rather, what *they* would be like. And she definitely didn't expect to find that they'd have anything in common.

May, Jessa and Shannon had been on the squad full time since their freshman year, and they weren't so much students who happened to cheer, as cheerleaders who went to school. But if they were the headline-hitting A-listers of Oak Ridge, then Hayley wasn't even on the same page. In fact, she was usually the one who wrote it: on the side lines clutching her notebook while the three of them struck a pose for the camera.

So it was a shock, actually spending time with them. Take Jessa, who seemed so achingly cool from a distance with her funky twists and designer sunglasses, perfect toe-touches and crowd-pleasing splits. Hayley had barely dared to breathe around her when she'd turned up at her first practice. But it had been Jessa who'd approached her, sweeping her into a hug, all 'call me Jessa' and 'don't worry, Shannon's bark is worse than her bite'. Jessa, who only ever drank soda and lime when they partied after the games on tour, who drove everyone safely home and quietly disappeared for two and a half hours on Sunday morning to find a local church while the others were still too hungover to get out of bed.

May had been less accommodating. She'd frowned when Jessa took pity on Hayley at that first practice and Hayley had found herself on the sharp end of May's tongue several times since. But who hadn't? It felt like you had to earn your way into May's good graces, and Hayley was about a decade behind the other girls.

But the biggest surprise was Shannon. It was hard to put her finger on what was so different to Hayley's expectations. Shannon was beautiful, popular and talented up close, just like she seemed from afar. But it was as if she didn't enjoy it, like it was all a job. Shannon didn't just drill the team at practice, she turned up with pages and pages of detailed, complex notes; she'd call at nine o'clock on a Friday night to discuss your dismount; her knowledge of other cheerleading squads and their routines was encyclopaedic. On the first Saturday of the tour, when the team had no games scheduled, she'd insisted on dragging them all to a local competition, silencing May's loud objections with a single *look,* while the guys used their day off to head to a local arcade. Hayley didn't only admire Shannon's conscientious approach, she recognised it. Shannon was just as driven in her pursuit of cheerleading excellence as Hayley was in her quest for an Ivy League entry ticket.

She'd never had any classes with Shannon, but she had tried to interview her once, the year before she joined the squad, on assignment for the school paper. There had been a huge party at someone's parents' beach house, and it had ended badly; the police were called and there were rumours that Chad Maxwell, the star quarterback from a private high school in Tampa, had been taken away in handcuffs. But apparently he was back at his school the next week and nobody at Oak Ridge seemed to be talking much about what had happened. Or at least, when they did, they weren't talking about Chad. They were talking about some girl who'd been working at the party, a waitress. How she'd been drinking on the job . . . caught Chad's eye and seen her chance. How she fancied bringing him down and getting a cut of the family fortune and five minutes of fame in the process. It hadn't worked, though, they said, with satisfaction, as they murmured about it in the oak-panelled hallways between classes. Police must've seen right through her.

So Hayley had pored over Instagram posts from the night until she spotted a familiar figure; Shannon framed in a doorway in a metallic silver halter top, Jason's hand draped around her hip. Hayley had visited the school office with a sob story about needing to lend notes for chem class to her lab partner and left with Shannon's address on a scrap of paper.

She'd figured Shannon would be less likely to give her the brush-off if she turned up on her doorstep. But Shannon hadn't been home when Hayley arrived outside a small, one-storey terraced house in Dillard Park. Cheap peach paint peeled around the windows and a bucket stood beneath a leaking gutter. There was a beat-up old sedan in the driveway and a greying Rottweiler barking half-heartedly at the end of a heavy chain. It occurred to Hayley that she'd never seen Shannon's car, though she'd assumed she had one. She'd only ever seen her hopping lightly into the back of Jason's Jeep, waving to a crowd of friends as they sped off. And, once, Jason reacting furiously as the metal buckle on Shannon's bag scraped his paintwork, shouting something that Hayley couldn't hear as he pulled away, Shannon's back rigid in the passenger seat.

Just as she rechecked the address, the door was opened by a quiet, mousy woman with owl-round glasses and an oversized cardigan clutched tightly around her; Hayley noticed her fingernails were all bitten down to the quick. For a moment something flickered across her face when Hayley said she was from Oak Ridge; Hayley thought it might have been relief, or pleasure, and she gave a little 'Oh', as if it was a surprise. She asked Hayley in to wait and led her into a modest sitting room with slightly faded pink wallpaper and a vase of plastic flowers in the empty fireplace. Hayley had just accepted a glass of iced tea when Shannon swept in, eyes flashing, refusing to comment on the party and insistent that she had no idea what Hayley was talking about. 'So, is that everything?' she'd asked, pointedly, and Hayley had found herself standing on the other side of the front door inside of three minutes, her drink left untouched.

She'd never got any further with the story – some other staffers on the paper poked around a bit without turning anything up except a furiously worded letter from the Maxwells, lawyer threatening a libel suit – but Hayley had been anxious the episode might count against her, when she came to try out for the cheer squad.

She needn't have worried, though. Shannon barked 'Name?' when she entered the audition room, and wrote it down blankly without a flicker of recognition. Like she didn't even remember having met her at all.

And in spite of Shannon's spikiness, in spite of her sharp tongue and stand-offishness, there's a part of Hayley that wishes she could break through that outer shell and just talk to her. Wishes she didn't feel so nervous and tongue-tied around her. Because deep down, she suspects they've got far more in common than Shannon knows.

They'd almost finished seven shelters when Jason and Brian returned disconsolately with only saltwater-soaked clothes, sun-singed shoulders and a sore foot to show for their troubles. 'Stood on a goddamn anemone,' Brian gasps, wobbling on one leg and squeezing his big toe with both hands.

'Not as easy as it looks?' Hayley asks, sympathetically, biting the inside of her cheek to keep from laughing.

Brian looks more and more aggrieved, his face contorting as he hops around. 'That's it, sorry, guys, I've got to pee on it. Look away now or don't say I didn't warn you.'

'Er, Brian?'

He hooks his thumbs into the swimming trunks he's been wearing for the past several days, and bends over, pulling them down in one quick motion.

'BRIAN!' Shannon steps towards him, not exactly averting her eyes. 'That's jellyfish.'

'Huh?'

'Jellyfish. You pee on jellyfish stings. Not anemones.'

'Oh. Well, okay then. Good. I'm gonna—' He pulls his pants up and hobbles off towards the campfire, arms swinging, neck glowing like a beacon.

Later, after picking unenthusiastically at her apportioned fruit and coconut, Hayley finds herself wandering along the beach, feeling the grainy resistance of the sand beneath her heels and listening to the soft swish of the waves. The sun is dipping behind the trees, sending long, waving shadows stretching towards the water's edge. For the first time in four days, she doesn't feel terrified or panicked. The reality of their situation is starting to set in. This morning for the first time she awoke without a fluster of disorientation. And there is space to breathe, now the immediate threat of dehydration and hunger has receded, loosening the squeezing cage of anxiety around her lungs.

Just for a moment, she lets herself follow May's example, and tries to trick herself into believing this is a free holiday; a wild adventure she'll tell her grandchildren about someday. She walks down to the edge of the water, letting it whisper over her bare toes. If she stands very still, with the warm breeze brushing her arms and the salt tang of the air on her tongue, she can almost imagine herself on a beach break, about to head back to the fluffy towels and crisp white sheets of an air-conditioned hotel room.

'Want to help?' Elliot has followed her down the beach, a battered backpack slung over one shoulder, a slender stick grasped in his left hand. He settles himself in the sand, pulling somebody's phone out of the backpack. For a moment, her heart jumps. Has he found a way to rig up the phone somehow, to send an emergency call? If anyone could, it would surely be Elliot. But the phone is dead, the screen dull and lifeless.

'E.T. phone home?' she asks, lightly, trying to ignore the lurch of disappointment.

'Better.' He grins, pulling the phone case open with his fingernails and starting to gently separate its internal components. 'E.T. catch fish.'

She watches closely as he peels apart the circuitry inside; the complex web of electronics that can power a thousand tasks in the palm of her hand at home, and yet lies completely flat and useless here. First, Elliot removes a mirror about the size of a credit card, which he turns over thoughtfully in his palm and then slips into his pocket. Next, he takes out a dark green circuit board, criss-crossed with silver lines like a tiny map and littered with gold and silver dots. 'It's very soft,' he explains, holding the thin wafer of metal delicately between his thumb and forefinger and gently scraping it back and forth against a hard stone. One corner quickly wears down and then another, until a knife-sharp, metal arrowhead rests gently in his palm. He pulls a pair of white headphones from the backpack and splits open their plastic casing, separating the fine, coppery wires inside. Taking a single, fragile strand, he binds the blade tightly to the long, thin stick.

'You really know your stuff, don't you?'

He shrugs. 'I've really been on that many camping holidays. But if you want to hear about shopping centres in Dubai or diving the Great Barrier Reef, you might want to ask one of the others.' He checks himself, perhaps realising how bitter he sounds. 'Want to try your luck?' He smiles at Hayley and hands her the spear; she tries not to notice the brush of his fingers against hers, and together they wade into the shallow water.

The sea rests motionless in that long, lazy, moment when late afternoon turns imperceptibly to early evening. The water is turquoise, so still that they can see the sun shining on the seabed like a silver net, irregular loops shifting and sliding across the sand. She watches their toes, sand seeping up between them to anchor their feet in position, sucking them into the fabric of the place. There's an exhilaration about feeling rooted in, a closeness to the sensations of the natural world that Hayley has never experienced before.

A silver flash ripples beneath the surface, breaking her chain of thought. It's gone before she can draw breath, but there's another, and another – a shoal of tinfoil scraps, darting and hesitating, pouring themselves between rocks and soaring upwards again like liquid smoke. They move as a single body, iron filings drawn by the same magnet, moving so swiftly that it seems impossible she could ever catch one. But she crouches, grips the spear tightly in her right hand, jabs it through the water as suddenly and quickly as she can, aiming wildly not at an individual fish but at the middle of the shoal itself. A silver firework explodes in the water, her hand at its epicentre; she stands, frozen, as the fish vanish in all directions. She draws back her arm. Nothing. The spear is empty, the tip clean.

They try again and again, standing stock still in the water, waiting until the fish swarm confidently around them before pouncing, holding the tip of the arrow to the very surface of the water to bring it as close as possible. Still, nothing. The fish are too fast, or the arrow too blunt. Elliot clicks his tongue.

'Why do you think nobody has found us yet?' Hayley asks, resting the spear in her hand as she waits for the fish to settle again.

Elliot sighs. 'There could be a million reasons. It wasn't a big, commercial flight with hundreds of passengers on board. Maybe there are fewer resources available to look for a private jet than the kind of massive searches when a big airliner goes down. Maybe they are looking, but there's bad weather somewhere affecting the search. My best guess is that whatever went wrong with the plane killed its communication systems and they have no idea where to start. Maybe the pilot flew off course to try and correct the problem and we're not where we should have been.'

'They could be looking in completely the wrong place,' Hayley whispers, horrified. But part of her has grimly noted the passing days and is not so surprised.

'That's not the worst of it,' Elliot says, quietly, glancing back towards the shore, where the others are starting to build up the fire, adding extra sticks in anticipation of nightfall.

'What?' Hayley asks, flatly.

'What if they've found the other part of the plane?' Elliot whispers, even though they are much too far away for anybody else to overhear. 'What if they've found it and it's completely mangled, or floating in the middle of nowhere, and maybe Erickson and the pilot . . . you know . . . and they assume the rest of us must be dead too?'

'You mean they might have given up looking altogether?'

'I don't know,' Elliot says, suddenly sounding weary and irritated. 'I don't have all the answers, okay? It's just a thought I had, that's all. But there's no point freaking everyone out.'

'Mind if I try?'

It's Jessa, standing next to the abandoned backpack with the remaining strands of copper wire in her good hand. She wades in to meet them, uncurls the fist of her injured arm to reveal a metal ring pull, taken from a drinks can. She has snapped one side of the metal loop, filed it down on a stone into a sharp point and bent it outwards slightly.

'A fishhook.' Hayley grins, impressed, grateful for Jessa's interruption, happy to push the conversation with Elliot aside.

Elliot stumbles sideways in the water as Jessa approaches, splashing awkwardly, water slopping up his front.

'I'll see you later,' he mumbles, and Hayley watches him go. For a moment, she thinks she sees disappointment flicker over Jessa's face, but she's soon smiling again, twisting the strands of copper wire together to create a single line and threading it through the ring pull.

'How did you—'

'My dad's taken me fishing every summer since I was seven. Elliot's not the only scout in the group you know,' Jessa says quietly, pulling a handful of coconut scraps from her pocket and delicately piercing one with the hook, wincing a little as she uses her injured arm. 'One year I forgot my rod and he showed me this. I'd have thought of it sooner but I was –' she glances down at her arm – 'distracted.'

She drops the hook into the water and gently pays out the wire, letting it trail deeper. Almost immediately, the wire goes taut, a rippling circle skidding over the surface of the water as something beneath pulls it from side to side. Jessa tugs on the wire and the hook flies up to break the surface, glinting emptily, the coconut gone. 'Cheeky nibbler,' she murmurs, spearing another piece of coconut and releasing the hook again. They watch the wire drift lazily with the sea's gentle movements, feeling the cool silk of the water caressing their calves. The fierce heat of the day has gone, replaced by a gentle, soothing warmth. Nothing happens.

Jessa frowns silently and Hayley sees her eyes flick down to her arm again. The swelling has subsided around her shoulder, but it's tightly strapped to her chest with a neon orange chiffon scarf she remembers May wearing on the last night of the tour, the deep cuts bulkily swathed in a bandage Jason found in the single first-aid kit to have survived the crash.

'Jessa,' Hayley asks, gently, 'is your arm okay?'

'It's fine,' she says quickly, 'I'm fine.'

Suddenly there's another jerk on the fishing line, and this time Jessa gently releases her grip, feeding more out instead of yanking it in, patiently waiting as the surface of the water seethes and froths. Another tug catches her off guard, the wire bumping against her injured arm and she lets out a single, high-pitched yelp of pain.

'Can I?' Hayley asks, and Jessa hands her the wire, putting one hand on top of hers.

'Slowly, slowly,' she whispers. Hayley gently starts to wind the line in, wrapping it around her left hand like a bobbin. She can feel resistance, something pulling determinedly in the opposite direction. It reminds her of flying a kite on the beach with her dad, running into the wind, feeling the pressure of the string like a wild thing pulsing in her hands.

With a little splash, the end of the line emerges from the water, a glittering peacock-blue fish the length of her hand twisting and whirling on the end. Hayley gasps and Jessa lets out a loud yell of triumph.

Beginner's luck.' She smiles, modestly, as they splash back across the shallows to deposit the fish in the backpack.

'It's weird,' Jessa says, quietly, glancing up. 'Everything's different somehow.' She laughs. 'I mean, obviously everything's different, we're stranded on a desert island, but—' she trails off.

'I know what you mean,' Hayley says. 'It's not just every*thing* that's different, it's every*one*.'

'Yeah,' Jessa agrees thoughtfully. 'I never thought I'd see the day that Shannon and Jason would be anything less than rock solid but now . . . who knows?'

'They've never argued before?' Hayley asks, curiously.

'Oh sure, they've fought, but not like this. Jason would fill the changing room with flowers, or he'd write some cheesy poem about Shannon and read it over the Tannoy while we were in the gym, or come in and sweep her off her feet in the middle of practice in front of everyone and it would always blow over, you know? She'd *have* to forgive him. But it's different here. She's different. And he is. It's like your parents falling out or something.'

'Do you know what started it?' Hayley asks.

'I wonder,' Jessa starts, almost whispering, 'if it's to do with how Shannon was at the party—'

'I doubt it.' May is suddenly there behind them, wading through the shallows, peering curiously at the makeshift fishing line. 'It wasn't a big deal, and I don't think Jason even saw, anyway.'

'Not a big deal?' Jessa sucks air through her teeth. 'I've never seen Shannon like that. She was wild. I wonder what got into her?'

May looks briefly unnerved, or maybe it's just the coldness of the water, but at that moment the line jerks again, then again and again in quick succession. The conversation is quickly forgotten as they rush triumphantly back to the shore with their treasure glittering in the old backpack.

While the others argue about how to prepare the fish, with May insisting they let it die 'naturally', and Elliot begging her to let him bash its head quickly on a rock, Hayley sits back, pleased to have been useful but wary. For the first time, today it feels like there is solid ground beneath them – food, water and shelter – but behind it, she knows instinctively that something is very wrong. And not just the pathetic amount of tiny fish to share between seven people and the terrible fear of not being found. Maybe it's just the pressure of the situation, but she has a nagging feeling that there's more to it than that. There's something 'off' about the fabric of the whole group. Like a jigsaw where all the pieces have been slightly reshaped and none of them fit together any more.

DAY 5

By the fifth day, Hayley's skin has darkened to a deep tan and her body is covered in bites, scratches and scrapes.

It's uncomfortably humid inside her shelter, the armfuls of leaves she spread to soften her sleeping mat adding an unpleasantly musty scent to the already clogged air. Shifting her body weight, she's uncomfortably aware of the smell of her own sweat, the stale sweetness that returns no matter how often she washes in seawater. Not that everyone is so concerned with hygiene: Brian can now be smelled from six feet away, as May disgustedly pointed out to him at dinner last night. ('All I'm saying is, you either need to wash, or sit downwind.')

When Hayley wriggles out onto the beach it doesn't offer much relief; her lungs feel hot and thick even outside, like they're full of cotton wool.

Shading her eyes with her hand, she looks out towards the sea. Elliot cuts a lonely figure, standing knee-deep in the water, silhouetted like a statue as he patiently pursues more fish. In the distance, she can just see May's head bobbing along as she swims the length of the island, a morning ritual she claims is keeping her sane.

The fish they caught last night were a success, of sorts, cooked over the fire on a sharp stick, eager fingertips singed as they scraped scales off soft white flakes and picked minute translucent bones from between their teeth. But there was barely a taste for each of them before the fish were gone, the heads and tails sizzling and spitting in the embers.

By mid-morning, they've run out of coconut water again, the bottles empty and the shallow pit they've dug in the shade of the trees to keep a supply of fresh coconuts cool emptied. Hayley hasn't kept track of how many they've consumed, and she didn't take an exact count of how many were scattered at the foot of the trees on the western coast of the island. But the supply isn't infinite, and as one long, hot day stretches into another, they've been getting through them fast.

'We're going on a coconut run,' Brian calls to nobody in particular as Jason charges into the trees. 'Going to try and get some of the green ones down, Elliot says they'll have more milk inside.' He circles his hands around his mouth, shouting through them like a loudspeaker. 'Yo, Elliot!' He gestures towards the other side of the island. 'Come show us what we're looking for.'

'But—' Shannon waves a hand dismissively as they disappear without waiting to hear what she had to say. 'Your funeral,' she mutters, going back to the damp grass she is carefully twisting into a new length of twine.

When she's finished, she ties one end to the top of the tall stake they've kept by the fire to split coconuts, and the other end to one of the closest of the palm trees, creating a washing line to hang up some sodden clothes she's rinsed in the sea.

'Any of the boys help with that?' May asks as she towels her hair with a dry T-shirt, rolling her eyes when Shannon quietly shakes her head and starts spreading the clothes out on the line.

The row of dangling shirts and pants hems the camp in neatly, creating a wall on the south side. To the west, the treeline is a few metres away, providing a natural windbreak and helping to keep the fire from being blown out. They've built up the fireplace with bigger stones, and around it odd tree stumps, rocks and airplane seat cushions have been placed in a rough circle, providing a focal point where they can gather for food and sit in the evenings.

A pair of overhead lockers that had been thrown clear of the plane has been dragged nearer to the fire, providing a largely rainproof makeshift cupboard. One side is filled with dry clothes and blankets, the other stacked with firewood.

When the tide is at its highest, the waves lap at the sand about twenty-five yards from the camp, and when it's low, the beach stretches out in a molten gold flood, the water so far away you almost can't see it at all. A little distance to the south, and close to the tideline, the twisted wreck of the plane remains, but it has become almost normal to them. In less than a week, it has morphed from a shocking reminder of their situation to a familiar landmark that Hayley almost doesn't notice any more.

The sleeping shelters stretch out in a line to either side of the camp, four for the girls on one side and three for the boys on the other, about ten yards between them, each leaning up against a sturdy palm trunk.

May and Jessa are sitting in the shade, both wearing black yoga pants and spaghetti strap tops, using white shells and stones rubbed in black soot from the fire to play backgammon on a board scraped into the sand with sticks.

'Double six,' May gloats, unfolding two scraps of paper she's picked out of the shoe that holds their makeshift dice.

'Oh really? Again?' Jessa narrows her eyes suspiciously while May flashes her an angelic smile and skips two of her shells to safety.

'How many sixes are in there, exactly?' Jessa asks, teasingly, and May quickly changes the subject.

'Does anyone else have their period? Mine's due soon and I have literally nothing to use.'

'Sorry,' Shannon says. 'I had tampons in my bag, but it hasn't turned up in the stuff from the crash.' The others shake their heads too.

'I *cannot* deal with *that* here,' May declares, dramatically. 'We are going to have to get rescued in the next . . .' she counts quickly on her fingers . . . 'nine days or less. We just have to. It's non-negotiable.'

'Right,' says Shannon drily. 'Because Jessa's possibly infected arm can wait, but God forbid we should still be here when your Aunt Flo arrives.'

'It's getting better, I think,' Jessa interrupts, with forced brightness. She flashes a smile that doesn't come close to her eyes. 'I think it's much better than it was, actually.' She turns to May, abruptly returning the focus to her best friend. 'We'll manage something, sweetie. Rags, or whatever. That's what they used to do in the old days.'

'Oh good. I'll look forward to it.' May pulls a face.

Jessa leans over to take the shoe and gasps, her face twisting in pain.

'Jessa!' May leaps to her side, shells and stones scattering beneath her feet.

'It's nothing, it's nothing.' But Jessa's breathing is heavy and she's biting down hard on her lower lip.

'Show us,' Shannon commands, and Jessa reluctantly loosens the scarf sling, groaning as her arm droops into her lap. Gingerly, she begins to unwrap the bandage, and as the layers peel back it darkens with a wet, seeping liquid. Hayley's gut twists as Jessa finally, delicately lifts the last layer from her arm, revealing a slick, pulpy mess that reminds her sickeningly of the fruit she ate for breakfast.

'Jessa!' May gasps again, and Jessa swallows hard.

'It's not as bad as it looks,' she says, shakily.

'Why didn't you say something sooner?' Shannon sounds almost irritated, but Hayley recognises the tone; it's the same disguised panic that crept into her voice when Coach Robinson cancelled a Saturday practice at the last minute because the gym roof was leaking; the tone that creeps in when something happens that is outside of Shannon's control.

'Hayley,' she barks, 'get the first-aid kit.' There's not much left of it: a battered red case that Jason dragged out from under the twisted metal remains of one of the plane seats. They've already used one of the bandages, but there's a tube of ointment, some gauze and plasters.

'Iodine, get the iodine,' Shannon snaps, and Hayley rummages through the box until she finds a small, shattered bottle at the bottom, shards of glass floating in a sticky pool of dark ochre.

'It's broken,' she whispers, helplessly.

'We need something else then,' May says, smiling reassuringly at Jessa, her voice about two notes higher than usual. 'Something else that's a disinfectant.' She casts around wildly. 'Alcohol,' she shouts. 'How many cop shows have you seen where they pour vodka into a wound when they can't get to a hospital?'

'Can I just say I am *not* reassured by how many of our survival attempts on this island have been guided by stuff people have seen on TV?' Jessa gasps, with a weak smile, though her teeth are gritted against the pain.

'It's actually not a bad idea,' Shannon says. 'We need to clean out that wound.' But they can't find any alcohol in the supplies Jason pulled out of the plane, supplies that have dwindled to some pieces of metal and plastic trays, a fire extinguisher and random plastic cutlery, piled neatly next to the overhead locker cupboard.

'There has to be something they missed,' Hayley says, cautiously approaching the metal carcass of the jet. 'What kind of a plane doesn't have those miniature bottles of spirits on board somewhere?'

She has to bend double to get inside, wriggling between jagged edges and deformed, unrecognisable shapes. She edges forwards on her knees, passing a pile of smashed glass, long, triangular shards sticking into the sand at odd angles like peanut brittle. And she has to stop for a moment, to let the familiar clench of pain pass, to clear her head of the image of making peanut brittle with her mom in a cosy, steamed-up kitchen, laughing more and more hysterically as it completely failed to set and started bubbling uncontrollably over the stove top.

Unclench. Breathe. Don't remember.

Almost everything that was inside the plane has already been stripped out. The one remaining overhead locker yawns empty, its door hanging wildly off a single hinge. Hayley reaches the tail, where the food would have been stored. A metal trolley lies on its side, its drawers lolling out like dead tongues, emptied of food trays by Jason. But there's another drawer at the top, a locked drawer that doesn't look as if it's been touched. Hayley pulls at the metal handle: something rattles inside.

With some difficulty, unable fully to turn around in the cramped space, she looks around until she finds a loose, thin piece of metal. She slides it into the narrow slit at the top of the drawer and begins to wiggle it back and forth, forcing the flimsy lock. The drawer judders open, revealing rows of shining glass bottles with brightly coloured labels and metal caps. 'Bingo,' she calls, grabbing a handful.

Jessa screams when Shannon pours the vodka into her wound. She can't help it. Her lips curl back from her teeth and tears spring to her eyes as her fingernails dig deep into May's hand.

The liquid runs black, then brown, then yellow, then red, like a grotesque rainbow.

'That's cleaned some of it out at least,' Shannon says, apologetically. She pours another bottle over her own fingers to clean them, then gently dabs ointment into the wound, pausing each time Jessa flinches. Then she carefully dresses it with the remaining clean bandage.

'We need to get you a drink,' Shannon says firmly. 'The boys should have been back with the coconuts by now. I'd say they've had long enough to attempt it on their own. Shall we?'

'Not you, sweetie,' May says firmly, as Jessa tries to get to her feet. She gently ties the orange sling back around her best friend's arm. 'You stay here and try to rest.'

'Don't tell the guys,' Jessa whispers, as they leave. 'They're not strong enough to take it. They think they are, but . . .' She sighs and closes her eyes.

The boys, when they reach the other side of the island, are a sorry sight. Brian is sitting in the sand, panting, nursing what looks like a split fingernail. Jason is clinging a few feet up the trunk of a palm tree, sweat beading his forehead, cheeks puffed, desperately clamping his knees together and pushing himself up a few inches only to slide back down several inches more. And Elliot is stripped to the waist, trying unsuccessfully to use his T-shirt as a makeshift catapult, flinging rocks towards the green coconuts clustered twelve feet above him, his missiles going nowhere near his targets but landing dangerously close to the others.

'Knock it off,' Brian shouts, angrily, as one of the stones whistles past his elbow. They're so wrapped up in their exertions that they don't even hear the girls emerging from the trees.

May takes in the scene and starts to laugh, a wicked, infectious cackle that shakes her whole body.

Hayley is starting to think that each person on the island has a 'tell', like in a game of poker. Whenever anyone mentions how unlikely they are to be rescued, Jessa's fingers worry at the little cross around her neck, without her even seeming to realise it. Jason goes quiet at first when he's worried, but then his silence builds up and builds up inside him until it bursts out in a fit of expletives, usually aimed at Elliot. Shannon becomes hypercritical, her sarcasm sailing off the charts. Elliot withdraws, back into his familiar, silent shell. Brian seems to swell, somehow, wrestling whole saplings out of the ground and pounding away at the coconut stake like he can smash his feelings away. And when May is scared, she becomes exuberant, a sparkling, bubbling stream of songs and giggles.

'It won't be so funny when you don't have anything to drink tonight,' Jason says, his low voice angry.

'I'm sorry,' May gasps, trying to catch her breath, 'I'm sorry. But it's just . . . has it not occurred to any of you guys that you have a group of people here with the exact skillset you need?'

'What are you talking about?' Jason slides irritably down from the trunk, rubbing his grazed palms.

Shannon cracks her knuckles and takes a deep breath. She flicks up her head, smiles widely and strikes a pose, beneath the palm tree, one arm in the air, the other hand jauntily on her hip. 'Go, go, Ridge Raptors, go,' she chants, and the boys look at her like she's crazy, but Hayley suddenly sees what she's doing and the same realisation is dawning on May's face too as she moves to stand behind her captain.

'Go, team, go! Get into formation!'

And as the guys watch, Hayley moves smoothly, lining herself up directly in front of Shannon, her feet planted shoulder-width apart, knees slightly bent, hands firmly on thighs. Ready and braced for the impact as Shannon leaps lightly up behind her, planting one bare foot in the crease at the back of her knee, the next in the small of her back and then pushing herself deftly up, placing first one and then the other foot on Hayley's shoulders.

'Steady now,' Shannon whispers, and Hayley grips the top of Shannon's calves as they both focus carefully on a spot out in front of them, thinking of nothing but balance, as May scampers, catlike, up Hayley's back, clasping Shannon's hands, using Hayley's wrist as a stepping-stone and finally emerges on Shannon's shoulders, straightening carefully, triumphantly to her full height, her bare toes curled in a tight grip.

Hayley hears the wild applause of the crowd rushing in her ears, feels the tingling sense of elation she had when they'd pulled off this formation at the end of the last game of the tour. They'd finished out the trip at Duke's Academy, a prestigious Texas private school packed with the children of elite oil oligarchs and banking bosses. It was a rush, that last game. They were five points behind coming into the last quarter, and Hayley saw the strained looks on the boys' faces as Erickson brought them in for the huddle. Sweat dripped from Elliot's face, Erickson was shouting something, his clenched fist smacking into his palm, Jason animated beside him. Shannon was vibrating in front of Hayley, her face alight with intense excitement, outlining their final routine, urging them to give it everything they had.

She felt the pressure ramp up as the whistle blew, forcing her high kick higher than she'd ever managed before, the roar of the crowd whirling her out of her handspring as Brian made a basket, followed quickly by a free throw from Elliot, closing the gap between the teams to just two points. And as she felt Shannon's toes dig into the back of her knee, as the last moments of the game ticked away on the clock, Jason took a long shot from outside the three-point arc, the ball sailing past May as she straightened on top of Shannon's shoulders, the triumphant climax of the routine perfectly coinciding with the ball swishing lightly through the net and winning them the game.

A wide grin spread across her face as the crowd noise surrounded her like a wave, aware of the tension in her every muscle as she strained to keep perfectly still. She felt better than she ever could have imagined this could make her feel. And as May and Shannon backflipped smoothly down to land, as they were enveloped in a chaotic, elated scrum of hugs and back-slapping and sweaty necks, she was, for a moment, one of the squad.

That had been when one of the Duke cheerleaders, a tall, pretty girl with curly red hair, had come over to congratulate them and invite them to a party at her house. 'To celebrate your last night on tour,' she'd said, with a wink. And Brian had laughed, saying something gross about how much action he could fit into one night, and one of the Duke players shrieked that it would be wild, and Shannon laughed, Jason suddenly there with his arm around her shoulders, his lips on her mouth. Meanwhile, Hayley's feeling of lightness and excitement quickly hardened into the usual foreboding that preceded any major social gathering – especially a house party with strangers – and she mentally flicked through underwhelming outfit combinations, already planning her excuses for slipping away early.

May lurches suddenly to the left, wrenching Hayley back to the present. 'OW! Careful!' Shannon shouts crossly from above.

'Sorry, mosquito!' May gently prods at the bunch of coconuts now immediately in front of her and frowns. 'Well, are you all just going to stand there *gawping* or is somebody going to pass me something to cut them down with?'

Elliot hands the cutting stone over wordlessly, Hayley passing it without looking to Shannon, who reaches up to May, who bends slowly down to get it, one arm out wide for balance.

'Well, we did not think of that,' Brian mutters, sheepishly, as May begins to cut delicately through the stalk of the first coconut.

'Catch!' She tosses it in Elliot's direction and he jumps forward, arms outstretched.

The young coconuts are different: their husks are shinier and tougher, and opening them is harder work. It takes Brian almost half an hour of carving and swearing at one before he finally reaches the hairy brown shell inside. But it's worth the effort. The meat of these coconuts is less developed, a jelly-like layer almost like underboiled egg whites that clings to the tongue with a rubbery wobble. 'It's like sick flavour blancmange,' Brian whinges, letting it drip out of his mouth into the sand. But there's at least twice as much water inside these nuts, its taste far sweeter and fresher than what they've become used to. They won't need to worry about thirst again, at least not for a few days.

It's ironic, really, that the rain clouds don't begin to gather until they arrive back at camp with the fresh coconuts. Elliot is already working on the shelters, adding extra layers of leaves and even tucking in pieces of plastic and metal from the plane here and there in an effort to make them waterproof.

The sky is swollen. Greys quickly deepen to heavy, hanging purples and angry browns, reminding Hayley unpleasantly of the wound in Jessa's arm.

But the rain doesn't come. They busy themselves, finding extra clothes for warmth, moving their supply of fresh fruit and remaining equipment into the shell of the plane to keep it dry. They move quickly, not talking much. There's something in the air, a kind of electric tension, that makes Hayley feel on edge, like she's holding her breath, waiting for something awful to happen.

Brian and Shannon disappear into the treeline, hurrying to find as much wood as they can, planning to stash some in the shell of the plane. Jason returns a few minutes later with more palm leaves for the shelters, his eyes darting round immediately, calculating, counting.

'Where's Shannon?' he barks, and when Hayley tells him she's gone to fetch wood with Brian, Jason disappears after them at a loping run. They re-emerge shortly afterwards, Brian's arms piled with wood, Jason's hand vice-like around Shannon's.

'Doesn't want her to be alone even for a moment in this place,' Jessa whispers to Hayley, with an admiring sigh, as if this only confirms Jason's perfect boyfriend credentials. But Hayley, studying the white tips of Shannon's fingers, is not so sure.

When there's nothing left to do, Hayley sits in the sand at the mouth of her sleeping shelter, scooping up handfuls then letting the grains trickle through her fingers. The methodical, repetitive movement helps her to feel anchored, slowing her racing heartbeat and brain. May is humming under her breath the same few notes over and over, a little ditty that makes the hairs on Hayley's arms stand on end. Not because there's anything about the tune, particularly, but because she's heard it before. An innocent trill of notes that might sound absent minded, coming from someone else, but that means something completely different when it's May.

It was about half an hour after that last triumphant game had ended, and the guest-team changing rooms were cloudy with steam as some of the girls finished up their showers. Shannon was dressed already and standing at the mirror, drawing on cherry-red lipliner with a perfectly steady hand. Behind her, May's wet hair swept almost to the floor as she towelled it, head hanging down between her legs. Hayley was tying her shoelace when Shannon blotted her lips and said: 'I asked

Coach Robinson to film us through the last quarter so we can do a quick play-by-play – pick up our mistakes and look at where we can tighten up that finale routine. I'll see you all in my hotel room in thirty minutes.'

May snorted, still rubbing vigorously with her towel. 'Good one, Shannon,' her voice came, slightly muffled. 'Like you're going to drill us on the last night of the tour.'

Shannon's gaze was icy in the mirror. 'We need to look at it now while it's fresh in our minds. This is about putting us in the strongest possible position going into next semester's competitions.'

'Hmm,' May mused, a sarcastic edge to her voice. 'What's going to put a team in the strongest position to win ... a chance to let their hair down and relax with a well-earned night off, or an insanely intense captain who never gives anyone the chance to recharge?' She snapped upright, tousled damp hair falling around her flushed cheeks.

'Don't worry, May, you'll still make it to your precious party on time.'

'Well, I'd like time to get ready as well. And you'll need ...' May glanced at the clock, pretending to do a calculation in her head. 'I'd say a good two hours at least to remove the stick from your ass.'

'C'mon, May.' Jessa's voice was soothing, ever the peacemaker, as she appeared between them. 'We've got plenty of time to do both, it won't take more than half an hour to go through the tape, right, Shannon?'

'I guess we can do it quickly,' Shannon assented, smiling gratefully at Jessa. And Hayley watched irritation flash across

May's face as she bit her lip and said nothing, wondering if it was really the half hour that bothered her or the fact that Jessa took Shannon's side against hers. May started yanking a comb through the tangles in her wet hair, humming a trio of notes over and over again.

They're still waiting for the storm when they hear the engine. At first, Hayley thinks it's the thunder arriving, a distant, stuttering purr that comes and goes. Or the sea; the sound of the waves crashing more wildly as the wind starts to whip them higher. But it gets louder, until it's unmistakeable. A plane, or a helicopter, perhaps very close, perhaps quite far away – it's impossible to tell between the rising wind and the thick, grey clouds.

'It's a plane! It's a fucking plane!' Jason laughs maniacally, screaming 'I fucking told you! I fucking told you so!' at no one in particular.

Jessa's face is flooded with relief, tears pooling quietly in the corners of her eyes. But Elliot looks worried.

'I think it's coming from the north-west,' he says, in a low voice, his eyes on Jessa.

'What does that mean?' Hayley asks him, quietly.

'They might not see the SOS. And the fire's almost out.'

Hayley looks at the fire. Nobody has fed it for hours. It's only white powder and scattered ashes, not a single wisp of smoke rising up into the pregnant air.

'Can we stoke it up?'

'Not fast enough.'

Jason has overheard; the elation on his face quickly turns to consternation, then to anger.

'Build it. Build the fire up NOW. Get it smoking,' he yells, assuming the same commanding tone he uses to bark out plays on the court, a tone nobody argues with.

But Elliot spreads his hands.

'I can't. There isn't time.'

'You idiot. You fucking idiot.' Jason is face-to-face with Elliot, his chest puffed out, his whole body bristling with rage. 'You think you're such a smart little boy scout with your clever water-bottle tricks and your little fishing lines? But when we actually need a fire, where the fuck are you?'

The engine is getting louder, throbbing like a physical presence in the air around them.

'What good are you?' Jason's eyes are aflame, spittle flying into Elliot's stricken face. 'You think you're such a big man, taking over, seizing control, eh? But you can't even keep your stupid campfire burning, you asshole.'

'We have to do something,' Jessa gasps, desperately.

They stand there, frozen, staring up at the sky. Hayley is caught by a frenzied desire to start throwing things in the air, as if she could possibly throw anything high enough to catch the attention of a pilot, even in a low-flying plane.

Elliot is patting his pockets, frantically searching for something. He pulls out the mirror he extricated from the phone yesterday.

'We can signal them!' he yells, setting off at a run, crashing into the trees. 'If we can get to high enough ground, we can signal them.'

And after a split second, the others throw themselves after him.

Elliot runs without looking back. He turns sharply to the right, pushing through the trees, and for the first time Hayley approaches the steep incline where the ground rises up into a kind of hill, the trees becoming slightly sparser. They are halfway up when the rain starts, fat drops that penetrate Hayley's clothes and soak her hair, somehow wetter than any rain she has felt before. The noise is louder at the top of the hill, a motorised roar that sounds as if it must be directly above them, but all Hayley can see are rolling black clouds, the raindrops whizzing down faster now, stinging her eyes when she tries to spot the plane.

Elliot has the mirror in his palm, tilting it this way and that, but Hayley can see that it's useless, there's no sun left to reflect, no glinting beam to force whoever is flying above to take notice of them. The clouds are so thick, hanging so close as if weighed down by the weight of water, she would be surprised if the pilot even realised there was an island below at all. What might have been left of the sunset has been swallowed up completely, dark strangling the island faster and more completely than it ever has before.

Still Elliot strains his arms out, holding the useless mirror above his head like a shield. And even though the others can see it's useless too, they crowd around him, the ground in front of their feet falling away in a sharp twenty-foot drop. They screech and wave their arms shamelessly, voices grating hoarse in desperation, hands stretched up to what little moonlight penetrates the clouds. They are drowning, screaming their fear at the dark, bruised sky.

*

Nobody could say, later, exactly how it happened, or even at what moment, except that one minute they were hanging there, suspended in the clammy, hot and cold air with the rain slicing sheets around them, their own harsh voices filling each other's ears. And the next moment, Elliot was falling, his body U-shaped as his arms and legs floated up towards them, plummeting in slow motion into the welcoming jaws of the bushes and rocks below.

DAY 6

It's not actually as easy to carry a body as you might expect.

Just disentangling Elliot from the greedy claws of the bushes that ensnared him and yanking him back up the rocks takes what feels like hours. Hayley shudders at the unwelcome thought that the island seems glad to have claimed him, that it doesn't want to give him up without a fight. Like it demands a blood sacrifice for their trespass there, a price to pay for the vines they've trampled and trees they've torn, the unwanted footprints they've left in the sand.

The battered face of Elliot's wristwatch, now hanging limp above his splayed fingers, shows that it's after midnight before they begin the dejected journey back to the camp.

First, they try carrying him slung between them like a sack of potatoes, four of them taking a limb each, bumping him roughly along the ground when their grip slips. But it's awkward and impractical to move that way. The thick undergrowth and narrow spaces between bushes and trees make it hard to travel two abreast, let alone with an extra person hanging immobile in between. So Brian and Jason start taking it in turns to heave Elliot over their shoulders, clutching tightly to the backs of his thighs, his head hanging limply down behind. The group spreads listlessly out in a scattered, dejected procession: Shannon silent and taut; Jason spitting out swearwords like he's releasing pressure from a gasket; May singing again, a perky, flippant pop song about embracing your booty, starting again from the beginning every time she runs out of notes as if she's scared to stop; Brian has gone very quiet, his head hanging low, his breath coming in short, jagged gasps. Nobody speaks about the plane. Hayley moves close to Jessa and realises she is repeating a prayer over and over under her breath, saying the words so fast Hayley can't even make them out.

'Shut up, Jessa. That's not going to make any difference,' May snaps at her, irritably, and Hayley sees Jessa flinch and recoil, hurt painted across her face.

'Well, Meghan Trainor's not about to swoop in and save us either,' she replies, with uncharacteristic anger. 'But I don't see you keeping your mouth shut.'

'It can't be good for him,' Hayley frets, watching Elliot's cheek bashing unceremoniously against Jason's back. Following closely behind, she can hear Jason's heavy, rasping breathing. Elliot's face looks serene and somehow innocent, mouth slightly open so she can see the glistening shell pink of his inside lip.

'He's lucky to be alive,' Jason replies curtly, pushing his sodden hair out of his face. 'I don't think he's going to be too worried about the odd bruise here or there when he wakes up.'

'If he wakes up,' says Shannon, sounding terrified. She's

worrying at the edges of her nails with her teeth, more openly panicked than Hayley has ever seen her.

There's a stark, eerie flash and the trees around them are suddenly illuminated in bright white, the cracks and whorls of their bark standing out in sharp relief, before the cold, gunmetal-grey night sweeps in again. It's darker than before, making it harder than ever to see where they're going. It tastes of metal too, a bloody tang that coats the sides of Hayley's tongue, setting her even more on edge. A few moments pass between the lightning and the angry drumroll of thunder that follows. The thick blanket of leaves above holds off the worst of the rain, but now and then they step into the path of a mini deluge, where the water pours furiously down through a gap in the canopy like a waterfall. The air smells like peat and electricity. Hayley watches Elliot flopping around like a doll.

'I'm tired,' May complains, petulantly, flopping down to the floor and crossing her arms as if they're not in the middle of a midnight thunderstorm.

Jason stops and unceremoniously deposits Elliot in a heap. 'Oh, *you're* tired? I'm so sorry, you poor thing. Can I interest you in taking a turn with this hundred-and-fifty-pound weight so you can see what actual tiredness feels like?'

May scowls.

'Maybe we should just leave him here,' Jason mutters, angrily.

'Are we sure we should all be going back to camp?' Brian's voice is flat, subdued. 'Shouldn't somebody stay up there, in case the plane comes back?'

'It's not coming back,' May whines. 'It doesn't know we're here.'

'Which probably means they'll cross this area off the map and never come back,' Jason adds, darkly.

'Is he definitely breathing?' Hayley bends over Elliot, relieved to feel his warm breath flutter against her cheek.

May gives an exaggerated sigh and Brian turns on her. 'I don't know what you're complaining about. If you lot hadn't left the camp this afternoon the fire would still have been burning and they would have seen the smoke.'

'Oh, come on,' cries May. 'If it had occurred to you that the girls might actually be good at something physical, or maybe even – shock horror – *better* than you guys, then we could have finished collecting the coconuts hours ago and got back in time to get the fire going again.'

'It's my fault,' Jessa says, her voice tight. 'I was resting in the shade, my arm . . .' She sighs heavily. 'I should have kept the fire going. I'm so sorry.'

'There's no point fighting about it now,' Hayley says, feeling a cold jolt as a stream of water unexpectedly finds its way down the back of her neck. With Elliot out of action and the plane gone, she feels utterly defeated. Thoughts about being stuck here forever, about starving here, about never seeing her parents again: all the thoughts she's been trying so hard to block out since the day they arrived are crowding back into her head. Thoughts so heavy she feels like Jason isn't the only one lugging around a deadweight.

'It's my mom's birthday tomorrow,' Jessa whispers and begins to cry.

'Maybe they did see the island,' Hayley says, with an effort, though she doesn't really believe her own words. 'Maybe they saw us and they've gone to fetch help, and they're going to come back when the storm has passed.'

'Yeah, right,' mutters May.

Shannon is sitting quietly, her legs crossed, staring fixedly into the dark forest.

'We're never getting off this island, are we?' Jessa's voice is beginning to rise, half sobbing. 'If they were going to find us they'd have done it by now ... they're going to decide that we're dead, and then they'll stop looking ... and they'll hold our funerals and bury empty caskets ... and everyone will forget about us ...' She is talking faster and faster, her voice increasingly shrill as the words start running into one another.

'Jessa, we're not going to die of old age here,' Brian says, and she looks up hopefully, sniffing. 'We'll die way sooner of starvation or thirst or, like, an in-growing tick bite. Or something stupid like a cut that gets infected and we don't have the basic antibiotics to treat it.'

Jessa looks up in horror and Hayley's isn't the only voice that rises in a scream of 'SHUT UP, BRIAN.'

'Jeez, touchy much?' Brian takes his turn, hoisting Elliot up around his neck like a bizarre muffler, head and arms hanging down over one shoulder, legs over the other. 'C'mon,' he grunts, starting to head back towards the camp, and the others have little choice but to heave themselves to their feet and trail after him. May and Shannon wordlessly lace their arms behind Jessa's back while Hayley follows, alone.

On the beach, the wind is much wilder, whipping their hair across their faces and flinging the gritty sand into their eyes. The rain is torrential, drumming hard on their scalps without pause and streaming down their faces. It is too dark to see the sea, but they can hear it, like some hideous monster tethered nearby, guttering and snarling in its throat, threatening to break its shackles, to leap up and devour them. And with each lightning strike the crests of the waves surge forward, foaming and boiling towards the sky. Jessa has already taken refuge in her sleeping shelter, and the others scramble to do the same, Jason first shovelling Elliot unceremoniously into his own, his head propped sideways on a folded jumper, with Shannon promising to check on him regularly.

It's at least a bit drier inside her makeshift tent, Hayley thinks, realising with a tightening feeling in her chest that she might not get the chance to tell Elliot how well his shelters worked in the storm. But it's harder to control her imagination in here, lying on her own in the dark. Just the wet-dog smell of the rain on the sand, the crashing of the waves and the incessant drumbeat falling on the plastic meal tray that Elliot had wedged into the branches above her to keep her dry.

She closes her eyes and tries to control her breathing, a trick her mom taught her years ago to calm her nerves before exams.

She can hear her mom's voice, soothing and cool.

'Breathe in for one. Hold for one. Breathe out for one.'

Her thoughts flit wildly like grains of sand caught in the storm.

'Breathe in for two. Hold for two. Breathe out for two.'

'You'll be valedictorian one day, you know that?' Grandma, neat hands curled around the tortoiseshell handle of her walking stick, smelling of lipstick and soap. 'But don't work too hard, my sweet girl, save something for you.'

'Breathe in for three. Hold for three. Breathe out for three.'

The sea fizzes and hisses. A boiling kettle.

Elliot lying unconscious. Jason's face, angry and taut. Jessa's arm, heavy and useless, hanging from her body. The sticky remains of the iodine sparkling with slivers of glass.

'Breathe in for four. Hold for four. Breathe out for four.'

'*C'mon,* Hayley, come *out.*' Nella, the girl who used to live next door, shaking her tight, blonde curls, clutching a pair of walkie talkies, perched astride her red bike with the stabilisers. Pouting. 'You never come *play* any more.' Going back to her spelling homework, turning up the volume on her headphones.

'In for five.'

Standing quietly in the entrance at the South Florida Science Center, on the fifth-grade aquarium trip. Trying to blend into the glass tank behind her. Watching the others easily obey the teacher's command to 'get into pairs.' Knowing she would be the odd one out.

'And six.'

Smoothing out the *Oak Ridge Tribune* and staring, staring at her first-ever front-page byline. Smelling the fresh, crisp paper, the cheap ink transferring to her palms. Stroking it over and over.

'Now seven.'

'Come on, Mom. Do you think Woodward and Bernstein had time to go to their eighth-grade Spring fling? Believe me, I'm missing *nothing.*'

'Breathe in for eight. Hold for eight. Breathe out for eight.'

Ninth-grade prize day. Kids shuffling up to the stage to collect their awards. Most improved. Best effort. Then the list.

An unbearable seven subjects long. 'Math, English, History, Biology, Chemistry, French, Geography ... outstanding academic achievement in every single one goes to ...' *the longest pause in the world* ... 'Hayley Larkin.' The sniggers. Pride and shame. Bite the inside of your cheek. Walk up, shake hands, look straight ahead. Don't listen.

She never could get past eight.

The wind howls and a few sticks shift, leaving a gap above Hayley's head. The sky is a deep, menacing grey. She can just make out the leaves of the palm tree whose trunk her shelter leans against, thrashing and writhing like wild things, trying to take off into the storm.

A squall buffets the side of her shelter and a cold spray of rain stings the side of her face.

Her eye smarts and burns. Hayley blinks, trying to dislodge a grain of sand, feeling it scratch painfully against her eyelid. She wishes she had some fresh water to wash it out.

Fresh water!

Without thinking, without pausing, she is out of the shelter and running full pelt along the beach. The storm is still howling in the distance, but it's getting quieter here, muted, and the clouds have lifted enough for a little moonlight to leak back in. Her sneakers slop and slap against sodden mud, its stickiness seeping inside, her feet squelching.

The stumps crouch like squat sentinels in the gloom. She can see the plastic slung low between them, bulging now, stretching closer to the ground.

She plunges her wrists into the icy water. Three inches, maybe. Cool and silky on her skin. She cups her hands and brings a scoop to her lips: it tastes somehow sharper and cleaner than she remembered. She gulps another mouthful, feeling the chill race into her chest while the rainwater drips from her nose and earlobes, like she's being cleansed inside and out at the same time.

When she gets back to the beach, the wind has dropped and it isn't raining any more. She can see the pinpricks of stars piercing the velvet. There's enough moonlight to make out the shape of Elliot's shelter, his sneakered feet just visible at the entrance.

'It worked, Elliot! It worked!' She pats his ankles, awkwardly, wanting him to wake up, needing him to share this, to let him feel the same rush she does now that something positive has finally happened.

'Okay, okay, you don't need to shout,' comes a grumpy voice.

'You're awake!' She shrieks it so loudly that heads poke out of other shelters. The others gather around, grinning, as Elliot shuffles out like an ungainly caterpillar. They all look as bedraggled and soggy as Hayley feels.

'It worked, it worked! Elliot built a rain reservoir in the trees to catch water and it worked – there's a few litres in there at least!' Hayley garbles, excitedly.

'I'm glad,' Elliot says slowly. 'But it's not our first priority.' He is carefully scanning the faces around him.

'What are you talking about? What else is more important than water?'

Elliot looks at her.

'Finding out who pushed me.'

*

They can't get the fire to light on the wet sand, so there's no warmth and there aren't enough dry clothes to go round. They sit in a shivering circle, lit weakly by the grey beams of the moon, apart from May, who returns immediately to her bed after saying they're all being ridiculous, and nothing will change before morning so they might as well get some sleep.

'Tell us again, Elliot,' Shannon says, with the tone of a sceptical but patient teacher trying to get to the bottom of what she suspects might be a tall tale. 'What happened, exactly?'

Elliot sighs, frustrated, and rubs a hand through his unruly curls, leaving them even wilder than before. 'We were at the top of the hill. I was looking up, trying to spot the plane, doing everything I could to get the mirror to reflect and signal the pilot. It was loud and windy and it all happened really fast, but I felt a pair of hands shove me, hard, in the small of my back, then I was falling. The next thing I remember is hearing Hayley's voice and waking up here.'

'Elliot,' Jessa speaks slowly and gently, like she doesn't want to upset him. Hayley notices that she's cradling her arm, sitting very still, trying to avoid any sudden movements. 'Isn't it possible that you just slipped?' she asks, calmly. 'If everything happened so fast?'

'Yeah, it was super chaotic up there,' Jason latches eagerly onto this explanation. 'I couldn't hear myself think, everyone was shouting at once and the weather was crazy ...'

'No. No.' Elliot shakes his head irritably. 'I felt it. I felt somebody push me.'

'Okay, but we were all looking up, all trying to get the

plane's attention,' Brian chimes in. 'Maybe someone did push you, but by accident? Like they sort of banged into you or shoved you by mistake?'

Elliot starts to shake his head, but Brian is in full flow: 'I mean, most of us had never been up there, we didn't know the lay of the land ... I totally didn't realise that drop was so steep ...'

Elliot gets to his feet and turns around. 'I felt two hands, here and here.' He balls his fists and places them on either side of his spine, just above his shorts. 'It was hard, and quick ... *definitely* deliberate.'

He sits heavily back down.

'That's silly.' Jessa says, eventually. 'Why would anyone want to hurt you?'

'I don't know,' Elliot admits.

'I mean, totally apart from anything else, you've basically been saving our asses since the day we got here,' Brian chimes in, with surprising warmth. 'It's not like we'd even have survived this long without you.'

Jason gives a tiny snort.

Suddenly, something else occurs to Hayley. 'Could it have been about the mirror?'

Elliot frowns at her. 'What do you mean?'

'What if they weren't trying to hurt you, but they wanted to stop you from signalling the plane? Someone who didn't want us to get off the island?'

'This *is* ridiculous,' Jessa sighs impatiently. 'Why are we talking about this as if it's an unsolvable mystery? If one of us shoved Elliot, they should own up.'

There is a long, uninterrupted silence. Hayley feels gooseflesh rising on her forearms that has nothing to do with the cold.

'So ...' Brian raises his eyebrows and jerks his thumb towards May's shelter. 'Then I guess ...'

'Oh, shut up, Brian,' snaps Jessa. 'May would never do something like that.'

'Well, someone did,' Brian says. 'Apparently,' he adds, looking at Elliot a little sceptically. 'Sorry, man, but you did bang your head hard enough to pass out. Maybe you're just imagining it.'

'Or maybe someone was so angry with me they wanted to punish me,' Elliot says, quietly, and everybody turns to look at Jason.

'Oh sure, just because I pointed out his idiocy with the fire, I must have tried to murder him,' Jason says, bullishly. 'Yeah, that makes loads of sense, I'm definitely guilty.'

Hayley recalls the fury that had passed over Jason's face, the spittle in Elliot's eyebrows, and doesn't know what to think. Could Jason really have been so pissed at Elliot, so desperate that the plane wasn't seeing them that he'd lash out? Surely not. Jason was all charm and bluster. He wouldn't actually hurt somebody ... would he?

They talk each other around in circles, Elliot continuing to stick stubbornly to his story, the others trapped between his certainty and their own unwillingness to believe that one of them could have done what he describes, Jason angrily maintaining his innocence.

'I've had enough of this,' he finally explodes, stumbling

to his feet. 'It doesn't even matter whether you believe me or not, does it? It's not going to change the fact that we're never getting off this goddamned island.'

The silence he leaves behind is heavy, loaded with each of their fears and unspoken anxieties. Hayley runs her fingers over and over the deep cut on the back of her wrist, sealed over now with a thick scab. What if Jason's right? What if that plane was their one real chance of rescue? She picks at the edge and feels the wetness seeping out.

One by one, tiredness catches up with them and they traipse off to try and sleep. And as Jessa settles in for the night, it is the first evening that Hayley doesn't hear a soft, rhythmic murmuring of prayer coming from inside her shelter. Only silence.

The last thing Brian says before they leave the campfire does nothing to raise anyone's spirits.

'Guys. I've been thinking about it every which way. My man Elliot says he was pushed.' Elliot raises his eyebrows, looking like he doesn't know whether to be amused or grateful that his accident has suddenly made him far more popular with his teammates.

'Okay, so he was pushed. And each of us says we didn't push him, right?' There's a pause, some nodding. 'Well, there's another possibility, isn't there?'

Hayley watches the others' baffled faces. She thinks she knows what is coming; she's been trying not to think it ever since Elliot's bombshell.

'There might be someone else on the island.'

DAY 7

The morning doesn't begin well. Hayley makes an early pilgrimage through the trees, enjoying the peaty, rich smell that rises up from the wet ground after last night's deluge. The birds are noisier than ever, shrieking exuberantly as if to celebrate their victory over the storm. A beautiful golden yellow blur flutters to a stop on a branch just yards away from Hayley, its shining black eye fixed on her with bright curiosity. She holds her breath, marvelling at the richness of its feathers, drenched in colour, the buttercup hue gleaming against its delicate black-and-white wings.

For one ridiculous moment she entertains the fantasy that it has come to tell her something: to warn her, perhaps, or to help her. There is such intelligence in that fierce little eye. 'Who did it?' She almost asks, out loud. Then it tilts its head to the other side, as if to chide her silliness, and is gone as quickly as it came.

She walks on, eagerly, an empty water bottle grasped in each hand, glad to have a purpose to distract her from the murky fears and questions hanging over the camp. The memory of the clear, cool water she gulped down last night dances tantalisingly on her tongue, pushing her forwards, stumbling in her eagerness.

But when she reaches the shady clearing, she stops dead.

Rocket the raccoon is floating on his back in the water, his body horribly bloated, his eyes milky and unseeing. Hayley cannot bring herself to touch him, although she knows she should remove the carcass and discard the contaminated water. She trudges disconsolately back to the camp.

'Not Rocket,' May wails, while Jason smashes his fist into a tree trunk in frustration when Hayley breaks the news.

'We'll try again,' Elliot says, quietly. 'At least it worked.'

Brian has decided they have to check the island. He's calling it a search party, which May says is stupid, because how can you search for something if you don't even know what you're looking for? Elliot says it's stupid too, but for different reasons. He doesn't think someone could have slipped out of the trees and shoved him and then melted away again without anybody noticing, even in the chaos of the storm.

Jason says looking will give them an answer, once and for all.

Hayley can't decide what's worse – the threat that there might be someone else hiding on the island, waiting to launch another attack, or the idea that one of them could hurt Elliot so badly and then lie about it. She looks over at him, a purple bruise protruding from his temple. It could have been so much worse. But he looks different somehow, more alert, his eyes darting here and there, jumping a little when someone bumps into him from behind. Like he can't relax, because he doesn't know who to trust. And Hayley can't blame him. She's starting to feel the same way herself.

She takes in each of the others, one by one, as they pull on shoes and drag random items of clothing out of the locker, getting ready to head out on what they all know is probably a wild goose chase.

May sniffs cautiously at the armpits of a yellow T-shirt before wrinkling her nose and throwing it to one side in disgust, choosing to pull one of the boys' jerseys over her head instead. It swamps her, but that seems preferable to wearing clothing that's stiff with someone else's encrusted sweat.

Brian is thumping the bottle of sunscreen, trying to get it to spit the last dregs out into his palm. His nose has started to peel so violently it looks like he's permanently shedding scraps of white confetti. Shannon is readjusting Jessa's sling, tying the orange scarf tighter and trying to find a more comfortable position. Jessa's face is rigid with concentration: she's staring down at the sand as if she can't actually see it.

Jason is sketching something in the sand with a sharp stick, pointing to different areas and murmuring to himself. Elliot is hunched at the edge of the trees, a stubborn frown etched into his features, decanting the milk out of the last of the brown coconuts into small water bottles he's scratched their initials into, making sure they all get an equal share. He's shaking his head and muttering about not getting dehydrated on a pointless mission.

Nobody looks like they're hiding anything. Hayley feels a stab of annoyance at herself. She ought to be able to figure out what's going on. She's an investigative journalist, for goodness' sake, or at least one in training. But nothing's jumping out at her like it should. Someone ought to be looking guilty, making excuses, trying to avoid detection. But there's nothing. Absolutely no clues at all. She watches them bustling around the camp, clearing away their breakfast things, fetching fresh wood to build up the fire. She watches Jason the longest. He's the only one with something approaching a motive. But he does nothing to give himself away.

Could there really be someone else on the island after all?

'Okay, guys, huddle up.' Jason waves them all over, wiping his hands on his bright red vest.

'I've divided the island into quarters.' He points with the stick, a rough circle drawn in the sand in front of him. 'This is the crash site and the camp, along the beach here. We've spent most time in this area, and the trees immediately adjacent to the beach, collecting wood. And we haven't seen anybody. So we can assume this area is clear. But here . . .' He stabs to the left with the stick, indicating the southernmost quadrant. 'This is the most densely wooded area, where the girls found the fruit trees. We haven't searched that whole area yet and it's possible someone could be hiding amongst the trees. Jessa, you can show us the way. Hayley, you're with us. And you, babe.' Jason slides an arm around Shannon's shoulders and pulls her tightly to him. 'I'm not leaving my girl alone with some lunatic running around the island trying to kill people.'

'Jeez, overexaggerate much?' mutters May under her breath.

Jason pretends not to hear and slides the stick over to the opposite side of his map. 'Meanwhile Elliot, Brian and May should go sort out the water tarp then head back to the north, to the hilltop, and search the area around there. Elliot can try to pinpoint exactly where he was when he felt the push: see if you can work out where someone might have taken cover.' Elliot rolls his eyes but seems to have decided that there's no point arguing.

'Then head to the beach where the coconut trees are,' Jason continues, 'and search for any sign of a shelter or someone hiding out.'

Hayley grabs one of the water bottles Elliot has prepared from their makeshift 'fridge' pit. She takes a sip. The liquid is unpleasantly warm, with an overpowering sweet aftertaste, a bit like a compost heap.

'I know,' Elliot says, seeing her grimace. 'Sorry, they're quite strong. I think it's because the coconuts were left out in the sun. We'll get some more green ones tomorrow.'

Hayley follows Jason as he strides off to the south, Jessa and Shannon close behind her.

'I swear, if we ever get out of here, I'll never moan about my little brother again,' Jessa pants, as they start picking their way through the undergrowth. 'He'd love all this. Desert island … jungle adventure … it's like his idea of heaven. I can't stop thinking about him.'

'We're going to get out of here.' Jason says it firmly, like his word is the final say on the subject. Hayley wonders if he's ever experienced what it's like not to get his own way. It's an open secret that at the end of sophomore year, Jason told his guidance counsellor he wanted to take AP Latin after the Princeton Review recommended it as a good way for law school applicants to boost their admissions prospects.

The trouble was, Oak Ridge only offered eight AP courses, and Latin wasn't one of them. But a week later, a Latin tutor miraculously joined the staff and a fortnight afterwards it was announced that a generous endowment had been made for a new classics wing in the school library. The *Angel* Wing. As in Jason Angel.

In fact, she suddenly realises, even their current situation is partly down to Jason always getting what he wants. Hayley had heard a rumour that the off-season basketball tour might be cancelled this year because of funding issues, before Jason's parents stepped in with their offer of private jets and free accommodation. None of them would even be here if it wasn't for Jason Angel and his charmed life.

'Have you guys thought about what our families must be going through?' Jessa asks, breathing heavily as, clambering over a particularly knotty vine, she uses her one good arm to grab a tree trunk.

'I've been trying not to,' Shannon admits. 'It's easier that way. We can't do anything about it, so it's best not to think about it.'

'I know it's stupid,' Jessa says softly, 'but I have this idea, this hope, I suppose, that somehow my mom just knows . . .' she sniffs, 'like she knows I'm okay. Because we're so close she'd have some kind of a sixth sense if I was dead. It's dumb, I know.'

'It's not dumb,' Shannon says, quietly.

'I got my brother one of those stupid touristy cowboy hats, at the airport,' Jessa whispers. 'I was gonna write "my sister went to Texas and all I got was this stupid cowboy hat" on the back in magic marker.'

Hayley swallows hard. She really, really doesn't want to think about how her mom and dad must be feeling. Partly because it hurts too much. Partly because, on a good day, she can almost trick herself into thinking that things aren't so desperate . . . that they're on a crazy adventure rather than trapped in an incredibly dangerous situation they might actually not survive.

She needs to think about something else. *Anything* else. So, as she automatically scans the ground ahead for tangles of vines and treacherous rocks, her brain is scanning too, going back over everything that has happened, trying to make sense of Elliot's fall, of his certainty that he was pushed.

If he's right, if someone pushed him, they must have had a reason. They'd have been acting differently, maybe, not seeming themselves. Hayley sighs. That could describe all of them. Nobody has been themselves for a week, and who could blame them? But then Hayley thinks back further. It isn't just being on the island that's changing people, is it? Not entirely. She remembers that stupid cowboy hat. Suddenly an image pops into her head, Jessa snapping at May when she knocked it onto the floor as they waited to board the plane. She'd thought it was weird at the time. People have been behaving oddly since *before* the island: ever since the morning of the crash. The night after the party.

The group assembled at the airport terminal that morning had been uncharacteristically quiet. Brian had sat on his own, excusing himself repeatedly to go to the bathroom. Elliot was hidden behind his sketchbook, Jason leafing through the same few pages of a sports magazine over and over again without seeming to take in a word. Hayley had tripped and spilled a takeaway coffee over May's white sneakers but she'd barely looked up, preoccupied and biting her lip, none of her usual spiky attitude on display. Jessa had seemed on edge somehow, drumming her fingers annoyingly on the armchair of the uncomfortable, plastic terminal chair. Shannon arrived at the last minute, her face hidden behind a huge pair of sunglasses, and swept onto the plane without a word to anyone.

Then there were the little moments on the plane: things that seemed meaningless on their own but looked like something more substantial now. Shannon and Jason sitting apart. May and Jessa's whispered conversation. The way people reacted when Erickson mentioned the party – right before the plane went down. Had something happened that night?

They are deeper into the trees than Hayley has ever been. The sunlight filters down in long, glittering bars. It feels still here, like the island is trapped in this single moment. The golden light is like amber, preserving everything for eternity, as though they've somehow slipped outside time. Hayley wants to be able to examine other moments, frozen, like this one, to turn them over in her fingertips and look at them from every possible angle.

'What did you guys think of the end-of-tour party?' She asks Shannon and Jessa, casually, walking a little faster to catch up with them. Jason is still ahead, out of sight, though the occasional rustle of a bush or crack of a stick makes him easy enough to follow.

'Why?' Jessa asks, immediately, shooting Hayley a suspicious look. 'Has someone said something about it?'

'No, no. I was just wondering, that's all. I didn't stay to the end,' she says. She'd escaped back to the hotel just before she was drunk enough to make a fool of herself.

She tries to think back to that night. It was only a week ago, but it feels like a lifetime.

It was stuffy in the living room. The windows were open, but it was a warm evening and there were bodies crowded in; thighs pressed against each other, elbows knocking, the loud, throbbing beat of the music pressing in close. And laughter, crashing over her like a wave as she came in from the kitchen, her red plastic cup of stronger-than-she-really-wanted vodka orange clutched tight like a talisman against her insecurity. Hayley couldn't have said how it compared with other parties, because she didn't really know. Did everyone usually just sit around like this? Sandwiched together and chatting, trying to look casual while sweat dripped a slow, uncomfortable path between their shoulder blades? Laughing too loudly at the loudest person's jokes? Was that what you did to show you were part of it all, in the zone, one of the crowd? She remembers wondering whether everyone else at the party was spending as much time as she was thinking about whether she looked like she was enjoying the party.

'It was pretty standard,' Jessa says, dismissively. 'Not much happened, right, Shan?'

'Mmhmm.' Shannon nods, focusing on her feet.

'There was a lot of alcohol, right?' Hayley asks, thinking back. 'There was that keg the Duke guys set up in the front yard, and the cheerleader, the redhead … her name was

Sasha, right? She'd set out all her parents' liquor in the kitchen with mixers and things.'

'I wouldn't know,' Jessa says, dismissively. 'I don't drink. May was acting a little weird, though, now you mention it. Like halfway through the evening, she suddenly seemed all jittery and nervous. I don't know why. Then she started acting pretty *extra*, even by May standards. Dancing on the tables and all sorts. Like she was trying too hard to have fun.'

'Elliot could tell you how much liquor there was.' Shannon smirked. 'I found him in the bathroom towards the end of the night, getting pretty cosy with the toilet bowl, if you know what I mean.'

'That wasn't his fault,' Jessa protests, 'did you *see* the concoction they made him drink during Truth or Dare? It was gross.'

The game had come later. The atmosphere was different by then, the living room smudged somehow by the blur of alcohol and sweat and awkward excitement. Hayley should have been terrified of Truth or Dare, but it actually came as a relief. There were obvious pitfalls: dares that could expose her inexperience or questions that could reveal gaping holes in her pop culture knowledge, but at least it was organised. It had rules, structure, a pattern she could follow.

Brian had already stolen a gnome from the next-door garden, one of the Duke cheerleaders had toilet-papered a mailbox and Shannon had begun to perform a pretty explicit feat with a banana and a can of whipped cream, at least until Jason had yanked her down from the table she was standing on, shouting 'Show's over, folks.' Elliot, who'd been hovering awkwardly on the edges of the party, had downed a disgusting concoction of every spirit in the house mixed together with a squeeze of toothpaste stirred in. Hayley didn't know whether to be relieved or disappointed that her turn never seemed to come.

'Right, how close are we to the fruit?' Jason asks from up ahead, crashing out of the trees and interrupting Hayley's train of thought.

'They're over this way.' Jessa moves forward confidently, pointing at some nearby tree trunks. 'I tore bark and branches off trees on the way last time so we'd be able to find our way back.' Now she knows what she is looking for, Hayley can see the snapped-off, splintered ends and scratched sections on several of the trees they walk past, their green muscles bristling through the torn skin. She remembers what Jessa said about Elliot not being the only scout in the group.

'So what are we supposed to be looking for exactly?' Hayley asks.

Now that they're actually in amongst the trees, Jason seems a little less confident than he had with his simplistic sand diagram on the beach. The tree trunks are choked with vines so thick they've calcified like bones, the ground uneven and cluttered with small plants and bushes underfoot, their visibility restricted to just a few metres because the vegetation is so dense. Hayley finds it pretty hard to believe that anyone could be living in amongst all this, but if they were, she's not convinced they'd be able to find them anyway. It wouldn't be difficult to stay hidden, dodging behind trees, hiding in bushes, cutting back behind them once they'd passed – especially given the amount of noise their search party is making as they crash and stumble along.

'We're looking for any evidence of someone living here,' Jason hisses. 'A shelter of some kind . . . probably a camp setup.'

'Nobody else had picked up the coconuts,' Hayley says suddenly, stopping so abruptly that Shannon bumps into her from behind. 'The ones we found on the other side of the island – if someone else had been living here before we arrived surely all those brown coconuts wouldn't just have been left lying there on the ground, would they?'

Shannon is frowning. 'That's a good point. It's a small island – they'd have covered it within a week. If they'd been here any time at all they'd have needed those coconuts. So can we just agree this is completely absurd?' she asks, hands on hips. 'It's a massive waste of all our time and energy, combing a clearly deserted island looking for a phantom pusher when the *obvious* explanation is that Elliot had an accident.'

'Maybe he doesn't want to admit that he slipped,' Shannon continues. 'He's quite enjoyed playing the hero these last few days. And falling down a steep drop and knocking himself out doesn't exactly fit with the skilled hunter-gatherer image, does it?'

Jason grunts approvingly.

Hayley doesn't know what to think. It does seem unlikely that anyone else could have survived for a long time on this island – and even if they had, why wouldn't they have made contact with the new arrivals after the plane crash? Why would they have wanted to hurt Elliot?

After another hour of searching through the untouched

undergrowth, they've seen nothing untoward. Nothing suspicious or strange at all. Until they get back to the camp.

At first, Hayley thinks May is just joking around.

'We found ... NOTHING!' She shouts it loudly as she comes crashing back through the trees with the rest of her group, attempting a drumroll on a tree trunk and missing. 'Nothing like a dasted way hey?' She frowns, chews the words in her mouth, tries again: 'Wasted day! Way hey!'

She does what Hayley thinks is supposed to be a sarcastic celebration dance, but it looks like her arms and legs are getting messages from completely different brains. As she whirls wildly, she sings at the top of her voice, something about mixed messages or a wild goose chase, but the notes don't seem to be coming out in the right order and the words are all garbled and slurred. Eventually she becomes tangled up in her own limbs, lurching to the floor and subsiding into silence.

'She's been like this half the journey back,' Elliot says, uneasily.

Hayley takes a step towards May, watching her closely.

'Ss'allright Hayleys?' May attempts to stand up and give Hayley a hug, but almost misses and ends up sort of hanging around Hayley's waist, her face level with Hayley's belly button. May dissolves into helpless giggles and slides back to the floor.

'Ow,' she says, thickly, trying to sit up and falling over again.

Jason is laughing, clapping her on the back like a clown and whistling. But Hayley feels sick. Something is very wrong.

May has never voluntarily hugged her in her life. The more Hayley stares at her, the more she notices the slack jaw, the slightly glazed, unfocused eyes.

'What's going on?' Shannon crouches down next to May, looking uneasy.

'May, can you look at me?' May spins around, her gaze landing on a spot somewhere over Hayley's right shoulder.

'May. Focus.'

'Hmmm?' May's starting to look less confident now, Hayley can see her eyes starting to flit quickly from side to side. A look of panic is creeping in.

Jessa comes back from a bathroom trip and takes in the scene, her eyes widening in horror.

'Jessa, whaddami . . .' May takes a breath, shakes her head heavily like a dog and tries again: 'Wasssa . . .' her speech slurs and her eyes lock onto Jessa's, shining with fear. A tear escapes and slides slowly down May's cheek.

'It's okay, May.' Hayley tries to keep her voice steadier than her jangling nerves. 'I think . . . have you guys eaten anything? Berries or roots? Or drunk something?'

Elliot shakes his head.

'Mayday, Brian, have you guys been drinking without me?' Jason raps the words out accusingly, sounding more team coach than team captain.

Brian looks surprised. 'No, I swear!' He holds up his hands like he's protesting his innocence. 'Honestly – we've been trawling along the beach the other side of the island looking for a hut or signs of a fire or something – the only thing we've drunk is that disgusting coconut water.' He holds up his half-full bottle. 'We really need to get some more green ones,' he adds.

'Where's May's bottle?' Hayley asks. They look around. There's an almost-empty bottle lying on the floor by the campfire, the initial 'M' just visible scratched into the side. 'Is this it?' She takes off the lid and cautiously sniffs the contents, then takes a small sip. 'That doesn't taste the same as mine,' Hayley says, sipping from her own bottle to compare. 'I think there's something in it.'

May is limp now, her head resting on her knees. Without warning, she lurches forwards, vomiting into the sand.

'Is there any fresh water left?' Shannon snaps into action.

'There's half a bottle. That's all we've got until it rains again.' Elliot hands it over and Shannon crouches next to May, rubbing her back reassuringly. She helps her sip from the rainwater bottle while Jessa looks on, helpless and aghast.

'Guys.' Elliot has been poking around in the overhead locker. He holds out his cupped hands. He's holding seven of the vodka miniatures they'd found in the back of the plane. They're all empty.

'May!' Jessa shrieks, whirling to face her. May lets out a muffled groan and waves her off weakly. 'What were you thinking? What, you just felt like a party? All by yourself?'

'You could've shared at least,' Brian chips in, resentfully.

'Yes, because getting drunk and dehydrated is a fantastic idea in a survival situation with very little drinking water.' Elliot frowns.

'I DIDNNN,' May drawls angrily, sweat standing out along her hairline. 'Didnknow. Didn't know.' It takes her a supreme effort to separate the words, frowning as she forms them carefully and deliberately with her lips. She points vaguely in the direction of Elliot's hands, before slumping over again, cradling her head and groaning.

'Is she saying what I think she's saying?' Jessa asks. The bottles clatter together noisily as Elliot hurries to put them down, like he doesn't want to be the one left holding them. 'Did someone spike May's drink?'

'Uh yeah: *May* spiked May's drink.' Jason shakes his head: 'Can't believe I didn't think of it myself – those bottles were just lying there for the taking.'

'Yeah,' Brian says, but Hayley can see he's uneasy. 'She is kind of a party girl ... look how wild she was the other night ...' He trails off sheepishly. 'You can't exactly blame her for wanting to forget –' he waves his hand around vaguely '– all this, can you? She probably just overdid it.'

'What, overdid it by seven bottles?' Jessa sounds sceptical. 'Drinking fourteen shots of vodka isn't exactly something you do by mistake, Brian.'

'Well, what other explanation is there?' Brian asks. And his question hangs heavy in the air, because everybody knows the answer, but nobody wants to be the one to say it. Except Elliot.

'Maybe it was the same person who knocked me out.' He looks around at the circle of faces, slowly and uncompromisingly making eye contact with each of them in turn. 'That coconut water was strong and sweet – the taste was so overpowering May wouldn't have realised it was spiked until it was too late.'

'And everyone's bottles were labelled with their initials,' Shannon says slowly, running her finger over the rough 'M' scratched into the plastic.

Rain starts to fall again, big fat droplets splashing onto Hayley's face. But she can't enjoy it, can't let herself bask in the relief of the tarpaulin filling again, not while the creeping idea of sabotage is slowly seeping into the camp like poison.

Elliot takes a deep breath, with the expression of somebody who is about to take a dive off the highest diving board and knows there is no going back. 'Someone is hurting people. And since we've searched the whole island and found no sign of anybody else . . .'

Hayley finishes his sentence for him. 'It has to be one of us.'

DAY 8

Of course, nobody owns up. Even when May wakes up with a horrible hangover the next morning and swears blind she had no idea there was vodka in her drink. 'Yes, I know it tasted weird,' she snaps at Brian when he questions her. 'But that damn coconut stuff always tastes disgusting. I just thought it was grosser than normal.'

They look at each other, the accusation hanging heavily over the camp.

'Was it you, Brian?' Jessa, blurts out, directly.

'What?' His voice is squeaky with indignation. 'Why are you accusing me?'

Jessa squirms. 'I'm sorry, it's just ... it seems like the kind of prank you might play. You did fill half the team's water bottles with washing-up liquid on that second tour game ...'

'Yeah, for a *joke*!' Brian splutters. 'And don't pretend you weren't laughing when bubbles started coming out of Tom Allen's nose, Jessa.'

'So was just this another joke?' she persists. 'We won't be mad, if you tell us. It'd be much better to own it.'

'No. Jesus. I wasn't even the one who filled up the bottles: that was Elliot.'

'And why would I want to get May drunk?' Elliot asks, immediately. 'Besides, if whoever did this was also the person who pushed me then that puts me in the clear, doesn't it? I wouldn't exactly give myself a serious head injury on purpose.'

Hayley watches him closely, the tense narrowing of his full, dark eyebrows, the cut on his cheek all but completely faded now, the bruise on his temple faded to a faint, dark yellow, trying to sense whether or not he is lying.

'But you *were* the one that filled the bottles,' Shannon says, slowly, narrowing her eyes at Elliot. How did the vodka get in there if you didn't put it in?'

'We were all rushing around getting stuff ready,' Elliot protests. 'The bottles were left in the trees to keep cool, anyone could have slipped something in while they were getting wood or going to the bathroom. We all had the opportunity.'

Hayley watches him closely, the tense narrowing of his full, dark eyebrows, the cut on his cheek all but completely faded now, the bruise on his temple softened to a faint dark yellow, trying to sense whether or not he is lying.

'But who wanted to?' May whines, furiously. 'If you've got a problem with me, say it to my face,' she shouts, defiantly.

But nobody says a word. And eventually they fall into a dissatisfied silence.

Hayley can't stop thinking about it all. The party. The more she tries to connect the dots between what happened to Elliot and May, the more convinced she becomes that the party is the key to unravelling it all. And though she wouldn't admit it, there's a part of her that feels energised, almost buoyed up by finally feeling that there's a role for her on the island. So she wasn't cool under pressure in the first days. And she doesn't have any particularly useful survival skills. But uncovering the truth? Getting people to reveal more than they intended? This is Hayley Larkin's wheelhouse. If anyone can work out what is going on, she can. Ideally before anyone else gets hurt.

The only problem is, none of it adds up. The only person with a clear motive to hurt Elliot was Jason: jealous of his new leadership role in the group. But why would Jason want to hurt May? Why would *anyone* want to hurt May? One thing is certain: Hayley can cross Jessa off the list of suspects. Elliot says he was pushed with two hands, and Jessa's injured arm is practically immobile. And there's no way Jessa would ever do anything to hurt her best friend.

There is always something that needs doing. It's laborious repetitive work, but it distracts them from arguing about whether Elliot's attacker was real or imagined, whether May was deliberately poisoned with alcohol, or stole the vodka herself and lied about it.

The main jobs are collecting and boiling any rainwater, catching fish, picking fruit and coconuts, and keeping the fire burning from dawn to dusk. If another search party comes close, they'll be ready.

They've decided not to worry about keeping the fire burning after dark, since rescuers would be less likely to be out looking at night anyway. Elliot is convinced the island would be too small to support any predators so there doesn't seem to be much need for a night-time guard, and that was a disaster the only time they tried it. (Or at least, as Elliot darkly adds, they don't need guarding from anything *outside* the camp.)

But keeping the fire burning during daylight means collecting firewood. Lots of firewood. Hayley, whose family has one of those neat little electric fires behind glass for the rare winter night that's cold enough to turn it on, had no idea that woodfires gobbled up so much fuel. Within the first week, they've gathered and burned every piece of driftwood and most of the obvious, large sticks in the trees that line the beach. Which is why Hayley finds herself deep in the dense, wooded central part of the island with Elliot on the afternoon of the eighth day, her back and thighs aching, her forearms ribboned with livid scratches, painstakingly adding piece after piece of wood to the backpack she has slung across one shoulder.

'I think my splinters have splinters,' she grumbles, inspecting her reddened palms. The cuts and bruises left by the crash have almost all healed, but they've been replaced by other sore spots, souvenirs of a week on the island. There's a half-healed cut where she accidentally gouged herself with a fishhook whilst trying to bait it. A scrape down the side of her shin, grazed by tripping over a vine on a fruit-gathering expedition. A nasty bruise on her left thumb from taking aim at a coconut with the cutting stone and accidentally bringing the blunt side smashing down on her hand instead. And a little, smooth blister on her right index fingertip from a cooking accident.

They have started to attempt slightly more sophisticated 'cooking', of a sort. Elliot showed them how to make a mini stove with a Coke can. He cut a hole in the side of the can to allow hot stones and tinder to be pushed inside, and the top provided a stable base for a kind of cooking container made of half another tin can to stand on. They've boiled sea snails, plucked slimily from rough rocks at low tide, and steamed pieces of white fish (more of them caught with Jessa's hook than Elliot's spear), wrapped in supple, green leaves.

Everything is an effort. They don't eat, drink or rest without working for it. It can take an hour or more to catch a single fish. By the time they've scraped off the scales and pulled out the hundreds of bones each one is barely a mouthful. And there are seven hungry mouths to feed. By the time they've prepared the fish, collected wood, made the fire, eaten, cleaned up again, it's time to start scavenging for the next meal immediately.

Hayley sighs and adds another stick to her bulging pack. 'Can you believe we've been here over a week already?'

Elliot has his back to her, bent over a dead tree trunk, trying to break off some pieces of dry wood. But she can hear the care in his voice, like he's trying not to scare her. 'It's not a very good sign,' he says, slowly. 'If they had any means to find us easily – like if our radar had been working until the last minute, or we hadn't strayed very far from the planned flight path – then we should have been found in the first couple of days, tops.'

'So not being found quickly means we might not be found at all?'

Elliot nods, apologetically.

'No.' Hayley is embarrassed by the hot prickling behind her eyeballs. She can handle this. Just because Elliot's been camping a lot, doesn't make him the final authority on all things desert island. He's guessing, just as much as anyone else.

'They'll keep looking until they find us,' she says firmly, trying to keep a wobble out of her voice. 'It doesn't matter how long it takes. Our parents aren't going to stop. And you can bet Jason's parents will pay for a private search, even if the authorities give up. May's too, come to think of it.' In fact, the combined wealth of the families of the cheerleading squad alone could probably finance a round-the-clock rescue operation for months, before you even started on the boys.

'Yeah, I can believe there's not many of those booster club parents who'll take no for an answer,' Elliot says, drily. 'I guess we should think ourselves lucky it works in our favour this time around.'

'This time?'

'As opposed to, say, when we're applying for college places and our recommendation letters are being written by the school, but we're in competition with classmates whose parents can afford to fund a new library.'

Elliot wrenches at the dead wood, twisting great clumps of it off and piling them beside him.

'Or competing for basketball scholarships with kids whose parents have been paying for them to fly around the country playing in the off season for years, sending them on pricey summer camps since they were in elementary school. Kids who basically bought their ball skills instead of spending a thousand hours late into the night shooting at a single rusty hoop screwed into their backyard wall because they can't afford to go out anywhere anyway.'

He breathes heavily, concentrating on the stump, not meeting Hayley's eyes. She has no idea what to say. She feels a strange mixture of embarrassment and irritation that Elliot so often manages to make her feel like a naïve child. She likes to think of Oak Ridge as her beat – prides herself on knowing it inside out. But she's never heard a story like Elliot's before. Partly because she's never spoken to a scholarship kid. Not because she's avoided them … just because, she suddenly realises, she's never known who any of them are. And she's beginning to understand why.

Hayley's parents aren't off-the-scale wealthy, not by the standards of a lot of her classmates, but they live comfortably, managing the school fees with enough left over to take a nice holiday every few years if they budget carefully enough. Somehow she's always just assumed her peers' lives were all broadly similar … apart from the significant handful whose gold-plated existence revolves more around private pools, skiing chalets and Dior clutch bags, that is. And, she is slowly beginning to realise, being around those kids has always made her think of herself, by comparison, as … normal. But talking to Elliot, she's beginning to realise just how lucky she is. And just how little she's ever really stopped to appreciate it.

'Elliot,' Hayley begins, hesitantly, 'Do you really, honestly think someone pushed you off those rocks?'

He sighs and turns to look her directly in the eye, wiping

his hands on the same scruffy khaki shorts and thin grey T-shirt he's been wearing since the day they arrived, only taking them off to rinse them in the sea once or twice.

'Come here,' he says, walking over to her, until they're so close that she can see a slight dusting of freckles across the bridge of his nose. Elliot takes her shoulders and gently spins her around so she's facing away from him. Then suddenly, before she has time to realise what he's about to do, he shoves her, hard, in the back with two fists, sending her crashing to the floor.

'OW!' Hayley protests, rubbing her elbow and picking leaves out of her hair. 'What did you do that for?'

'Do you think you could have "imagined" that?' Elliot asks. 'Might you have just tripped over? Could you be confused?'

'Okay, okay, I get your point,' Hayley mutters, grumpily, dusting herself down.

She looks at him for a moment, weighing him up. Out of everyone on the island, he's the person she probably knew the least before they crashed. But somehow, now he feels like the one she's most willing to trust.

'I think maybe something happened at the party and that's why someone pushed you, and maybe why they spiked May's drink as well.' She lets it all come out in a rush before she changes her mind about confiding in him.

Elliot looks troubled. 'At the party? Why?'

'Think about it. Everyone's been acting weird ever since the morning after, we just didn't really notice because the crash happened. Shannon and Jason haven't been the same, Jessa says May was acting strangely that night, nobody seems to want to talk about it . . .' She runs her hands through her greasy hair, frustrated. 'I can't explain it, exactly, I just feel sure that whatever happened that night holds the key to what's going on here.'

Elliot thinks for a while. 'I guess you could be right,' he says, thoughtfully. 'It was kind of a crazy party. But it was Shannon who was acting the weirdest, if you ask me.'

'What do you mean?'

'It was like she was high or something, the way she threw herself into that game of Truth or Dare, the way she was dancing with that Duke player later, them grinding up against each other like that . . .'

Hayley remembers the sweaty, heaving, swaying mass of bodies, arms coiling and necks arched, hands twisting and finding flesh, colours whirling and legs rubbing and hair sticking to the side of your neck. By that point, Hayley had been comfortably numbed by the vodka, sliding into that sweet spot where her knees tingled and a cloak of somebody else's confidence was softly draped over her shoulders. Not yet at the point when her tongue started to grow rubbery and floppy so she had to concentrate hard on her words in order to avoid tripping over them. Surrounded by an invisible force field of protection from her own constant inner monologue of self-consciousness. The whispering voice in her head – *you don't know what you're doing, you're totally out of your depth, everyone's looking at you* – finally quietened. And it hadn't hurt that really nobody was looking at her, at all. Brian was huddled in the corner, in a sort of sweaty, pulsing ecosystem of his own with two of the Duke cheerleaders. Jason seemed to have disappeared. Shannon, head thrown back and nostrils flaring, was dancing like her life depended on it with the tall, muscular Duke basketball captain, his light blond hair elaborately gelled into place. May was dancing alone, throwing beautiful, angular, unpredictable shapes and somehow completely pulling it off as only May could. She couldn't remember seeing Jessa. And Elliot was on the table, feet splayed and propped on one arm, his top ripped off, humping the air, his groin plunging and arching to the music. Surrounded by a chanting crowd of faces, a buzzing muddle of admiration and mockery.

Hayley had slipped out, shutting the door gratefully against the wall of noise and damp heat, writhing bodies and pulsing music. She walked slowly back to the hotel in the moonlight, going over the night the way Shannon would analyse her performance in a complicated routine. It had been a solid non-disaster as far as Hayley was concerned. Which, for her, was a big success. And as she snuggled down between the crisp hotel-room sheets, relishing the night's final rebellion of slowly sucking the chocolate on her pillow even though she'd already brushed her teeth, she'd whispered quietly to herself. 'You went to a party. An actual party. And you didn't totally suck.'

'So what about you?' She looks sideways at Elliot to gauge his reaction as she continues picking at the wood on the stump. 'Shannon wasn't the only one who let her hair down that night, was she?'

Elliot flushes. 'If by letting your hair down you mean being forced to drink the most disgusting cocktail known to man, then I suppose you could say that. I don't remember very much after that if I'm totally honest.'

'Shannon said she found you on the bathroom floor.'

'Oh God.' He cringes. 'That was much later, I think. She sort of flew into the bathroom and collapsed over the sink, spitting into it and rinsing her face with cold water. That was when she spotted me. But then she disappeared again, I don't know, I think I passed out.'

'You guys need any help?' Jason appears behind Elliot, flicking a bug off the sleeve of his grubby white T-shirt.

'Yeah, thanks,' Hayley answers quickly, wondering how much of their conversation Jason has overheard. 'We're trying to break down this stump for firewood.'

It occurs to Hayley, absurdly, that this might be one of the only times Jason Angel has addressed her directly. Unless you count him making her feel extremely uncomfortable in her first-ever cheer practice, which she doesn't, since he didn't even bother to find out her name. Not that he deliberately ignores her, exactly. It's more like he just never seems to notice her. On tour, he'd talk to Jessa and May in front of her, and he was always with Shannon, of course, turning up to collect her from practice, shepherding her from their changing rooms onto the court ('so everybody knows you're my girl ... don't want any of those opposition fans getting ideas ...'). But it's like he's never really *seen* Hayley. It's the way she imagines famous people just don't notice the aides who buzz around them getting things done every day. Jason's not the sort of person who needs to notice everybody around him. Everybody else takes notice of him instead.

He took notice of Shannon, though. The day she arrived as a transfer student, halfway through ninth grade, Jason picked her out. People were a little surprised, actually, back then. Jason could have chosen almost anybody, and Shannon wasn't the most obvious. She had a regal poise and pale, dramatic looks. But she wasn't the stereotypical prom queen type, not like May with her exuberant, butterfly popularity, or Jessa with her dimples and her massive brown eyes and eyelashes that went on forever. But there was something about Shannon. And on Jason's arm she walked into the world of cheerleading royalty with every door swinging open in front of her. That was a long time ago, though. Now Shannon is cheer captain, with her extra practice sessions and drills run like military exercises, it's hard to remember the coltish, shy girl who turned up in second-period math and slid quietly into a seat next to Jason.

Jason gets his nails into a crack in the stump and starts to heave, ripping off a substantial strip and sidestepping as a stream of tiny bugs with shiny black shells swarms out from underneath it. He's just starting to heave at a second piece when he stops suddenly.

'What was that?' Jason sounds uneasy.

They all stop and listen.

The noise comes again: a cascade of descending notes like tinkling laughter. The skin on the back of Hayley's neck start to crawl. She tries to slow her breathing, standing frozen, straining in the direction the noise seemed to come from.

It comes again, like a silvery waterfall of noise, so quick and light that it seems to slip through her fingers. But this time there's a pause and then a dry rustling noise, which sounds like it's coming from the trees behind Elliot.

Jason looks absolutely terrified. He quickly takes a few steps towards Hayley, putting Elliot between him and the noise.

'I think it's a bird,' Elliot whispers, breathing heavily.

A flurry of dry leaves puffs into the air and a bird the size of a rooster struts confidently out of a bush just yards away from them. Hayley's hand flies to her mouth, the shock of its unexpected appearance making her heart leap in her chest.

The bird is beautiful. At first, Hayley thinks it's a peacock, with its powder-blue head and long, decorative feathers, darker at the back but shining all over with a petrol sheen. It has a little red comb on the top of its head and a red ring around each eye, with small decorative lumps like red and yellow baubles clinging to its face. Its pink scaly legs end in sharp claws that scratch and scrabble sure-footedly through the debris on the forest floor. A moment later it has seen them, and it stops, cautiously, looking more curious than afraid, cocks its wrinkled face to one side and fixes them with its little currant eye.

'We have to kill it,' Elliot breathes, barely even moving his lips.

'What?!'

'We need the food,' Elliot replies immediately, his eyes darting around the clearing, already making calculations for a hunt.

'It's stunning,' Hayley hisses, 'and defenceless … and it's probably never seen humans – it won't even know how to run away – it's not fair!' And what she wants to say, but doesn't, is that she feels, somehow, that the island will never forgive them if they kill this beautiful, majestic bird. Bad enough that it has been forced to accept their rough intrusion without them spilling blood as well.

'All the better.' Jason grins, moving quietly into a crouching position, his arms outstretched.

The bird flicks its head to the other side, staring unblinkingly at Jason. With a quiet whoosh, it fans out its tail feathers, a gorgeous array of intricate black-and-white patterns, each feather tipped in blue and gold as if it has been dipped in a shimmering ink pot.

'It's like some kind of turkey,' Elliot whispers, as the bird puffs out its green wing feathers, glinting mermaid-like, and extends its neck. It gives that beautiful call again, the pure notes scattered carelessly through the trees.

Elliot is cautiously moving to his right, blocking off a gap between the trees. 'Jason, block its escape that way. Hayley, see if you can get round behind it so it can't go back the way it came.'

'Uh uh. No way. I am not involved in this.'

'Hayley,' Elliot whispers out of the corner of his mouth, never taking his eyes off the bird. 'Do you and your family celebrate Thanksgiving?'

'Well, the holiday is problematic, but . . .'

Elliot cuts her off. 'Do. You. Eat. A. Turkey? Yes or no?'

Hayley sighs. She can see where this is going. 'Yes.'

'Okay, then. This is no different than that. Actually it's a lot more honest. We are killing this bird for survival. It is absolutely necessary. It's not a cranberry-filled, sentimental celebration of American ego and invading brutality. It's not cruel. It's biology. It's life and death. Survival of the fittest. It's nature.'

Hayley crosses her arms and tries not to look the turkey in the eye.

'Do you want to eat something other than fruit and fish bones in the next month? Or is going to the bathroom five times a day a hobby you're quite happy to continue?'

She grimaces reluctantly. 'Okay, okay. Fine. But I'm not participating. I'm conscientiously objecting.'

'You're not going to eat any of the meat then? The juicy, tender white breast meat, barbecued over a smoky fire? Or the flavoursome, tasty dark leg meat that slips off the bone?'

She feels her mouth start to water in spite of herself.

'You don't get to eat it if you aren't prepared to help catch it. It's dishonest. It does the animal a disservice. Those sterile, bloodless packets we pick up in the supermarket distance us from the reality of our food chain – they separate us from respecting and acknowledging the animals we sacrifice for our survival—'

'Dude, can we please just get on with it?' Jason hisses, as the turkey starts to move again. 'Rock on with your natural-world philosophising and all that but it's going to get away if we don't shut up and catch it.'

'Fine. I'll do it.' Hayley starts inching to her right, trying to creep around behind the turkey. But it's too clever for her, or she's too unskilled a hunter. As soon as she moves towards it, it starts to panic, kicking up the leaves and scrambling to run, letting out a horrible, screaming gobble, lurching towards the gap between Elliot and Jason.

Jason and Elliot both dive towards the bird like line backers, Jason half crushing it beneath his body, its feet clawing helplessly in mid-air, its body writhing, still making that awful squalling screech, so different from the melody of its earlier call.

'Kill it,' Jason squeals, panting, twisting his face to the side just in time as the bird arches its neck backwards, trying to peck him with its sharp, curved beak. It rears and its beak dives again, scalpel-like, finding its target this time as it sinks into Jason's forearm.

'Argh!' He screams and rolls to the side, and the bird half rises, scrambling straight towards Elliot now, blind with panic, its shining feathers dirty and stuck with leaves, some broken and twisted, sticking out horribly at the wrong angles.

'It's suffering,' Hayley screams, and she finds herself lurching forward, her hands reaching out for the bird's neck, thicker and firmer than she'd anticipated, muscular beneath her fingers. And without really knowing what she is doing, without letting herself think too clearly, she twists with all her might, wrenching the gleaming blue softness to the side with a sickeningly muffled crack.

There's quiet. Its body lies grotesquely spread and broken, legs sticking comically up in the air, robbed of its grace and elegance. Its beady eye, it seems to Hayley, is trained on her still, reproaching her.

'Come on,' Jason mutters, and there's a kind of shame on his face as he grabs it up by the neck, so its heavy body dangles limply by his leg.

'Oh man,' Elliot groans, pulling a single, blue green feather from his hair. 'May is *not* going to like this.'

Her tirade begins the moment they trudge back into camp with the dead bird. 'What gives you the right to take away its life? You're murderers, you know that? Murderers. I just hope you can live with yourselves after you've picked its greasy carcass clean.'

'May.' Elliot takes the bird, sits down and calmly starts to rip out great handfuls of its jewelled feathers, twisting and bracing against its body as he wrenches them out of the skin. 'We have to eat. Okay? You literally wouldn't be here if your ancestors hadn't killed animals to survive. Humans are carnivores. Get over it.'

'Humans also used to live in caves and walk around naked,' May retorts, spikily. 'Are you suggesting we do that too?'

Brian raises a hand: 'I would just like to say for the record that I for one would have no objection to that.'

It turns out plucking the bird is the easy part. Disembowelling it and removing the wings, feet and head are far more of a challenge with only sharp stones to help them. Hayley has to turn away as Elliot hacks at the bird's neck, flecks of blood and chunks of raw flesh spattering out in wet bursts. When it's finally done, he pulls out the slick, shining mess of its innards, saving them carefully in a plastic airplane food tray to use for fish bait.

But when it is finally prepared, threaded onto a long spit over the fire with two forked sticks to rest it on, the rich, smoky smell of meat and sizzling golden skin calls irresistibly to her tastebuds. Hayley's stomach growls and clenches like a wild thing as drops of translucent fat drip down to crackle in the embers.

'For the first time ever,' Brian says, watching hungrily as Elliot turns the stick to roast the bird's pale belly, 'I can honestly say this is the kind of spit roast I am most excited about right now.'

Jason guffaws, while Jessa and Hayley exchange embarrassed looks but say nothing. Suddenly Hayley is powerfully reminded of an afternoon in the seventh grade, when she'd sat uncomfortably in her plastic chair while the boys in her science class excitedly passed a novelty pen along the lab bench, taking it in turns to turn it upside down and watch while the skimpy bikini slowly disappeared to reveal a nude, busty model grinning blankly back at them. She wishes she knew what to say now just like she wished then, but somehow the words to describe how gross it makes her feel just won't come. And she knows, like she did then, that she'd be called a prude or accused of being uptight if she tried to object. So she says nothing at all.

They eat the bird the moment it's cooked, crouching in the sand around the fire, tearing off pieces of meat with their fingers and stuffing it into their mouths, the crispy skin melting away. The meat is deliciously, satisfyingly chewy after a week of sinking their teeth into soft, yielding fruit. May watches them from a safe distance, throwing them the occasional accusing glare while she chews sourly on some strips of coconut they've experimentally dried in the sun.

Hayley's brain plays tricks on her. There are moments when

she feels almost normal, as if this life is something she knows, something expected. Her body cannot sustain the sensation of shock and fear, not for days on end. So there are times, even whole hours, when life just goes on. Even in the strangeness of the situation they can almost mimic normality, for a few suspended moments here and there.

'That wants cleaning,' Shannon says, nodding at the greasy plastic tray they used to serve the turkey, which is exactly what Hayley's mother would have said, and Jason nods, and sits still, which is what her father would have done. Shannon picks it up and takes it down to the sea and Hayley sees her mother's back curved over the sink as she bends to scrub it.

DAY 9

At first, Hayley thinks it's just the birds again.

The screeching of their morning calls, so shocking that first time, has almost become as expected as the morning light filtering through the leaves, tickling her eyelids open.

But this is something different. It's a male voice, urgent and angry, the words coming so fast she can't make them out. Hayley scrambles out of her makeshift bed, scattering sand everywhere in her haste, and waits impatiently for her eyes to adjust to the usual shocking brightness.

The boys are gathered round the campfire, where Elliot is attempting to re-use yesterday's spit to cook some fish for breakfast. (Not very successfully, if his frustrated expression and the number of blackened fins charring in the fire are anything to go by.) Shannon and May are emerging from the trees with yet more firewood, and Brian is standing in front of Jason, frowning like he's trying to make sense of what he's shouting. Hayley hurries over, still half asleep, Jessa stumbling after her, drawn by the rumpus.

'I'm telling you, there's a fucking psycho on this island!'

Jason is apoplectic, his usually placid face reddened with panic, a vein pulsating in his neck as he gesticulates wildly at the sand around his feet.

'Great shards of glass, sticking up all around my bed like knives coming out of the beach,' he shouts. 'I almost cut myself to ribbons when I woke up, I only just saw them in time. It's a threat, some kind of sick game someone's playing.' He breaks off, chest heaving, looking accusingly around the circle as if he expects somebody to apologise.

'Sorry, you're saying someone surrounded you with pieces of broken glass in the night?' May stifles a yawn, not bothering to hide her unconvinced expression. 'Broken glass from where, exactly?'

'From the plane crash,' Jason yells, a ball of spittle flying from his lips. 'They must have taken them from the wreckage – huge, sharp, jagged pieces—'

'Could they have blown in there or something?' Jessa looks as confused as Brian.

'They didn't *blow* there,' Jason explodes, looking like he's about to have an aneurysm. 'They were planted! It was like waking up in the jaws of a glass crocodile. Oh, for Christ's sake, look, I'll show you.' And he grabs Jessa by her uninjured arm and drags her along the beach with the others trailing behind in various stages of wakefulness, their expressions ranging from perplexed to bemused to politely sceptical.

The sand around Jason's makeshift tent is smooth and soft, unblemished by glass or any other debris for that matter. He stops dead, staring at it in disbelief.

'It . . . it was there.' He looks around, taking in May's smirk and Jessa's sympathetic smile. 'It was all *right* here, I swear.' He gestures helplessly at the empty beach. 'Glass everywhere, sharp pieces . . .'

'Maybe you had a bad dream, J.' Shannon puts a supportive hand on his back, rubbing it soothingly. 'It wouldn't be surprising after everything we've been through, to have a vivid nightmare like that, get confused . . .'

'I'm feeling pretty compos fucking mentis actually,' he roars, and her hand drops like a stone.

'COME ON, YOU GUYS!' Jason shouts, his eyes swivelling wildly from one face to the next. 'Are you seriously telling me this doesn't fit in with all the other weird shit that's been going on? Elliot gets pushed off a cliff—'

'Bit of an exaggeration, it was more of a small hill—' May holds up her hands as Jason eyes her as if he's about to explode: 'Sorry, sorry, go on.'

'Then someone practically gives May alcohol poisoning . . .'

'Oh, so now you believe me?' May cuts in, sounding aggrieved. 'The other day it was all May's a drunk, May can't hold her liquor, but *now* you think I was telling the truth, do you?'

'Well, I didn't know it was a pattern then,' Jason protests. 'But look at it – add in blades of broken glass surrounding my bed and you've got a pretty obvious spate of attacks.'

'Nobody actually did anything to you, though, right?' Jessa asks. 'I mean, they didn't cut you or attack you with the glass?'

'They could have done,' Jason splutters. 'It's a threat, don't you see? They're letting me know they could have stabbed me to death in my sleep if they wanted to.'

'Who would want you to know that? Who would have any reason to threaten you?'

'I don't know. But I did *not* imagine it. It was *not* a dream. Someone was trying to scare me, or threaten me, or cut me,' Jason hisses between clenched teeth. 'Not that I am scared,' he adds quickly, 'I'm just angry. This is getting stupid and dangerous and it needs to stop.'

Privately, Hayley thinks that Jason's rage-fuelled outburst sounds exactly like fear. A particular, male kind of fear. But this doesn't seem like the best moment to mention it, so she keeps her mouth shut.

'This is getting pretty damn weird, bro,' Brian says, uneasily. 'What the hell is going on?'

Hayley thinks about it all day. She mulls over everything that has happened while she stands knee-deep in seawater, her arms aching as she scrubs the few pieces of clothing she's worn in rotation for the whole of the past week. She takes herself back to the moment Elliot fell, the confusion and shouting, the feeling of the wind whipping her hair into her eyes, the straining, desperate hope for a miracle from the sky. She tries to make herself step into the memory, to look around for signs of anything unusual – to recall a shadow, or a figure that might have slipped into their midst quietly, at the edges of her vision. But there's nothing except her imagination. Sometimes it shows her a masked figure, hovering in the trees. Sometimes one or other of her teammates: Shannon, shiftily looking around before her fists shoot out to shove Elliot in the back, or Brian and Jason nodding silently to each other and pushing him over in unison. Sometimes her feverish brain even shows her own scarred hands reaching out, forcing Elliot over the edge. Could she have done something like that, in the trauma and the shock of the storm and forgotten it? Her mind feels like it's spinning out of control, trying to find something real to grip onto.

She picks at the problem while she stands for hours on fishing duty through the afternoon, her feet slurping into the wet sand, the hot sun beating down unforgivingly on her shoulders, the limp line trailing off into the water, catching nothing.

She turns each of her teammates each like stones, trying to identify possible suspects and motives, none of them convincing. Could it be Elliot? Finding ways to hurt the classmates he's clearly had hostile feelings towards for years, taking revenge for their life of luxury and the advantages it gave them? But he was the first one to be attacked. Could he have faked his own accident to divert suspicion away from himself? It doesn't seem very likely, considering how badly he could have been hurt. None of it makes any sense.

'Any luck?' May splashes out towards her wearing just a black sports bra and a pair of cut-off shorts, on her way to the daily swim she swears is keeping her sane. ('And fit, because you *know* the press is going to want to talk to us when we get out of here,' she airily informed everyone on the third day, when she started the regime.)

'Not much.' Hayley shows her the backpack she has slung over one shoulder, containing just one small, grey fish. 'Hey, May, this might seem like an odd question, but …' She shields her eyes, watching May closely. 'Do you remember anything strange happening at the end-of-tour party?'

'Strange?' May freezes, her neck muscles tautening. 'No, definitely not. It was just a normal party.'

'Did anyone seem to be acting strangely?' Hayley presses, and May's eyes dart from side to side as if she's trying to work out what to say.

'Well, I guess everyone was relieved the tour was over, and happy to celebrate our win, right?' she replies, cautiously.

'Shannon was certainly in a celebratory mood,' Hayley says, watching May closely. May takes a step back and loses her footing, splashing down into the sea and swallowing a mouthful of saltwater. She gets to her feet, coughing as water streams out of her nose.

'Sure, but Shannon deserved to have a good night. So what if she decided to have a few drinks? And doesn't she have every right to have a bit of fun once in a while like the rest of us? It's not easy being head cheerleader, you know.'

May runs a hand over her face, wiping saltwater out of her eyes. 'Anyway, why is it always all about the girls at parties? Brian was all over those Duke cheerleaders all night, but I don't see anybody giving him a hard time about it. Not that I necessarily respect their judgement,' she mutters, 'considering what he was up to earlier.'

'What do you mean?'

'Oh, you know, those stupid running jokes he had going with those guys from Duke.'

Hayley frowns and takes herself back to the party again, the crush of people and the hot, uncomfortably humid living room. She was perched on the edge of an armchair, trying to look like she was part of the conversation of a bunch of Duke girls standing near her. A great splash of laughter erupted around the sofa where Jason and Brian were sitting swigging beers and rippled out around the room. She remembers the half smile on her lips, like she could catch the wave and ride it, using the shared appreciation of a joke to unite her with the other partygoers. But she never heard the actual joke, or the ones that followed as the laughter swelled and crashed. It was lost in the din.

'Let's just say he wasn't exactly being complimentary to women,' May says, tight-lipped. 'Quite how he managed to attract several of them at once is a total mystery to me.'

'What did he say?'

'I'm not repeating it, Hayley, it was disgusting.' And before Hayley can ask her anything else, she splashes off into the deeper water, launching into a rhythmic crawl.

After a few more minutes, Hayley decides to give up and wades in from the shallows. Any fish that might have been tempted have probably been scared off by May's splashing anyway. Further up the beach, she can see Jason lying in the shade, still glowering. She stops next to his sleeping shelter and crouches down, running her hand over the warm, smooth sand.

Hayley gasps and cries out as a sharp, clean pain flashes through her finger. She sucks it, tasting metallic blood, and examines the fresh cut, bright and wet alongside the scabs of the scratches she got in the crash. Cautiously, she sifts through the sand with the end of her fishing stick, and uncovers a long, razor-sharp sliver of glass. Hayley picks it up between her fingertips and examines it, eyeing the distance to the rest of the plane debris. There's no other glass nearby, nothing to suggest it was thrown from the wreck during the crash.

She digs out a plaster from the first-aid box, and finding the 'fridge' empty, fills the skirt of her pale blue sundress with empty water bottles and sets off through the trees to fill them from the fresh water supply. It rained torrentially a couple of nights ago, leaving the island smelling of earth and secrecy the next morning, and there should be enough water left for another round of bottles, at least.

When she steps into the shaded clearing, someone's already there. Shannon, standing over the tarpaulin, staring at her own reflection, quietly sobbing.

She's suspended there in her own private world, and Hayley feels like she's intruding. As if the island has somehow accepted Shannon and is holding her in its embrace. Hayley has crashed unwittingly into this tender scene, where she isn't wanted or needed. She's about to turn and leave when Shannon looks up and sees her, quickly wiping her eyes.

'Sorry,' Hayley whispers.

'Don't be. Sometimes you forget for a few hours, you know? And then . . .'

'Yeah. I know.'

And they stand side by side and push the empty bottles into the still water.

Later, after she's forced down yet another meal of dry, bony white fish, Hayley is pushing through the bushes to find a quiet spot to relieve herself, when she overhears hushed voices, whispering in the trees ahead. She pauses behind a tree, every nerve ending tingling, every muscle clenched on high alert.

'—didn't want everyone to know—' a voice hisses furiously. And Hayley's stomach drops as she realises it is Elliot, standing next to a tree a few metres away with his back to her, fists clenched with frustration.

'I didn't say that,' comes the other voice, and Hayley leans out very slowly from behind the tree and sees Jessa, hurt and anger playing across her face, standing opposite Elliot.

'I can see how it might tarnish your perfect image,' he spits, bitterly, and Jessa snaps at him.

'Oh, shut up, it's got nothing to do with that and you know it.'

'Then why haven't you told your friends? Because you know exactly what they'd say if they found out.'

Hayley leans further, trying to see Elliot's face, and curses herself as a twig snaps under her foot with a loud crack. Jessa jumps and turns towards her, as Hayley crashes through the bushes towards them, as if she's just come from the beach.

'Oh, hi, guys,' she beams, as the sweat pools in the small of her back. 'Nature calls!' and she strides cheerily on, pretending that nothing is wrong, that she didn't hear anything, that the two people she thought were the least suspicious on the whole island haven't just jumped right to the top of her suspect list.

DAY 10

There's almost no conversation as they pick at their fruit and fish the next morning. Hayley, sick with unease, just swigs at a bottle of water. She tastes it carefully first, an automatic check she's taken to performing on everything she consumes, just to be safe.

A lethargy has settled over the group. The survival skills that seemed dramatic and exciting in the first week have become monotonous. Their immediate fears of acute thirst and hunger have been allayed by the supplies they've built up, at least for the time being. In the first few days, there was always someone scanning the sky, checking for any sign of rescuers, stiffening in excitement when they thought they heard a faint noise that might have been a distant engine. But every day that passes without any sign of relief blunts their hopes. Nobody is looking skyward today.

Jessa and May are sharing a coconut, taking it in turns to scrape unenthusiastically at the white flesh. May is humming under her breath as usual, something upbeat and poppy, and Jessa's nodding along to the beat, but Hayley sees how her eyes dart sideways towards Elliot every now and then. Could Jessa and Elliot be working together? What did Jessa do that Elliot knows she is keeping secret? Could it really have been Jessa who spiked May's drink? But why?

Hayley is still mulling it over when the girls set off on yet another a fruit-picking expedition, leaving the boys rattling around the camp like aimless marbles. She considers just coming straight out and confronting Jessa, telling her what she overheard and asking what it was about. But something holds her back. Even though the crash has obliterated some of their social hierarchy, there are still deep-seated boundaries, unwritten rules she doesn't feel able to break. Jessa, May and Shannon are still *those* girls, still somehow distant and unreachable from Hayley's vantage point even though she's a member of their squad. Things are shifting, slowly, but she still can't bring herself to accuse Jessa of something outright. Not yet, anyway. And she doesn't want to scare people off, alert them to the fact that she's listening and watching, probing into the cracks, trying to put it all together. Her confidence is returning as she tries to solve this mystery, but for now, she's still more comfortable gathering pieces of the picture and weaving them together from her place in the shadows.

The weather is mercifully cooler today, with thick, low bands of grey cloud blocking out the worst of the sun's direct heat. But the air feels muggy and full, pressing in around them and making it harder to breathe. Everything feels quiet and mysterious. The light among the trees is dappled and dark green, the thick air muffling noise, as if they are swimming in a deep lake. Even the bird song is silenced today, and Hayley wonders if they know another storm is coming, if they're holed up in their nests and crannies, waiting for it to pass in safety. Wondering what's coming next.

Suddenly May shrieks, her piercing voice ripping through the cotton-wool air, and Hayley's head snaps in her direction, her chest pounding. But it's just a bug, scuttling over May's hand as she steadies herself against a tree trunk.

'Ugh, ugh, ugh, get it *off* me.' She shudders, shaking her hand frantically and spinning around.

'Aren't you supposed to be an animal-loving vegan, May?' Shannon can't resist asking, with a sly smile.

'Vegan. Does. Not. Equal. Bug. Lover.' May gasps disjointedly, jerking around as if she can feel its scratchy legs clinging to her skin.

They walk on, the forest grasping at Hayley's sore ankle every few steps like an insistent child that will not be denied, clinging and encumbering her every step. In the quiet, close stillness, she notices the beauty in the trees around her for the first time. One trunk is enrobed in a fine mesh of thin red vines, the colour so deep and lustrous it looks like a network of pulsating capillaries. A bush she has always avoided because of the long, vicious spikes that protrude amongst its waxy green leaves is sprinkled, on closer inspection, with the tiniest powderpuff pink flowers.

'I have the weirdest feeling we're being followed,' May says under her breath, breaking the silence. 'Like someone is watching us.'

'Someone is watching us,' Shannon says, almost dreamily.

'What are you talking about?' Jessa looks alarmed, spinning round to peer through the trees that press close on every side.

'The island is watching us. I've felt it since the first night we arrived. We're not supposed to be here.'

'I've felt that too,' Hayley says, aware of the vibrancy of the trees, alive and listening, the vines and plants crushed beneath their feet.

'It's judging us,' Shannon says, looking up into the canopy.

May laughs uncertainly. 'I don't know about that. But I do feel very free here.' She sighs, picking her way carefully between two bushes, one crawling in shiny, black lacquered ants.

'Free? We're trapped!' Jessa speaks lightly, but Hayley recognises the note of fear, never far from the surface.

'I know. I know it's a strange thing to say. I'm worried about getting off the island, obviously. But in those moments when you let yourself focus on the present, it just feels so different from home.' May looks like she's trying to find the words to explain. 'There's such freedom in being able to explore a forest like this . . . or walk down the beach alone in the middle of the night . . .

'I know what you mean.' Jessa nods. 'I thought about it that first night, when the boys were so preoccupied about wild animals and protection. And I was thinking, this would be the safest I would ever feel camping out, knowing for sure that my body wasn't going to be found in some ditch the next morning.'

'It's funny, isn't it?' Shannon sounds pensive. 'The things that scare us are so very different from the things that scare them.'

'Well, until now, anyway.' May's voice is low and serious. 'Now I'm not sure how safe any of us are any more.'

'Do you guys really think there's someone going around deliberately hurting people?'

'I think the boys have vivid imaginations.' Shannon is curt and to-the-point. 'Like May says, feeling exposed and threatened is a new experience for them. It's not for us.'

'I don't know what to think,' Hayley admits. 'That whole thing with the glass . . . it'd be such a weird thing for someone to do . . . but on the other hand it would also be really odd for Jason to make it up. Do we really think he could have had a nightmare that vivid?'

'Don't look at me,' Shannon says, as the others automatically turn to her. 'My sleeping shelter isn't even next to Jason's. I have no idea what he is or isn't dreaming about.'

'What's going on with you guys, Shan?' Jessa asks, gently, curiously.

Shannon sighs. 'I don't know,' she says in a small voice. 'Everything just feels different, somehow.'

'Did something happen?' May asks, with characteristic bluntness.

Shannon shakes her head. 'It's hard to explain.'

'But you're Jason and Shannon.' Jessa smiles. 'You're the real deal! My world wouldn't make sense without you guys together.' She's speaking lightly, but Hayley senses a real, childlike fear underneath.

'Did something happen at the party?' Jessa asks, and May stops in her tracks, staring at Shannon as if she already knows the answer.

'He got mad at you for dancing with that Duke guy,' Jessa says, sympathetically, 'is that it?'

'No,' Shannon murmurs, vaguely, shaking her head. 'No, no, that was nothing. Jason had a headache, he'd already gone home before the dancing started.'

'Where did you guys go?' May asks, looking uneasily between Shannon and Jessa. 'When the party moved out into the back yard, I didn't see either of you. I ended up getting a cab to the hotel because I thought I must have missed you but when I knocked on your room doors, you weren't there. And your phone was off as *always*,' she shoots, reproachfully, in Jessa's direction.

'I was there,' Jessa replies, quickly glancing away. 'I went back to the hotel early: the whole party scene gets a lot less fun really fast when you're the only sober one left. I must have already been asleep when you knocked.' Hayley notices that Jessa doesn't meet May's eyes.

'I was with one of the Duke girls,' Shannon says. 'I went up to use the bathroom and found her in there sobbing. I stayed with her for about an hour, we went into one of the bedrooms to talk.'

'About what?'

'She'd had a ... bad experience,' Shannon says, lowering her voice as if she thinks they might be overheard.

'What do you mean?' May asks.

'Well ...' Shannon pauses as if she's not sure whether to continue. 'She'd been ... I think ...' She stops and then says, uncertainly, 'I think maybe she'd been raped?'

'You think?'

Shannon shrugs. 'She said she'd been making out in a bedroom with some guy and it was all moving really fast and she thought it was what she wanted but then at some point she panicked and changed her mind.'

'So she had sex with him and then regretted it?' Jessa asks.

'No, she changed her mind before the sex started, but he just carried on and did it anyway.'

'That's awful,' Jessa gasps. 'Did she go to the police?'

Shannon shakes her head. 'She said she had a boyfriend and she didn't want him to find out what had happened.'

'She had a boyfriend and she was making out in a bedroom with some other guy?' Jessa holds up a hand. 'Was it because she was worried about what the boyfriend would say that she called it rape?'

Hayley feels as if Jessa has reached out and squeezed her stomach with an ice-cold hand, but she continues, with sincerity: 'You know, they call it buyer's remorse, right? When a girl has sex but then regrets it, so she says she was raped.'

'Jessa!' May shoots her a shocked look.

'I don't think that's an actual thing, Jessa,' Shannon says. 'And she seemed pretty upset.'

'Well, did she actually tell him no?'

'I don't think so. She said she just kind of froze. She said he was heavy, that his body was pinning her down. But he must have been able to tell she wasn't into it, right?'

'Maybe,' Jessa says, slowly. 'But isn't there a difference between rape and having sex with someone who's not that into it?'

'Not really,' May says, firmly. 'It depends what you mean

by "not that into it", I guess. If he doesn't know whether she consented or not I'd say that's rape. You need an enthusiastic yes or you stop.'

'What, like you have to get the other person to stop and sign a contract before you begin? Sounds sexy.'

'What would you know about what's sexy, Jessa?' Shannon asks sharply. Jessa stops in her tracks, as startled as if Shannon had actually slapped her across the face.

'Nothing, I guess,' she says, slowly, cheeks flaming.

'Actually,' Hayley interrupts and it's as if the other girls had totally forgotten she was even with them, 'it depends where you are when it happens.'

'What? What are you even talking about?!'

'The law on rape. It varies by state – I looked into it when I was writing an article about that house-party arrest of that guy, Chad Maxwell.' She glances quickly at Shannon, but there's no flicker of recognition on her face when Hayley mentions the case. 'We were in Texas the night before the plane crash, right? Texas is one of the ones I remember, because it really shocked me. In Texas, it's only rape if the rapist uses force or violence or threatens it. Or if the person is unconscious or unable to fight back. In other words . . .'

'She'd have had to try to push him off her,' Jessa finishes.

'Yeah,' Hayley admits. 'It's completely messed up.'

'But in the guy's defence, how did he know she thought he was raping her? She was kissing him,' Jessa protests again.

'You'd never say that about anything else,' Shannon says. 'You'd never say, well how was he supposed to know she didn't want him to take her phone, it was right there in her pocket, he might have thought she wanted to give it to him – that's why he robbed her. Why are we so keen to give a guy the benefit of the doubt when it's rape?'

'And why can't he take the time to damn well check?' May adds, hotly. 'If you're not sure, it should be on you to make sure. The onus should be on him to know for certain she wants it, not on her to find a way to fucking protest.'

'Amen,' Hayley says, and Jessa rolls her eyes but doesn't say any more.

They walk on, the silence awkward at first. But at some point, May announces that this road trip needs a soundtrack and starts belting it out with gusto, flipping between Kesha, vintage Dolly Parton and Beyoncé with wild abandon, Shannon and Jessa occasionally joining in on backing vocals. Their singing is harsh against the silent undergrowth, and Hayley feels like they are breaking something sacred, like they should apologise and muffle their voices. But she doesn't know how to ask them to without sounding mad, so she says nothing and follows quietly in their wake.

Picking the fruit is harder work than Hayley had imagined. The guavas are the easiest to harvest, with their smooth, slightly textured skin turning from green to yellow as they ripen. She targets those the shade of tennis balls, twisting the stems gently until they pop off into her palm, trying not to wonder whether she'll ever feel a real tennis ball in her hand again.

She stubbornly blocks out the memories that come flooding in, summers at the court with her mom, Dad arriving to pick them up and honking from the parking lot, stopping for ice cream on the way home. When she'd told her parents about the tour, her mom had pointed out that it'd take up half the summer holiday. 'It's my last chance to beat you at tennis, kiddo,' she'd said lightly, ruffling Hayley's hair, trying to keep the catch out of her voice. 'You'll be heading off to college next summer, far too busy to hit the ball around with your old mom.'

And Hayley had dismissed her. Or at least, she'd been impatient, focused on her Ivy League dreams and getting the cheer squad on her applications. 'We'll play when I get back, Mom, I promise,' she'd said, carelessly. Not 'I love you, I'll always have time for you.' Not 'Mom, I'll never be too busy to come back for a game, wherever I go to college.' Just 'when I get back'. And now . . .

No. She isn't letting herself do this. Hayley Larkin is in control. She can't control the weather, or the island, or the bugs, or whichever one of her teammates is playing stupid, dangerous pranks, but she can and she will control her own brain. And she is not going to break down now. On the flight home, Hayley has promised herself, she'll let herself break. Let herself acknowledge for the first time how terrifying and lonely this ordeal has been. Not. Yet.

The low-hanging fruit isn't difficult to reach, but they soon run out of easy pickings. Hayley stands, legs apart, knees shaking in spite of herself, as May sits on her shoulders, reaching for ripe guavas and complaining that Hayley isn't steady enough.

'I'm doing my best,' she fires back, through gritted teeth. 'You're not exactly the sugar plum fairy, okay?'

May leaps down, landing light on her feet, catlike. She grins. 'It's taken a month of practice, a fortnight's tour and over a week stranded on an island for you to stand up to me, Hayley Larkin. I like it.'

And Hayley's smile might be a little uncertain, but it definitely reaches her eyes.

The brownish fruit that Hayley thought looked like an avocado is firmer on the tree than the wrinkled specimens she has eaten so far, tapering gently to a point like an overgrown, slightly squashed kiwi. These are harder to reach than the guavas, the tree trunks slender and tall, their leaves and fruit only appearing several metres off the ground. But May wriggles up the trees like a monkey, her skinned shins more than compensated for by the abundant bunches of fruit she finds, clinging together like clusters of dark, golden eggs. She picks them one at a time and drops them gently into Shannon's waiting, cupped hands.

'Did you ever think about becoming a baseball catcher?' May asks, with a low whistle of appreciation as Shannon dives for a stray fruit and catches it in the outstretched fingertips of her left hand.

'I'll keep it in mind as a backup.' Shannon grins.

They eat as they go along, digging their teeth into any fruit that splits or bruises as they pick it, letting the juice run down their chins and congeal stickily on their arms. Hayley is just piling the last mango neatly on the heap they've collected when she hears the faintest noise; something at once strange and deeply familiar.

'Can anyone else hear that?'

'Hear what?' Jessa panics immediately, shrinking closer to the others.

'It's not a person, or an animal or anything.' Hayley cocks her head. 'Keep still a second.' They all stand frozen, ears straining. Hayley hears the noises of the forest; a tree creaking slightly, a scuttling in the undergrowth, the rustle of leaves overhead. Then, in a moment of stillness, she catches it again: the faintest trickling noise, like somebody has left a tap on in another room.

'Have you heard that before?' The others shake their heads. 'It's always been windy when we've been here before,' Jessa explains. 'There was a lot more noise from the leaves.'

Concentrating hard, Hayley tries to follow the sound. Every few steps she has to stop and listen again, creeping forwards painstakingly, the noise almost out of reach, her ears clinging to the very edge of the sound.

Even when she's standing right on top of it, she doesn't see it at first. The forest floor is so overgrown, and there is so much debris and clutter: vines and dead leaves sprawling over one another. But she can hear it, a soft trickle, and as they scrape away moss and mud with their hands they find it, a little spring, bubbling up amongst some rocks and flowing for a few metres in a shallow stream before trickling away between some bushes.

'It must run down from the top of the hill and under the ground.' Shannon traces the path with her finger. 'But it only comes up here in this one spot – it's so quiet and small, it's no wonder we never spotted it before.'

'Well, I'm glad we found it,' Jessa grins, pulling off her

shoes and socks and sighing in pleasure as she dips her hot, sandy feet in the cool water.

'Never mind washing our feet, we've got water!' Hayley feels elated and buoyant, like a huge weight she didn't even realise she had been carrying has lifted from her shoulders. 'We won't have to rely on rain and coconuts any more. We can collect water from here and boil it to clean it.' She's surprised that nobody else seems to be as excited as she is. Don't they realise how precarious their situation is?

'Ew, ew, ew, ew!' Jessa jumps up, scrambling to put her shoes and socks back on, physically recoiling from the stream.

'What, what?' May scans the water for some horrifying predator.

'Sorry, nothing major, but there are leeches in there.' Jessa points and they all lean forward, spotting the slug-like brown creatures glistening in the water.

'Just when you thought this island couldn't get any creepier.' After her morning brush with bugs, May looks like she is taking the leeches personally. But her outraged face is so funny Hayley can't suppress a giggle, and before she knows it, she is crying with laughter, infecting them all with it, giddy with the relief of that tight, tight knot in her stomach unwinding just a little.

That afternoon the girls lie on their backs in the shade of the fruit trees. The clouds have lifted and a light breeze has swept away the thickness of the morning air, leaving Hayley feeling fresher, less constrained. She watches lazily as the dappled sunlight plays across her forearm, highlighting the soft, dark hairs.

At home, she'd have been worried about them. For years she's fought a pitched battle with her mom, who doesn't believe in arm waxes, and calls her body hair 'a beautiful part of my beautiful daughter'. A beautiful part she's been teased about since grade school, leaving her self-conscious and always pulling sleeves down over her wrists. 'Just because you've never seen them before doesn't mean they're not normal,' Grandma used to say, stroking her hands with long, papery fingers. 'You just haven't seen them because all we see are white models with blonde, invisible hair.' She ran a gentle palm down Hayley's arm. 'It doesn't mean this is any less beautiful, just because they choose not to show it to us.'

'I know that, Grandma,' she'd moaned, cutting her off quickly before she launched into the tirade about who 'they' are. 'The problem is, nobody else does.' The breeze strokes her arms, gently, and she closes her eyes, yearning for her grandmother's touch. The hair doesn't seem to matter so much here.

She has almost drifted off to sleep when Jessa speaks in that small, almost childish voice. 'Is it any of you? Honestly? Look, no judgement, I swear, and I won't tell the guys, but I'm scared, and I just want to know what's going on. So ... is it? Any of you?'

Hayley glances around. Jessa is looking determinedly straight up at the clumps of green mangoes huddled amongst the leaves above her head. There's liquid pooled at the corner of her eye. She and May are curled around each other like squirrels, May's arm slipped loosely over Jessa's hips, Jessa cradling her bad arm with her good one. They're breathing slowly, as if they're using each other's heartbeats to tether themselves.

Shannon is like something out of a classical painting, her dark waves of hair spread out across the floor, her slightly hollow cheeks still, tiny veins visible under her translucent eyelids. It looks like she's already asleep.

Nobody answers.

When Hayley wakes, disorientated and warm, the sun is much lower and the forest is striped with slanting shadows. She gently rotates her cricked neck, propping herself up stiffly on her elbows. Her eyes are still heavy with sleep, her scalp damp and hot.

The others are stirring too, Jessa yawning and blinking and Shannon sitting up, pulling her hair back into a ponytail. It's Hayley who sees them first, but the shock hits her so hard she can't even speak. She sits there, frozen, feeling ice rush through her veins. But something in her face makes Shannon look down, and her scream is enough to send the others leaping to their feet.

'What, what is it, where?'

'Our legs,' Hayley manages, in a strained whisper. They all look down.

'Get them off, get them off NOW!' May is high-kicking, thrashing her leg around like a can-can dancer. But it doesn't make any difference. The leeches are stuck fast.

Four or five fat, globular bodies clinging to each of them,

dotted from their thighs to their calves, their pulsating, balloon-like stomachs swollen, suggesting that they have been feeding for some time.

Jessa is doubled over with what Hayley thinks are silent tears, until she draws a trembling breath and lets out a shriek of laughter. 'I'm sorry, I'm sorry,' she wheezes, her shoulders shaking. 'You just look so funny. It's like you're trying to make your own foot fall off.' And she dissolves into tears of helpless laughter again.

'I'm. So. Glad. This. Is. Entertaining. To. You.' May speaks through gritted teeth, each word punctuated with another wild flail of her legs. When the leeches remain stubbornly in place, she squeezes her eyes shut and reaches down to try and pull one off. 'Grossgrossgrossgrossgrossgrossgross . . .'

'Wait,' Jessa shouts, grabbing May's hand to stop her. 'I had a leech bite when I was river fishing once; you can't just pull them off. They can regurgitate bacteria into your bloodstream or leave their mouth parts behind in the wound and get it infected.'

'*MOUTH PARTS?*' Shannon looks utterly disgusted. And something about her outrage, about the way she says 'mouth parts', tips Jessa back over the edge, until she's wheezing with laughter.

'You just have to use your fingernail – slide it under the mouth to break the suction, then you can flick them off.' Jessa demonstrates, her fingernail nudging under the thin end of one of the leeches that is gorging on her thigh. It subsides, reluctantly, leaving a horrible little wound that immediately starts to trickle blood.

'It'll bleed for a while,' Jessa says, matter-of-factly. 'When leeches start feeding they release something into your blood to stop it clotting so they can get full quicker.'

'I think I'm gonna be sick.' May gingerly starts to prise off her leeches, copying Jessa's technique.

Hayley looks down at her own unwanted passengers and almost gags. 'Don't think about it, don't think about it, don't think about it,' she whispers to herself, as she slides her fingernail under the end of one, feeling the slight release as the suction breaks and flinging it as far away from her as she possibly can. She shudders and wipes her hand on her dress.

A few minutes later they stand, panting amongst the shadowy trees, their legs striped with long, narrow trickles of blood.

'Remind me *never, ever* to fall asleep near a stream again.' May shudders, trying to stop the wound on her thigh from bleeding using the edge of her tattered violet cheerleading skirt. 'I still feel dirty.'

Jessa has stopped laughing. She's standing very still. 'I don't think the leeches made it from the stream on their own,' she says, suddenly.

'What do you mean?'

'The last time I got bitten by a leech, it was only because I was wading thigh deep in a river for two hours trying to catch a fish. They aren't exactly speedy creatures. Look where we are. The water is at least fifteen yards away. I find it very hard to believe that two dozen leeches somehow made it out of the spring and across all these leaves and rocks and vines and then evenly divided themselves up between us . . .'

Hayley's stomach feels cold. 'What are you saying?'

Jessa looks angry. 'Someone did this. No way it just happened by coincidence.'

Shannon looks from the stream to the clearing and back again. She slowly starts to nod. 'I think you're right. I didn't believe it before, but I'm starting to think something really creepy is happening on this island.'

'Well, who was it?' May sounds furious, like she's reached the absolute end of her tether. 'Which one of you bitches put a blood sucker on my leg?'

They're all staring at each other. Hayley feels her cheeks getting hot, feels a prickle of shame and fear, as if they might see guilt written on her face, even though she knows it wasn't her. The others look just as panicked as she does.

'It wasn't necessarily one of us,' she points out. 'We all woke up at the same time. What if it was one of the boys?'

'Yeah, we *think* we woke up at the same time.' May narrows her eyes suspiciously. 'But how do we know one of us didn't sneak up, get the leeches, then lie back down and pretend to be asleep again until we all woke up?'

'What, and cover her own legs in leeches too?' Jessa has a point.

'Well, yes, obviously,' May storms. 'To cover her tracks.'

'We don't have any way of knowing, do we?' Shannon automatically takes control. 'So let's get back to the camp. If someone is really trying to sabotage us, it's better if we're all together.'

Hayley likes the idea of safety in numbers. But it isn't lost on her that they might also just be running right back to the person who attacked them in the first place. Everything is so uncertain. It's like trying to find her way through fog. Suddenly, something else occurs to her.

'What if something happened to the boys while we were away?'

They crash back through the forest, ignoring the thorns and branches that tear at their hair and skin, jostling the fruits they're carrying in haphazard armfuls.

But the camp is quiet, the boys subdued There's fresh fish cooking over the flames and a huge pile of firewood nearby.

Jason freaks when he sees Shannon's legs.

'You're not just messing with me now,' he shouts, at nobody in particular. 'You're messing with my girl, and I will destroy you. Whoever you are, you don't mess with me or what's mine, you hear me?'

'Were you guys together all day?' Jessa asks, seriously.

'No,' Elliot answers at once. We were fishing and fetching firewood and stuff. Between that and, you know, bathroom breaks, we all went off into the trees at some point. It could have been any of us.'

Jessa raises an eyebrow.

'Not that I'm saying it was me!' he stutters. 'It wasn't me, I swear. But it could've been. I mean, except that it wasn't, obviously. We all had the opportunity is all I'm saying. On the upside, really great news about the spring, though.' He trails off nervously and turns to tend the fish.

Hayley and the others race to the sea, scooping up handfuls of water and rinsing their legs over and over again. But somehow no matter how much water she douses her skin with, no matter how much she welcomes the sharp tingle of salt in the wounds, Hayley still feels gross, as if the leeches have left behind slimy trails that won't wash clean.

She visits the plane in her dreams again that night. But everything is happening in slow motion. She's floating like an astronaut in a cloud of fruit pots, loose pages and pom poms, the others drifting past her with wide, unseeing eyes, terror frozen onto their contorted faces. She knows the plane is going down, knows there is nothing she can do about it, but still she tries to struggle, fighting against the heavy torpor of her limbs, wanting to make them move faster, wanting to run to the front of the plane, to help the pilot, or grab the controls ... something, *anything*. But instead it's happening torturously slowly, and she can't speed it up, can't speed herself up. There's nothing she can do but wait for the inevitable impact.

She's outside the plane now, watching it plummet towards the sparkling surface of the water, inch by inch. She tries to scream but her voice doesn't come out. She sees the island, and she's falling towards it, alone, so close now she can see every individual grain of sand, so close that she feels her whole body tense in terrified anticipation ...

And then it's gone, and there's just her mom's face, strained and fearful, her eyes boring into Hayley's, her fingers gripping Hayley's shoulders so hard it hurts. 'Hayley.' She's trying to tell her something, trying to warn her, but Hayley can't hear her properly, the wind is howling in her ears and her mom's voice is distorted. 'You're not looking hard enough.' Her mom is fading, her fingers are slipping away, she's being pulled in the opposite direction, they're back in the plane and the force is too strong, smashing them into the sides of the cabin ... 'You're missing something, Hayley ...' Hayley strains towards her, trying to reach her with every muscle in her body, but she's being pulled backwards, can't see or hear her any more, and she wakes in the dark with tears in her eyelashes and her mom's name on her lips.

DAY 11

It's Brian who first suggests they try diving for conch. He's the strongest swimmer in the group, a member of the water polo squad before he switched to basketball. He's been joining May on her daily swims and he says he's spotted some shells deep in the clear water off the island.

'It sounds dangerous,' Jessa warns, chewing her bottom lip. She's sitting on the beach, tipping a little of the spring water at a time into her hand from a plastic bottle, then gently working it into her twists, patting down the frizz that has started to grow at the roots.

'I've got this.' Brian swaggers, pulling on the tattered pair of old shorts he always uses for swimming. 'Want to guess how long I can hold my breath?'

'Why don't you show us?' May teases. 'Give us all a few minutes of peace and quiet.'

'Those conch might look close because the water's so clear here, but I reckon they're at least twenty feet down. No way you can get down to them and bring one back up all in one breath.'

'Watch me.' Brian strides confidently off towards the water, his swagger slightly undermined by the peeling patches of red sunburn on his back.

'That sunscreen run out, did it?' May calls after him, laughing. He pretends not to hear her.

'Just you wait,' he calls, over his shoulder. 'You'll be thanking us when you're eating fresh conch for dinner!'

'Ugh,' May mutters. 'Do I need to remind you that I'm a vegan?'

'NO!' Everybody shouts in unison, and Hayley cracks up at the affronted look on May's face.

'I'll come with you a way,' she shouts, hurrying after him. 'I could use a dip.'

Hayley's been waiting for a chance to get Brian on his own to ask him about the party, but this is the first time he hasn't been shadowing Jason. Now they're almost completely reliant on Elliot's fish to eat and his fire to cook it and stay warm after sunset, Hayley feels like she's watching Jason's grip on the group get looser every day. And he isn't taking it well. He's surly and withdrawn, snapping at anyone and everyone, making fewer attempts even to approach Shannon. And he relies on Brian more and more to be by his side, like still having his right-hand man to slap on the back and share the odd dirty joke helps to mask the vulnerability of losing his authority. But today Jason's out of sight, crossing the island to collect fresh coconuts, finally leaving Brian alone. And Brian is the only person left who she hasn't asked directly about the party, Hayley realises, apart from Jason himself.

'Want to know my secret?' Brian asks, as they walk down

the beach side by side, leaving a parallel path of footprints, his nearly double the size of Hayley's.

'Huh?'

'I practice holding my breath every morning. Nearly doubled my lung capacity that way,' he says, proudly, patting his chest. And I've read loads of online forums that say it increases your sperm count, too. Makes you last longer, if you know what I mean.' He glances sideways at Hayley. 'Something to do with physical control, I guess.'

'Oh.' It suddenly occurs to Hayley that there is nobody within earshot. She glances casually over her shoulder, back towards the camp, but the others must have gone looking for firewood or fruit, because there's nobody in sight. She suddenly feels very exposed. Very aware of how close to her Brian is, how few clothes they are both wearing. She hears May's words again as if she's whispering them in her ear. *'Let's just say he wasn't exactly being particularly complimentary to women . . . It was disgusting.'*

Almost imperceptibly she shifts her shoulders slightly, angling her body away from him. She lengthens her strides just a little, extending the distance between them. *Don't be stupid,* she tells herself, sternly, trying to calm her swiftly accelerating pulse. *Nothing's going to happen.*

'So, Brian,' she says casually, as their soles meet the slap of the wet sand. 'Did you have a good time at the party? The night before the crash?'

He stops dead and looks her straight in the eye. 'Why, what did you hear? You talk to one of the Duke girls?'

She stumbles backwards, then starts walking again.

'No. I was just making conversation. What did you think I'd have heard?'

'Nothing. Nothing.' He seems relieved, falling back into step beside her. 'I was just wondering what you meant.'

'So you didn't see anything out of the ordinary that night?' Brian glances immediately back up the beach, towards the camp, before his eyes flick back to Hayley.

'Why are you asking now?'

'I'm just . . . testing a theory. Humour me.'

'Well . . .' He looks conflicted. 'There was one thing, but I don't know if I should say.'

'I won't tell anyone.' Hayley speaks in her most soothing, reassuring reporter voice, usually reserved for reluctant sources in the school administrators' office. 'It'll stay between us, I swear.'

He looks to the beach again. 'It was after Truth or Dare finished. I'd gone up to the bathroom and as I walked past one of the bedrooms, I saw the door was ajar. I wasn't peeping, I swear,' he looks panicked, like he's regretting the conversation already.

'Of course not.' Hayley smiles, reassuringly, nodding encouragingly.

'Well, I saw Jason and Shannon, through the strip of the open doorway, having a major fight.'

Hayley is careful not to act surprised. She says nothing, letting the silence stretch until he feels compelled to fill it with more details.

'I dunno what they were arguing about, but he had her hotel key card: he pulled it out of his pocket and kind of flicked it at her, hard, so it clipped her right in the face.' He looks guiltily at Hayley. 'He must have had good reason to be so pissed.'

'Sure.' Hayley nods. 'Sure. Did he say anything?'

Brian scrunches up his face like he's trying to remember. 'He sort of hissed "walk yourself home then", and then he stormed out so fast he didn't even seem to see me, and he charged downstairs and slammed the front door behind him.' He shrugs as if it's all beyond him. 'Okay, well those conch aren't gonna pick themselves. See you later, Hayley.'

And she feels her whole body relax as he wades splashily through the shallow waves, leaving her alone.

Out of everyone she's spoken to, Brian is definitely the worst liar. But if he was willing to break his best friend's confidence to tell her about the fight, then what else is he still hiding? And what exactly was he joking about that night?

Hayley watches as he begins to swim, his head little more than a bobbing dot against the glimmer of the sea.

She does a few hundred yards of breaststroke, watching the others scurrying around on the beach like worker ants. The water soothes and caresses her tired limbs. Hayley is more active here than she has ever been in her life. The constant fetching and carrying, crossing the island and climbing trees has produced muscles where she never had any before. By the time she falls asleep each night she is thoroughly, achingly exhausted.

Eventually, she drags herself out of the water and heads up the beach, towelling herself off on somebody's spare jumper and pulling on a newly rinsed tank top and a pair of shorts.

They've been dried in the sun and their salty stiffness chafes against her skin, but at least they don't smell, which is more than she can say for the boys recently.

There's work to be done, as always. Hayley starts trying to cover a hole in one side of her shelter, where some of the sticks have shifted and the wind has started blowing in. She swears in frustration as the sticks she tries to shove in slip through her fingers and fall to the floor. She needs more of the long narrow palm leaves to plait together and make a kind of base.

It occurs to her that she could borrow some leaves from a pile Jessa had kept near her sleeping shelter, weighted down by a few large rocks. But as she reaches the leaves, everything happens at once. May emerges at the edge of the treeline, not seeing Hayley where she kneels, stooped, half hidden behind Jessa's lean-to. She looks both furious and terrified, a strange sort of panic on her face that Hayley has never seen before. And she is speaking, in a low voice trembling with emotion, to somebody in the trees behind her.

'You could have killed me, I hope you realise that. I easily could have slipped and hit my head on a rock with that much alcohol inside me. I could've gone for a drunk swim and drowned! I know it was you. And I know why you did it. I'm sorry, okay? I shouldn't have done what I did and I'm really, really sorry. I don't even know what got into me. But two wrongs don't make a right.' She pauses, like she's listening to somebody speaking too quietly for Hayley to hear. 'You know perfectly well I can't tell everyone what you did without them finding out what I did first. But if you're the one who's behind all the other things as well, you have to stop, okay? You have to stop before someone gets really hurt.'

And Hayley half rises, ready to sprint towards her, ready to crash into the trees and unmask whoever May is talking to, when a cold, thin, horrifying scream slices the moment in two. And she turns, instinctively, and stumbles towards the noise, and suddenly they are all there, in a jumble of people that happens so fast she doesn't know where each person comes from: May and Jessa and Elliot and Jason and Shannon, all wearing the same expression of sheer panic, all fumbling to count heads, all turning in unison to the sea and realising at the same moment that the awful noise is coming from Brian.

Hayley screws up her face, trying to see amongst the flashes of light that bounce up off the water. The sea swells and shifts restlessly, distorting her perspective.

'Is that him?' She sees a bobbing smudge that might be a head and next to it a hand, flickering upwards, jerking, writhing almost. There's no further sound, except the soft shushing of the water, no more screams or cries for help, yet somehow there is something frantic and desperate about the movement of that figure in the water. Suddenly the head seems to jerk, then snap backwards, and, for a horrifying, endless moment, it slips under the water and disappears. Then it surfaces again, barely moving, a floating speck, and Hayley knows, looking at it, that something is terribly, terribly wrong.

Elliot has already started pulling off his shirt as he runs towards the water and Hayley follows him, not thinking, not asking questions, just gripped by a terrible sense of dread.

Dimly, she hears the others also racing behind them, hears a voice she thinks might be Shannon's rise in a question, but there isn't time to stop, she is running, her feet pounding across the hot, soft sand, her legs splashing into the shock of the cold waves, wading out as quickly as she can, pushing against the firm resistance of the water.

They're closer now, though still at least twenty yards away, and she can make Brian out, starting to swim towards the shore, towards Elliot, who is a few yards ahead of her. Brian's face is awash with terror, his eyes skating across the surface of the water, his head jerking frantically as he scans the water around him.

'Elliot, move!' Brian's voice crackles with urgency as he glances over his shoulder. 'Get to the shore, NOW.'

Elliot doesn't listen, his arms driving through the water like pistons until he reaches Brian, who throws his arms around Elliot's neck, his face drained of all colour, coughing, through the spray. 'Hayley, get back to the beach, get back as fast as you can.'

May has reached Brian too, supporting him from the other side, helping him swim faster, murmuring something reassuring that does nothing to ease the stricken look on Brian's face. So Hayley turns and pounds back towards the beach, salt stinging her eyes. Half expecting at any moment to feel something grab at her legs, tear at her skin or pull her under the surface.

Elliot and Jason stagger out of the water, half dragging Brian between them. And it's only as they tear him from the clutches of the innocent, feathery surf that they see the trail of blood staining the sand a horribly vibrant red.

'Shark,' Brian gasps, his mouth opening and closing, his arms twitching as his face creases in pain. 'My leg.'

Shannon is white with shock, frozen next to him like a statue. It is the first time Hayley has ever seen her look truly helpless.

'Towels,' May screams. 'Fetch anything, any clothing, anything.' And Hayley is running, stumbling across the hot sand, feeling the searing pain as a sharp rock cuts into her foot, racing on, scrabbling frantically in the overhead locker for every item of clothing she can find and racing back across the beach, faintly wondering where the quiet whimpering sound is coming from before she realises it's in her own throat.

'It must've been at least four or five feet. Came straight for me.' Brian is gasping for breath, grimacing every time he shifts his weight. He physically braces himself, clenching his fists and gritting his teeth, before he lets himself look down and inspect what's left of his calf.

The leg is still there. It's attached, his foot unharmed, but there's a hideous groove of missing flesh, a cruel, gaping crescent like somebody has taken a great ice cream scoop from his ankle to his knee and simply carved it away. The blood is coming faster, gushing out into the sand and trickling down to mingle with the sea, visibly spurting in time with his heart rate.

'We have to stop the bleeding,' Shannon is panting, still rooted to the spot.

Hayley and May crouch in the wet, bloody sand, swathing Brian's leg as fast as they can in T-shirts, towels, everything they have.

'Pressure, put pressure on it,' Elliot urges, kneeling beside them and placing his warm, calloused palms beside Hayley's, forcing the sides of the gash together beneath the cloth, pinning the wound shut as Brian screams in pain and jerks away. Elliot's breath is warm on Hayley's neck, he smells of sea salt and coconut and something else she can't place.

'You'll have to hold him,' Elliot tells Jason, grimly, and for the first time, Jason nods and obeys, all his bravado stripped away as he kneels beside his stricken best friend, his face slack and uncomprehending.

'It's okay Brian, you're going to be okay,' he chokes, as he grasps him by his meaty wrists, forcing them down into the sand. And as Elliot rips a strip off a T-shirt and ties a tight knot above Brian's knee to cut off the blood flow, as more blood seeps out into the pool surrounding them, as Brian heaves and strains again to move away, Jason falls across him, using his whole body to force him still, and sobs. 'I'm sorry, man. I'm so, so sorry. This is for your own good. It's for your own good.'

The blood seems to slow. Brian lies still, his face ashen, tears trickling out of the corner of his eye to mingle with the blood and sand. The tourniquet is working. When Elliot discards the sodden layers of clothing saturated with blood and replaces them with a new white T-shirt, the bleeding is slower, visible but under control.

'Thank God,' Jessa repeats, over and over again. 'Thank God.'

Hayley doesn't know how long they sit there, keeping silent watch, as Brian drifts in and out of sleep, sometimes waking with a great, shuddering, keening cry of pain, only to fade into merciful oblivion again moments later. Once, he calls out for his mother, pleading for her like a baby, until Shannon eases his head onto her lap, tears in her eyes, and strokes his hair. 'Shh shh,' she whispers, her voice breaking. 'I'm here now. I'm here.' And he sighs a little and sleeps again.

It's a subdued group that gathers around the fire for a dinner of fruit, fish and no conch. Brian is asleep in the sand a little distance away, his head still on Shannon's lap. She won't leave him or swap with anyone else, refusing to take a break even to eat. She reluctantly accepts a bottle of water which she drinks with one hand, careful not to disrupt for a moment the gentle rhythm of her fingers stroking Brian's hairline. His absence hangs over the others like a heavy cloud, though the evening is calm and warm, the golden pre-sunset light lazily licking across the sand. The sea glitters close, mischievous and taunting. Hayley can't look at it. She doesn't think she'll ever be able to look at the sea again without seeing blood. Even now, she can't get it off her cuticles, from under her fingernails.

Long after the meal has ended, Hayley sits listlessly against the trunk of one of the palm trees, watching the fire die slowly down to a red glow, matching the first tendrils of crimson starting to leak into the sky from the edge of the horizon. She tries again and again to mentally reconstruct the scene near the camp earlier that day, trying to work out who might have come out of the trees behind May, who might have been the person May was accusing. But it's hopeless. It's all just a blur. May seems subdued, building a cracked pile of broken shells in the sand, the usual cloud of music that surrounds her noticeably absent. She's not even humming. Whatever the reason, she doesn't want everyone else to find out what she knows.

They examine Brian's leg in the warm, rose light of the early evening, the lips of the wound curling horribly like a snarl. The blood is beginning to clot, but the gash still gapes horribly, trickles still escaping at the bottom and turning his gym sock scarlet.

'We should sterilise it.' Shannon points out, gesturing to the remaining bottles of vodka from the plane.

'I think it needs stitching,' Jessa says, grimacing apologetically at Brian. You can't leave a wound that big open, it won't heal.'

'What are you gonna stitch it with?' Brian asks, through gritted teeth. And Jessa disappears into the jumble of supplies in the overhead locker and returns, apprehensively, with one of those miniature courtesy sewing kits from the hotel.

'No. No way. You have got to be kidding me.'

'She's right, Brian.' Elliot peeks again beneath the T-shirt swathing his leg. 'If we leave it open like that it'll be infected within days.' And nobody says it, but they're all thinking about Brian's stupid joke, about it being an infection that will kill one of them.

'The good thing is the cut is quite clean, like it slashed you instead of chomping down. The edges look like they could be brought together quite easily.'

Brian swallows heavily, turns his head away. But there's nowhere to go, no escape from this. 'Okay.' He grunts, and he lies back on the sand.

'Who's going to do it?' Jessa holds out the sewing kit and they all stare at it, trembling slightly in her fingers. 'Who knows how to sew?'

'Well, I'm out, obviously.' Jason shrugs.

'May makes her own clothes,' Shannon whispers.

May shudders. 'Yeah, with a sewing machine. I only do the buttons by hand.'

'That's still more sewing experience than the rest of us put together,' Jason points out, and they all turn to stare at her as she stands there, crowned with the gentle rose of the evening sun, opening and closing her mouth. It's the first time Hayley has ever seen her with nothing to say. May reaches out her hand reluctantly to take the needle as if she's in some kind of dream.

'Wait, put it in here first.' Shannon holds out one of the tiny vodka bottles and they stuff the whole lot in, needle and thread together, and Shannon puts the cap back on and shakes it for good measure. May takes another bottle and pours it all over her hands, scrubbing them together.

'Here.' Elliot hands two more of bottles to Brian, who takes them without hesitation and gulps them both down. 'This is going to hurt.' Elliot takes the last bottle and carefully empties it into the wound, sprinkling it over each section as if he's seasoning some grotesque cut of meat. Brian gasps, his face contorted in pain, and Jason and Elliot sit on either side of him, placing their hands on his shoulders and his thighs, ready to keep him still.

'I'll be as quick as I can,' May tells him. 'Move out of the light,' she snaps at the others. 'We've got to get this done before the sun goes down.'

But she stops, needle poised above the glistening edge of the flesh, and Hayley sees her throat move as she swallows over and over. 'You can do this.' Jessa is beside her, her voice low and steady. 'You are the strongest person I know. You can do this.'

And before she can change her mind, May has plunged the needle through the first slab of skin and into the other side, her fingers gripping the two pieces together, and pulled the thread tight.

Brian's screams are guttural and ragged, quickly giving way to wet, heaving sobs. It's not until he finally, mercifully passes out from the pain after the third or fourth stitch that Hayley takes a breath and realises she has been biting the inside of her cheek so hard that she can taste blood.

It's not pretty. But when May's finished, the lips of the wound are tightly drawn together, puckered and lumpy. There is a horrible purple bruise blossoming across Brian's calf, but it's no longer bleeding, at least. They wrap it tightly in the cleanest T-shirts they can find and elevate it on a pile of stones in an attempt to prevent swelling and keep the wound out of the reach of sand and insects.

And it isn't until Hayley's in bed that night that she hears a sound she never thought she would hear. The quiet, shuddering noise of May, crying into the night.

DAY 12

'What the hell?'

Brian has spent most of the day resting by the campfire, carried by the others to a nest of clothes and towels they've made up by the fire to keep him warm. But now he's struggling to prop himself up on one elbow, his voice alight with fury.

As they crowd around him he extends his outstretched hand, something wet and congealed hanging limply from it.

'What is that?' May wrinkles her nose: 'And why does it smell like it's dead?'

'Because it is!' Brian storms. 'It's a handful of the fish guts we've been using for bait. And I just found it in the pocket of my swim shorts.'

The others look at him, blankly, not understanding.

'Does someone want to tell me why they sent me out to deep water with literal *shark chum* in my pockets?'

'Woah, woah, calm down,' Elliot urges. 'Couldn't you have left it in your pocket from when you were fishing and forgotten about it?'

Brian is breathing heavily. He looks like a tethered bull about to rip the ring out of its own nose and go on a rampage. 'No, I couldn't. I always bait the hook before I go fishing and I leave the spare bait on the beach. Besides, I wasn't even wearing these shorts then. I've only been wearing them for swimming. Which anybody who had been paying attention knows.' He glares around furiously, his scowl etched deep into his forehead.

'Enough. Whatever the hell is going on here, it ends now. I could have freaking died.' His voice is shaking with fury. 'I still might, if we don't get out of here soon.'

There's deadly silence.

'Whoever you are, this needs to stop. Now. Before anyone else gets badly hurt.'

'We need to know what she wants!' Jason sounds hysterical, his eyes skittering from one face to the next.' Whoever's doing this. And don't look at me like that, May, because it's obviously a girl. Everyone who's been seriously injured is male.'

'Jason,' May deadpans. You weren't injured at all. My leech bites hurt worse than your sore feelings after you got scared by a few shards of broken glass.'

And before Jason can argue, Jessa steps between them, hands raised for calm.

'Jason's right. We can't stop it unless we know who's doing it, and why.'

'What do you want?' Jason shouts, half laughing, gesturing wildly around the circle. The silence is total. A log hisses and falls inside the centre of the fire and Hayley feels her pulse jump in her throat.

'We don't know for sure it's a girl,' May says, stubbornly. 'We've all had our blood sucked, too, remember. And I was almost given alcohol poisoning.'

'Yeah: I see your leeches and your cocktail afternoon and raise you *almost being killed by a damn shark*,' Brian yells, furiously, white flecks of spit flying out of the corner of his mouth.

'We don't know what species of shark it was,' Elliot says, in a conciliatory tone. 'It probably bit you by accident, Brian, because it thought you were a seal or something. If it had really wanted to attack you, you'd be dead. There are actually very few species of sharks that are dangerous to humans in these waters; it might have been a lemon shark or a sand tiger ...'

'Or a hammerhead or a blacktip,' Jason breaks in, angrily. 'We grew up in Florida too, Elliot. You might know more than most about your little fire-starter tricks, but you're not the sole authority on sharks.'

'So we're not doing this any more, okay?' Jason sounds commanding, but Hayley can hear the frustration in his voice. It's all very well making angry threats into thin air, but they fall flat when there isn't any response.

Hayley closes her eyes and tries to put herself in the shoes of whoever might be doing all this. And even though she isn't certain, she has a nagging feeling that whoever it is wants something.

Most of the attacks have had worse psychological than physical effects. If the attacker wanted Elliot dead, they could have finished him off while he was unconscious that night.

If they really wanted to hurt Jason, the glass shards could have been used to stab him, not to scare and confuse him. The leeches were more shocking and disgusting than actually harmful. Following the pattern, Hayley decides that the shark bait was meant to create exactly the kind of terror she saw on Brian's face in the sea, not to cause an actual attack. It's like somebody is trying to make them understand something, to send them a message.

If only they had the chance to communicate, Hayley muses as she wanders up the beach. If the person doing all this somehow got what they wanted, the attacks might stop. Suddenly, she is seized by an idea.

'Write it down!' Her voice comes out breathy and high-pitched, her cheeks flushed. She's digging frantically in a pile of stuff that's been left just inside the hollow tube of the plane, re-emerging triumphantly with a ballpoint pen and Elliot's dog-eared sketchbook. She races back to the group.

'Write. It. Down.' She repeats, urgently, her eyes shining around the expectant faces. 'I'll leave the sketchbook out tonight, away from the camp. Whoever is doing this can tell us anything they want. We'll check the book in the morning. And no tricks. Nobody keeps watch. No handwriting analysis – use block capitals if you like, whatever. Just take the chance to tell us what you want. Or what you want us to know. What we need to do to end this. okay? Please. We'll do whatever it takes – just tell us what you want.'

There's no answer except the incoming tide, which sounds like a mother soothing her baby. *Shush. Shush. Shush.*

*

Of course, Hayley keeps watch. She places the sketchbook far down the beach, away from their sleeping places, a good distance from the small glowing circle of sand lit by the campfire. Like the others, she pretends to go to bed, but she waits, lying in the silence of sticks and leaves for what feels like hours, her whole body tingling with excitement and anxiety, until the sky is black as soft velvet. She creeps out quietly, leaving some clothes bundled up in case anybody checks her shelter, then sets off, sneaking along the beach, seeing nobody. In spite of the danger, there's a small, irrepressible part of her that can't help bristling with excitement and tingling nerves: her first stakeout.

The sleeping shelters are dotted along the treeline: anybody who wanted to reach the sketchbook covertly could melt into the trees, make their way through the forest in the darkness and emerge onto the beach further along, unseen and unheard. Hayley continues through the dark gloom of the trees until she is beyond the book, which lies innocently on the sand, just visible in the soft moonlight. She finally emerges when she is level with a big rock, about twenty yards further along the beach, and she rushes to crouch in its shadow. She peeks around the seaward side so she has a good view of the book, but can't be seen by anyone walking towards it from the trees.

It takes about half an hour for her electric excitement to fade to a buzz. Then another hour for it to descend into stiff, unrelenting boredom. Her butt feels heavy and numb, her arms ache from pressing against the hard rock and her ankles are being bitten to pieces by sandflies. She shivers, wishing she had brought an extra jumper, and tries to shift her position quietly, lying down uncomfortably on her stomach, sand prickling her elbows.

After a few hours she feels stupid, freezing and exhausted. Had she really believed that someone who had managed to avoid detection so cleverly this far was going to just walk up and write down a full explanation of their actions?

Eventually, Hayley feels her eyes closing. She tries to fight it, digging her fingernails into her palms and training her eyes on the shadowy place where she left the sketchbook, but the weight of her tiredness presses gradually and unstoppably down on her until she can't fight it any longer. With a little sigh, she rests her head in the crook of her elbow and drifts off to sleep.

She wakes at dawn, unused to the thin, early light, her shoulder and hip aching. The beach is deserted. The fire is out, and the trees stand like silent witnesses to a motionless night. Still Hayley races to the sketchbook, grabbing it up and rifling through the pages with trembling fingers, clumsy in their haste. There's nothing but Elliot's drawings. A hastily sketched exterior of Oak Ridge, with its imposing bell tower and rolling lawns; a few drawn courtside during practice on tour; one of the squad on the plane just before they crashed. She flicks through it again, more carefully, to be sure. The pages laugh back at her, as smooth and blank as ever. Her heart rate slows to normal. She tucks the dog-eared book under her arm and starts to trudge back towards the camp.

The sky is fizzing orange at the horizon, fresh dawn waves lapping at the beach. And that's when she sees it. Letters four-feet high, scraped starkly into the smooth, wet sand.

JUSTICE.

DAY 13

A storm is brewing as they gather in the camp later that morning. The usual cacophony of the birds is strangely absent and the island feels still and silent. An unsettling heat weighs heavy on the camp, the humidity in the air almost beginning to crackle with electricity.

Hayley is pacing back and forth in front of the white, crusty embers of last night's fire, running her fingers through her salt-stiffened hair until it stands up wildly, waiting impatiently while the others assemble, some squinting and yawning, some wandering curiously over to examine the word carved into the sand.

She feels like everything is coming to a head. Finally she has her proof, confirmation that somebody has been trying to tell them something all along. That somebody has been trying to ask them all a question, or to answer one, perhaps.

'Justice?' Brian yawns widely, his eyes bleary, still sitting in his makeshift bed by the fire where he slept last night. 'What's that supposed to mean?'

'No idea, mate.' Jason shrugs.

'It has to be about the end-of-tour party,' Hayley bursts out, more loudly than she intended. The others look at her, all except Elliot confused or suspicious. Elliot is quiet and watchful. 'It just has to be,' Hayley rushes on.

'Look.' She points to the word in the sand. 'My question was "what do you want?" And the answer is: "justice". We know bad things happened that night. We have to work out who was involved and why.'

'The night of the party?' May looks slightly panicked. 'Are you still banging on about that? What makes you so sure that the party has anything to do with this?'

Hayley takes a deep breath. There's no byline to hide behind here. She has to speak up, to tell them everything. 'I've been thinking for a while that something must have happened that night but now I know it, and I think you all do too. For one thing, all this only started once we got here. The party was on the last night of the tour. The night before the crash ...' There's something else, too, something nagging at Hayley's subconscious. Something in one of the sketches in Elliot's notebook. She's missing an answer that's right there in front of her, but every time she tries to grasp it, it slips further away. 'It has to be connected. It's the only thing that makes sense.'

'Except it doesn't, does it?' Jessa frowns. 'If something happened that night and this is about revenge –' she glances uneasily at the letters on the beach – 'or, okay, "justice" – they'd be taking it out on the person who'd done that something, surely? But it's not just one person being attacked here, is it? We've all been targeted. We can't all be guilty, or lying, can we?'

'I don't know.' Hayley clenches her fists in frustration. 'I just ... somehow I just know it's all connected. But I can't prove it because ...' she pauses, awkwardly, her heart racing. 'Well, because I don't think any of you have told me the truth about that night. Not all of it anyway. It feels like everybody is hiding something.' There's a long silence, and nobody contradicts her. She sees Elliot and Jessa quickly glance at each other and then look away. May is chewing her lip, studying Shannon. Jason and Brian are both determinedly looking down at the sand.

'How can you talk about justice when there's absolutely nothing just about this situation?' Brian demands, frowning angrily as he shifts his position and his face creases with pain.

'At least what happened to you wasn't deliberate,' Elliot retorts, 'that stuff was probably just in your pocket by accident.'

'Says the kid who slipped down some rocks and started this whole thing by pretending he was pushed,' Jason interjects, scathingly.

'According to the guy most likely to have done it,' Elliot spits angrily back at him.

'I didn't push you, okay?' Jason is breathing heavily, his cheeks flushing. 'Stop putting me on trial!'

'That's it!' Hayley yelps, her voice electric with excitement. 'That's it. A trial. A trial to get to the bottom of this once and for all. To find out the truth. And to determine justice.'

'Okay, Nancy Drew, what are you suggesting exactly?' Shannon is sardonic, reclining in the narrow strip of shade thrown by a palm tree, looking supremely unconvinced.

'I think . . .' Hayley takes a deep breath and tries to sound authoritative. She's been thinking about this since she first saw the letters scraped angrily into the beach. 'I think we have to, sort of, testify.'

'Testify?' May chews a nail anxiously. 'Testify to what, exactly?'

'What happened that night,' Hayley lets the words rush out in a jumble, worried that if she doesn't win them over now her idea will come to nothing. 'We think we don't know the answer, but we each have one piece of the puzzle. We each saw different things, did different things at that party. If we put the pieces together, maybe we'll be able to see the bigger picture.'

She pauses, twists a foot in the sand, lets the warm grains trickle up soothingly between her toes. She closes her eyes for the briefest moment: she's on a family holiday, somewhere else, sometime else, relaxed and happy and only worrying about what kind of pizza to order for lunch.

Her eyes snap open and she takes a deep breath – 'I think, somehow, if we all try and work out what happened, we might be able to offer it. Justice, I mean. To whoever is asking for it. We work out what happened, we each admit the part we played that night and we come to a group decision. If someone is guilty, we admit that. We all agree. Like a jury. Maybe that will offer a kind of closure.'

The tide is still coming in, little rivulets of swirling, foamy water sliding into the grooves of the letters, already smoothing and flattening their edges, preparing to erase them completely.

'Sounds like you know an awful lot about what this

mystery person wants,' Jason says, eyeing Hayley suspiciously as he tears the flesh away from a mango stone. There is a large, stringy piece stuck between his front teeth, and it waggles up and down when he talks. 'How do we know you're not just trying to orchestrate your own weird revenge "trial", Hayley?'

Hayley sighs. 'I guess you don't. But does that really even matter?' She looks him straight in the eyes. 'I'm not the one who's been doing all these things, I swear. But whoever it is, we need to find a way to give them a sense of fairness, a sense that this is being resolved. Otherwise, I don't think they're going to stop. Somebody has been wronged, or they think they have been. They're angry. They're taking things into their own hands. And if we don't put it right ... I'm worried the next person might not escape with a concussion or a badly injured leg.'

'I'm scared,' Jessa says, suddenly. 'It's bad enough we're stuck here, not knowing whether anyone's going to find us, not knowing if the next storm or weird fruit or freak injury is going to be the thing that kills us. But add in someone actually going round hurting people? I agree with Hayley. We have to do something now, before it's too late.'

'Yeah, or it makes zero difference and we all get cannibalised in our beds next,' Brian helpfully offers.

'Say you're right.' Jessa completely ignores the cannibal comment. 'Say it makes no difference. We haven't lost anything, have we?'

'It's a stupid idea,' May says, mulishly. 'Why are we wasting time obsessing over a boring house party when we have no proof it's linked to what's happened on the island?'

'But maybe Hayley's right,' Elliot says. 'The timing does

fit. Whoever is doing this didn't know we'd be stuck on an island. If the cause of it had happened sooner, they might have started doing stuff while we were on tour. But nothing happened there.'

'Well, I don't want to talk about it.' May pouts, sounding like a petulant child. 'And you can't make me. What if this ridiculous "trial" (she sarcastically sketches quote marks in the air with her fingers) just creates more division and fighting, anyway?'

'Why would it, May?' Jason asks, suspiciously. 'You got something to hide?' She glares at him. 'You want to die next?'

May doesn't have an answer to this. She subsides into reluctant silence.

'Okay then.' Hayley nods excitedly, rushing ahead before anyone else can object. 'We'll need some ground rules. No interruptions. Each person gets a chance to take the stand. We can ask them questions, and they have to tell the truth. Don't leave anything out: you don't know what might be important, even a silly little detail.'

She is slipping into her role, feeling the comforting mantle of the reporter settling back onto her shoulders, handing out assignments like she would at an editorial meeting.

'And it doesn't leave this island,' Brian pipes up, looking suspiciously around at his teammates. 'Whatever we share here, stays here.'

Later that afternoon, the fire built up and the camp tidied, they find themselves sitting in a loose circle around Brian's makeshift bed. The hot, heavy air tightens around them as they all look expectantly towards Hayley, waiting for the trial to begin.

She starts, nervously. 'Elliot, you were the first one to get hurt. Why don't we start with you?'

'Wait.' Jessa steps forward, holds out her fine gold chain, the crucifix dangling and sparkling.

'Do you swear to tell the truth, the whole truth and nothing but the truth, so help you God?' Elliot looks taken aback, but Jessa gives him a little nod.

Elliot shifts nervously and then nods. 'Fine. If this is really what it takes to end this.' He looks at Brian, propped up on one elbow, his leg motionless. 'I'll tell you whatever you want to know.'

He reaches out to touch the crucifix briefly.

'Everyone,' Jessa says, firmly, offering it around the circle. Jason scoffs, but he looks at Brian's leg and he touches it too. 'We all swear,' May says, rolling her eyes.

'Elliot, when did you arrive at the party?'

'Late. I was shooting hoops by myself at the gym after the game ended. I went back to the hotel to take a shower and I didn't get to the party until around eight thirty, maybe nine. There were some guys outside trying to tap a keg – I remember it spraying all over one of them.

'I wasn't there for long before Truth or Dare started, and after I drank all that stuff they made me chug I honestly don't remember much of. At some point I made my way upstairs and I spent most of the night on the bathroom floor.'

Brian sniggers and makes a Loser sign with his thumb and index finger behind Elliot's back. It's actually kind of reassuring, Hayley realises, because if he's mocking Elliot he must be feeling a bit more like himself again. Elliot shrugs. 'Sorry. There's not much else I can tell you.'

'Then what were you and Jessa arguing about in the trees the other day?' Hayley asks, pointedly. 'I heard you – it sounded like you were covering something up.'

Shannon and May exchange a surprised glance: clearly this is the first they are hearing about it.

Elliot looks at Jessa in alarm. 'I—'

'That has nothing to do with anything that's happening on the island,' Jessa cuts in, firmly. 'We don't need to talk about it.'

'Uh, yeah, we do,' Jason counters. 'No secrets. That was the deal. Out with it.'

Jessa sighs. 'You know what, I agree with May. This whole thing is stupid. What do we really think is going to come of this, prying into everyone's privacy?'

Shannon laughs. 'Girl, could you make yourself sound any guiltier? You have to tell us now, otherwise we're all going to believe that you're the ...' She waves her hand in the air, gesturing vaguely towards Brian's leg.

'The attacker,' Brian mutters darkly.

'The psycho,' Jason adds.

'I'm not, I swear,' Jessa says, helplessly.

'Wow,' Elliot mutters under his breath.

'What?' She narrows her eyes at him.

'I just can't believe you'd rather let people believe you might be the one behind all this messed up shit than admit that we were together that night.'

Hayley's head snaps up.

'What?'

'Jessa and I were together, okay? After Truth or Dare, but before the alcohol caught up with me. I was dancing and I started to feel hot and dizzy, so I went outside to cool off and Jessa was out there, in the garden. And that has nothing to do with what's been happening on this island. Unless you tried to push me to my death so nobody would ever find out,' he says, with a sarcastic laugh.

'Of course I didn't!' she looks genuinely hurt.

'Well, I can't say it didn't cross my mind,' Elliot mutters. 'You weren't exactly keen to act like anything had changed between us after the party. You made it pretty clear you didn't ever want anyone to know what had happened.'

'Elliot,' Jessa says, quietly, 'you don't understand.'

'I think I do, actually. The scruffy scholarship kid doesn't fit in all that well with your usual crowd.'

May bursts out laughing and Elliot scowls at her.

'It's not about you, you idiot. Jessa's never been with *anyone*. She's taken a "vow of chastity",' May intones, in a sing-song voice.

'Hey!' Jessa looks horrified but May just shrugs.

'Oh, come on, Shannon and I already know and if we're doing the whole "total truth" thing it's going to come out anyway.'

'I didn't know,' Elliot mumbles, 'I'm sorry. I thought—'

'I didn't even know you were on a scholarship, Elliot, and it wouldn't have made any difference to me if I had,' Jessa says, quietly. 'But the other stuff is ... complicated ...'

He holds her gaze, his eyes warm and sympathetic, and suddenly he's crossed the circle and put a gentle arm around her, Jessa looking embarrassed but pleased, while May digs her in the ribs.

'You dark horse!'

Hayley stands a few yards away, glad of the warmth of the fire to disguise her hot cheeks, feeling herself gently deflate just a little before she rallies.

'All right.' Hayley's tone is brisk, business-like. 'Brian, you're up.'

Brian cracks his knuckles. 'Shoot.'

'You spent a lot of the evening with the Duke girls, right?'

'Right.' Brian grins at Jason and raises his eyebrows. 'And not just one of them, if you know what I mean.' Jason sticks his tongue into the side of his cheek, crudely mimicking a blow job, and Brian chuckles appreciatively while Jessa gives a loud tut.

'We don't need a rerun of your whole "routine", thanks Brian,' May says, sourly.

'What were you and the Duke guys joking about at the party, exactly?' Hayley asks, glad of the opportunity to get to the bottom of this.

'That? It was just me and a bunch of the Duke guys messing around,' Brian says, uneasily. 'Just banter, you know? And you have to admit, everyone thought it was pretty funny at the time.' He looks towards Jason for support.

'Yeah,' Jason says, staunchly. 'It was just a laugh.'

'Oh, it was hilarious,' May says, acidly. 'Really side-splitting. Go on, Brian,' she prompts, smiling a thin smile. 'Why don't you tell us one of the jokes again, give us all a lift, since it was so very funny.'

'All right, fine.' Brian says, defiantly. And I'm sorry if they're not woke enough for you, Comrade May, but they are pretty fucking funny actually.' He looks at Jason. 'Strawberry cheesecake, or bucking bronco, that's the funniest. Or the angry pirate . . .' He sniggers in spite of himself. 'Nah come on, May, the angry pirate is funny, it's just objectively funny.'

He turns to Elliot. 'When you . . . you know . . . *finish* in a girl's eye and then kick her in the shin so she hops around with one eye closed going "Arrrrr".' Jason is smirking and Brian lets out a snort. 'Like an angry pirate,' he chuckles.

May looks incandescent and Jessa is screwing up her nose in disgust. 'What's a bucking bronco?'

When neither of the boys volunteers, May turns to her, her voice low and gruff in a crude imitation of Brian. 'It's when you're having sex with a girl from behind and you take her in the . . . you know . . . without warning and see how long you can hold on.'

'Good grief.' Jessa sounds completely horrified. 'Are you guys saying these are things you've *done?*'

'No, God no!' Jason jumps in, looking at Shannon, whose face is impassive. They're just jokes, okay? May's not telling it right, it's not . . . it's not funny like that. It's a . . . party thing.' His voice peters out with uncharacteristic uncertainty.

'Did I tell it wrong?' May asks. 'Is that not how bucking bronco works?'

Brian frowns crossly. 'It's not . . .' He sighs. 'It's not *literal.*

Obviously, we'd never treat girls like that in real life, what do you think we are, monsters? It's just a fucking joke, okay?'

'What I don't understand,' May interrupts him, 'Is how, after hearing you making those jokes, multiple cheerleaders, all of them apparently in possession of their senses, actively made the choice to go upstairs with you. How did they know what was going to happen?'

'Jesus, May.' Brian isn't smiling any more. 'You don't have to make me out to be some kind of rapist just because I told a fucking joke. What, are you saying I might have accidentally raped someone without even realising it?' He says it like it's the stupidest thing he's ever heard and looks around the circle like he's expecting everyone to agree with him.

'Yes,' May says, quietly. 'That's exactly what I think.'

There is a long and uncomfortable silence.

'You and all those other guys were publicly joking about changing places with someone else midway through sex without a woman realising. About forcing things on a woman during sex that she didn't want or expect. That's rape. You all literally sat around laughing about rape. Describing rape and pissing yourselves. Talking about rape as if—'

'Can you stop saying rape?' Brian explodes.

'I need to say it,' May continues, defiantly, 'Because you didn't. Because you didn't use that word, and I don't think you necessarily even knew it was what you were talking about. What you were laughing about. I should have said it at the time. And every other time. So I'm saying it now, because it's better late than never.'

'There is a difference between talking about something or even joking about it and doing it,' Brian mumbles.

'Yeah? Well, we know one of the Duke girls was raped at that party.' May's eyes flash, as Brian looks in panic at Jason.

'What?' Elliot gasps.

All the boys look completely shocked. If one of them is faking it, they're very convincing.

'So how do we know you didn't rape someone without knowing it?' May demands, her eyes still boring into Brian's. 'Since apparently you don't even know what rape is.'

'Okay, fine,' Brian explodes. 'You want to know how I know I didn't rape anyone?' He pushes himself up into a sitting position, panting from the effort. 'Because there wasn't any sexual contact at all. Okay?' He is breathing heavily, a fine veil of tiny sweat beads trembling along his top lip. 'There. I've said it.'

'What do you mean?' Jason asks, slowly.

'I mean I couldn't . . . perform.' Brian gestures to his groin area, circling his hands exaggeratedly. 'It was a lot of pressure, okay? Those girls had ideas, and everything happened very fast and somehow it wasn't like I'd imagined it would be and nothing . . . came up.'

Jason lets out a raucous snort.

'You bottled it! You had the dream and you fucking bottled it. Two girls. TWO GIRLS. Oh man, you better hope we never get off this island because you will never, ever hear the end of this.'

'It is nothing to be ashamed of,' Jessa interrupts, flashing Jason a glare, though Brian looks ten times more scalded by her sympathy than by Jason's jibes.

'Can we. Please. Just. Move on?' he hisses.

'Right.' Hayley, who has watched open-mouthed through most of this exchange, tries to regather her scattered thoughts and take control again. 'Right.' She turns to Jason.

'You left the party early, is that right, Jason?'

'I had a bad knee,' he grunts. 'I'd twisted it in the last quarter of the game and I needed to ice it and rest up.'

'Huh.' Hayley looks at Shannon, whose eyes are glittering across the circle. 'Because Shannon said you went home with a headache.'

'Whatever. I wasn't feeling great, so I left. I'm not involved in whatever voodoo you're convinced happened that night,' he says, dismissively.

'And nothing happened before you left? Between you and Shannon?'

'We had a minor disagreement,' Jason says, stiffly. 'Which is not exactly unusual in a relationship as passionate as ours.' Shannon says nothing, simply gives the slightest shrug of her delicate shoulders. 'And anyway.' Jason bristles. 'I can't see how that's exactly relevant, since Shannon is obviously not the person running around pushing people off cliffs and trying to feed them to sharks.'

'How can you be sure?' Elliot mutters.

'Look at her,' Jason scoffs, grinning. 'Do you really think *she's* got it in her to be causing actual bodily harm?'

Hayley decides to move on quickly.

'May, you had a pretty wild night at the party, right?'

'Whatever you say, Hayley. I guess a fairly tame party where nothing much happens could seem "wild" if it's the first one you'd ever been to,' May fires back at Hayley, snarky as hell.

Hayley holds her hands up. 'So there's nothing you want to tell us? About the party? About anything else?'

'Nope. Someone else's turn??'

'Not quite yet. Because I think you do know something, don't you? Or at least you have a theory about who's behind all this?'

May freezes, her eyes locked onto Hayley's as if she's trying to work out whether she might be bluffing. 'I don't know what you're talking about.'

'I heard you. Two days ago. Just before Brian's accident. Accusing someone of poisoning you with alcohol. And saying you knew why they did it. Because you'd done something to them, hadn't you, May? Was it that night too?'

For a few moments, it looks like May is considering making a run for it. She actually glances around the circle as if she's looking for an escape route, her eyes lingering very briefly on each of them. Is she looking for permission? For forgiveness?

Finally she seems to accept that she is cornered. 'Okay, you got me. I did something that night that I never should have done,' she snaps at last. 'I was angry, and I acted in a moment of spite and I wish I hadn't done it, okay?'

'Done what, May?' Jessa's eyes are round and liquid, her hand on May's arm. 'What are you talking about? Why haven't you told me about this?'

'Like you told me about Elliot?' May retorts.

'What did you do, May?'

May's shoulders droop and her voice becomes very small.

'I spiked someone's drink. Sort of. She asked for a virgin cocktail but instead I gave her something very, very alcoholic mixed with syrups to hide the flavour, so she wouldn't realise until it was too late. I just wanted to prove a point, I guess, I wanted to force her to relax for once, to stop being such a priss, being on our backs all the time.' She looks up, defiance and embarrassment mingling on her face. 'She wanted us to skip the party to go over tapes of our performance ... a coaching session, on the last night of the tour!' She spreads her hands as if imploring somebody to agree with her. But she knows that it doesn't compare to what she did. She looks utterly ashamed.

'That's why Shannon was acting so weird!' Jessa exclaims, looking at May in horror. 'I can't believe you would do something like that.' The moment stretches thickly between them, the heat and humidity pressing down like a suffocating blanket as May sits there, trapped in her own shame and remorse.

'I wasn't thinking. I wasn't thinking about it like that, like "spiking" her drink. You know how I feel about that stuff, I didn't mean it like that, I was just so angry. I wanted her to just chill out for once, you know? And yeah, maybe a small, nasty part of me wanted to see her lose control, see her do something embarrassing or stupid for once. Anything to force her to let down that perfect, perfect exterior just for one night.'

May starts to cry.

'I'm sorry, Shan. I'm really sorry. It's hard being your friend sometimes, you know? I love you but you're so controlled and poised all the fucking time. It can feel exhausting just to exist next to you. It was so stupid.'

Slowly, one by one, heads are turning towards Shannon, who is sitting very, very still.

'Wait a minute,' Brian says slowly, his head swivelling from May to Shannon and back again. 'That's the same thing that happened to you, May. That day when we explored the island. You said your drink had been spiked . . .' he trails off, his eyes widening.

'And—'

'Then—'

'If spiking May's drink was revenge for her spiking Shannon's drink at the party, then that means the person who's been doing all this . . .' Elliot looks shocked.

'It was you?' Jessa whispers, turning to her captain and friend in disbelief.

They are all dumbfounded, staring at Shannon as if they've never seen her before. Jason is weakly opening and closing his mouth, his forehead deeply furrowed.

Hayley breaks the circle. It's like the last piece of the puzzle has finally fallen into place. Suddenly, she realises what she's been missing. It's been right in front of her since the very first day, when Elliot lit the fire. She moves across the sand to the overhead locker, and rifles through it until she finds his sketchbook.

'Exhibit A,' she says, softly, flipping it open to the picture of them all on the plane, moments before the crash. Elliot has captured the whole group as vividly as if it were a black-and-white photograph. May and Jessa tangled together in the back row. Brian looking like he's about to hurl. Jason reclining imperiously, earphones in. Hayley gazing out of the window, lost in thought. And Shannon. Shannon in a two-seat row on her own. Shannon with the faintest smudge of what could almost be a shadow beneath her left collarbone. Shannon's eyes, piercing and preoccupied. Shannon, before the crash, viscerally, visibly in pain.

'That bruise just under your neck, the day we landed. You didn't get it in the crash, did you?'

Shannon hesitates for the tiniest fraction of a second. 'Of course I did. We were all banged up.'

'But it was yellow round the edges. Not fresh.'

Gently, Hayley rips out the piece of paper from Elliot's notebook and passes it to her. 'You had the bruise before the crash.'

Shannon's whole face slips and her shoulders slowly sink. Her collarbones are like blades, pushing out through translucent skin. She lets out a long sigh. She almost looks relieved.

'Why?' Hayley asks her, simply.

'Chad Maxwell. All the Chad Maxwells,' she answers, straight away, her voice neutral, detached.

'Chad Maxwell?' It's not the answer Hayley was expecting and it takes her a minute to place the name. 'The guy from the beach party last year?'

'And every guy like him.'

'That guy who was arrested last year at Anastasia Wahlberg's house?' Brian is trying to keep up. 'What's he got to do with any of this?'

Hayley's head is whirling. 'But you said— I thought you didn't even know who he was?'

'Yeah, that's what I said. Because that's what everyone says. It's just what you do. You keep quiet. You protect the status quo.' She traces a pattern in the sand with her fingertips. 'Especially when it happens to someone else.'

'I don't understand.' Hayley is turning the pieces over in her brain, trying to get them all to fit together.

'Star athlete. A school champion. Probably going pro.'

The words echo in Hayley's head, reminding her of something. The letter the school paper had received from the Maxwell family's lawyer, warning them off the story. 'Star athlete ... bright future ahead of him ... spurious accusations ... ruin lives ... no foundation in truth.'

Shannon is still staring rigidly into the fire.

'That girl at Anastasia's party, she was drunk off her face. She was out of control. The whole thing was practically inevitable. If it hadn't been him, it might've been a car on the way home or God knows what else. She was a mess. Like I was a mess, the last night of the tour. Not the kind of person whose story stands up. Not against star power and a letter jacket.'

'But Chad wasn't in Texas ...'

'It wasn't Chad at the tour party. Obviously. But it might as well have been. Because the story is the same. Another star athlete. Same story. I wanted to, until I didn't. There was dancing. Everything was moving so fast. I was angry with Jason, wanted to punish him.' She doesn't look at Jason, who is gasping, as if he can't quite pull enough oxygen out of the tight, hot air.

'I walked upstairs on my own two feet. I wasn't in control, exactly, but I was conscious. I knew, even as we went upstairs, I knew it wasn't what I wanted. But I thought—' She breaks off, for a moment, scooping up handfuls of sand and letting it run through her fingers.

May is looking absolutely horror struck, tears rolling down her cheeks as Shannon talks.

Shannon sighs. 'I don't know what I thought. It was like I couldn't think, like my skin was electric and my brain was on a fairground ride and everything was spinning and I wanted to get off but I didn't know how and the music wouldn't stop.'

She runs a hand over her face, pushing her wild black hair, made wilder by the sea air, back out of her eyes. She suddenly looks exhausted, and very young.

'He was on me before the door closed. As powerful as he had been on the court. I didn't, couldn't say no. I didn't say yes, either. I didn't move. It felt like I didn't breathe. I didn't look. I didn't feel. It was like he was in there with nobody. He must have known I wasn't there. I don't know if he liked that, or if it just didn't matter to him either way. I tried to get up at one point, near the beginning. I tried to get away. But he had his whole body weight on me.' Her fingertips hover above the yellow stain of the bruise, as if she can't quite bring herself to touch it. 'The base of his hand, like this, and his fingers, near my throat.'

She takes her hand, spread wide, thumb straining one way and her four fingers together stretching in the opposite direction, and plunges it into the sand, knuckles taut. 'He was too strong.' She moves her hand and for a split second

223

there are five deep welts where her fingers have been. Then the grains of sand slide in, and the holes disappear. 'I waited until he was finished and then he left. And I just lay there and waited for the feeling to come back again. But it didn't.'

There is a stunned silence. Somewhere far away the first roll of thunder growls and an unpleasantly humid breeze moves across the circle.

'What?' Jason says, stupidly, his jaw slack, his eyes moving from Hayley to Shannon and back again as he tries to process what he has just heard. Like his brain desperately doesn't want him to.

'It wasn't some girl from Duke, was it?' May is catching on faster, nodding slowly as she starts to put it together. 'It was you. I'm so sorry, Shan,' she sobs, over and over again. 'Oh God, I'm so, so sorry.'

Shannon nods wearily. 'It was me. And no, Jessa, before you ask, I suppose I didn't fight back.'

And then the rain comes. In a rush of tropical fury, slashing across their faces like knives, punctuated by lightning so vivid it seems to split the sky in two, forcing them to scatter. A cacophony of noise and water, forcing itself into their mouths and eyes as they race to carry Brian to his shelter and each to dive into their own, huddling desperately underneath the plaited leaves, Hayley's mind racing to make sense of it all as the sky turns black and the storm rages on into the night.

DAY 14

Everybody has questions. So many questions it's difficult to know where to begin.

'You spiked May's drink,' Elliot says, cautiously, when the scattered circle reforms in the thin morning light. The tide is out, a vast glassy slick of wet sand stretching away towards the distant whisper of the waves, like the day they crashed. The sun has barely breached the horizon and the sky is soft and grey. The storm has cleared the air and the breeze is fresh and cool. Hayley can taste sea salt on the back of her tongue.

He says it quietly, like he's afraid Shannon might break into pieces if he speaks to her too harshly. Like she's suddenly an alien thing, a fragile exhibit in some bizarre story about female fury. 'So all the other stuff was you too? It's been you, all along?'

She doesn't answer, but she doesn't deny it either. Just looks down at her hands.

'You were raped?' Jason demands, bluntly. He's shaking his head like he can't accept it, like he's waiting for someone to tell him the punchline, tell him it's all been a stupid prank.

225

'You were raped.' He says it again, as if it will help him to understand. 'Raped by who?'

The hair that was shiny and coiffed when they'd arrived at the airport, just days and yet years and years ago, is greasy now, clinging to Jason's scalp in an oily slick. His face looks hollower, the usual sparkle in his baby blues replaced with a glinting metallic glare.

'It was you, wasn't it?' He moves towards Elliot like a predator advancing on its prey, arms outstretched, fury written in his tensed bicep as he draws back his arm. 'It was you,' he half shrieks, 'that's why she pushed you, that's why you were the one she started with, you dirty, thieving—'

'No!' Shannon is in front of him, eyes blazing, and for a moment it looks as if the blow will land on her instead, but with a visible effort, Jason halts, drops his arm.

'Then who?' His hands are on her shoulders, fingernails digging in, knuckles white. 'No more games, Shannon.' And there's a warning in his voice.

'Nobody. Nobody on the island. One of the Duke players at the party.'

Jason isn't the only one who looks completely floored.

'I don't understand, Shannon. You did all *this*? Because some other guy who isn't here –' he looks around at the others '– it wasn't any of us that hurt you?'

'I didn't say that,' Shannon says, quietly. And Hayley thinks she is beginning to understand.

'It was all of us,' she whispers. 'Wasn't it?'

'I thought I could bear it at first,' Shannon says, almost under her breath. 'Instinct kicked in, at the beginning when the crash was so fresh, and it drove everything else away. It was a relief, to be that person again, to play the role of that Shannon, the captain who would look after everyone else, would always know what to do. Like an escape. But later, when it all came back, when I realised we were trapped here, I thought I would die. I thought that I could not physically be here with this group of people who I realised had all been part of it, that it would end me.'

'And then, it was like . . .' She spreads her hands, looking up at the vast expanse of the sky as if she's searching for the right words to explain. '. . . like I slowly started to feel that the island was on my side, somehow. Like it knew. Like it would help me hold you all accountable, somehow.'

'Hold us accountable for what?' Brian snarls, and Hayley can tell that he has more to say, that he hasn't even begun to unleash his fury, but he's catching up too, slowly piecing it together like the rest of them.

'So what, you formed a plan, to create your own punishments?'

'No. No.' Shannon's eyes are liquid, her voice urgent. 'I never meant to – not any of it. It just sort of happened. It was that night, the night of the storm. We were there on the hilltop and everyone was shouting at once and the rain was slashing down and my hair was soaked and the airplane was roaring and it honestly felt like it might be the end of everything and then suddenly, in the chaos, there was this moment when I saw him, right there, in front of me, his back turned.'

'Elliot?' Hayley says. But before she can ask what Elliot

had to do with it, Shannon is rushing on, words tumbling out frantically, like she needs them to understand.

'And everyone else was looking up at the sky and I just, I don't know, something just coursed through me and it was like time slowed right down and I looked at him standing there for the longest moment, thinking about how he'd walked past me that night, how he'd left me hanging there, when all I needed was one piece of solid ground under my feet . . . one hand on my shoulder to stop me from falling . . .

'He *saw* me, Hayley. He saw me going upstairs with that guy, and he must have seen that I wasn't right, that I was out of it, and he just smiled. Smiled. What did he think was happening? And I tried to meet his eyes because there was still some part of me that sensed he could say something, disrupt the situation, somehow, and I tried to signal to him, I gave him a look, and his eyes just kind of slid over me and I swear it was like he almost winked at the guy. Like some kind of bro code or something.'

Her face darkens. 'Fucking Elliot. Elliot, who wasn't ever one of the guys. But that was the moment he chose to suddenly try and fit in? The one moment I needed him not to? And I just looked at his back, there in the rain, inches from the edge, and suddenly I realised he could feel it too. Feel what it was like to have somebody let him just slip over the edge. Feel the ground falling away underneath him and nobody put out an arm. He was almost there already.'

She's pleading, her eyebrows knitted together. 'He was this close to slipping by himself. He might have done, even. And I didn't plan it. I swear. But before I knew what was happening my arms had done it. They'd just done it and he wasn't there any more.' Shannon draws a deep, shaky breath, as if something has physically left her body and there's a void behind.

Elliot is standing in front of her, his arms slack at his sides, genuine hurt and confusion on his face.

'I never meant to hurt you badly, I swear,' Shannon addresses him directly for the first time. 'I didn't realise how steep it was, or that there were rocks. I thought you might fall a metre or two, have a scare, that's all. And once you were okay, once you recovered, and nothing too serious had happened, I couldn't stop thinking about it. I couldn't stop thinking about how I could make you others feel things, too. Things you'd never feel otherwise. Things you'd never have to feel at home. And it just took me over somehow. I never meant it to go this far. But I couldn't stop it either. I knew at any moment we might get rescued and it would be over and there was some urgent, hot part of me that needed it done, before we went back and I had to live with it, carry it with me. Like this could lighten the load.'

Hayley puts out a hand. 'Wait. Slow down. I'm trying to understand, Shannon, I really am. But you intentionally hurt everybody, right? You're going to have to walk us through this. Elliot left you hanging. You felt like he had a chance to step in and he didn't, I get that. I'm not saying I agree with you. I think Elliot was nervous and embarrassed at that party. He was trying to fit in and he'd drunk that disgusting cocktail ... but I get it. You wanted him to feel the way he'd made you feel ...' She frowns, thinking fast. 'And ... you spiked May's drink, because that's what she did to you?'

229

Shannon nods. 'When I thought back the next day, I realised she must have put something in that cocktail. It was the only thing I drank that night, so it was the only thing that made sense. I didn't realise it at the party, everything was happening too fast, it was like a dream. But the next day when I woke up, I felt so awful, my head was pounding and I could barely open my eyes. That was when I figured it out.'

May looks like she wants to sink into the sand.

'I'm so sorry, Shan. I'm so, so sorry. I didn't mean it. I never, ever wanted something like that to happen to you. I was just so pissed at you for forcing us to watch those stupid tapes when the tour was over, and Jessa was all "yes, captain, of course, captain, oh captain, my captain," and I guess it made me feel jealous. I never meant to hurt you. Or to let someone else hurt you.'

'I wanted you to see what it feels like,' Shannon says, in a low voice. 'To be scared, to feel out of control, like your own body won't do what you want it to do. To feel that confusion and terror.'

Hayley frowns, remembering May flopping around the camp the other day, the fear and frustration in her eyes. An eye for an eye?

'It was just one bad day for you,' Shannon goes on. 'It didn't lead to anything else. It won't affect you forever.'

'What about Brian?' Hayley asks, gently, and Shannon's face crumples in anguish.

'I never meant it to go that far. I just needed him to know what it felt like. To be really afraid of something bigger and more powerful than you. To feel physically vulnerable. To feel such visceral fear that you can't even move. He wouldn't make those jokes again if he'd ever experienced that. He wouldn't laugh about those things, not if he'd ever known that feeling. And I couldn't stop thinking about whether what happened later . . . about whether that guy would have felt so comfortable just taking what he wanted if they hadn't all been laughing about it downstairs just a couple of hours earlier.'

Jessa is shaking her head. 'But, Shannon, he could have been killed. And he didn't do anything to you, you know, *directly*.'

Shannon looks down at the sand, tracing patterns around her legs. 'I didn't really expect anything to happen. At worst, I thought he might see something small like a barracuda or a nurse shark or something.'

Hayley remembers Shannon's white face and shaking hands as they'd helped Brian out of the water. She hadn't been acting, Hayley was certain of it.

'I just wanted him to know what it was like, to feel that same fear. The fear we all feel practically every fucking day. A kind of fear he might go his whole life without ever once experiencing. And okay, I took a risk. But don't we play fast and loose with girls' lives every single day? I never really thought anything would happen, though, Brian, honestly I didn't.'

And for the first time she looks up and meets the fury in his eyes.

'Shannon.' His voice is shaking. Slowly, he starts to peel back the layers wrapping his useless leg. Rusty blood has oozed between May's amateur stitches and dried in dark clumps and patches. Around one stitch the flesh is beginning to swell, standing up hard and angry. The long, dark slit of the wound dominates his entire calf. He speaks very slowly, like he's struggling to keep himself calm. 'I will be scarred by this for my entire life.'

'Yes,' Shannon says, simply. 'Like me.'

'I DIDN'T DO THAT TO YOU,' Brian screeches, lurching forwards as if he would throw himself at her if he could stand up. 'I told some fucking jokes. You don't have a sense of humour? Fine, I can't help you. But putting someone else in danger? That is a completely different thing. What you did is unforgiveable. The only monster here is you.'

'And the glass?' Jason's voice comes, quiet and cold, as Shannon and Brian stare at each other. 'What was my "crime", please?' His voice is dripping in sarcasm.

For the first time, Shannon looks uncertain. She hesitates, her angular face turned slightly to meet the cool breeze as it blows in off the distant sea. She looks at Hayley.

'How did the glass make you feel, Jason?' Hayley asks.

'What are you talking about?'

'How did it make you feel, when you woke up that morning. And when you came back, with the rest of us, and it had gone?'

Jason doesn't answer. His eyes flit from Hayley to Shannon and back again.

'I think,' Hayley says carefully, not wanting to make things worse for Shannon, or put words in her mouth. 'I think it made you feel scared, and on edge, and paranoid. Like you were treading on eggshells and couldn't trust yourself. Like something awful could happen if you put a foot wrong. I think maybe those are things Shannon has felt in your relationship. I think maybe she feels them every single day. And I think maybe they came to a head that night.'

'You have no idea what you're fucking talking about, you nosy, interfering bitch ...' He lumbers furiously towards Hayley, but Elliot and Jessa leap forward, each putting a restraining hand on his shoulders.

'I think.' Hayley swallows, deliberately raising her chin, forcing herself to look him in the eye even though her heart feels as if it is about to break out of her chest. 'I think that something in her snapped when you treated her the way you did that night, when you argued, and if it hadn't, I don't know ... Maybe things would have been different. I think that's the part you played.'

Jason is about to protest again, but Jessa is tired of waiting for her turn.

'What about the leeches? I knew they didn't get out of that pool by themselves,' she says, angrily, and there's a hard edge to her voice. 'What the hell did I ever do to you?'

'I nearly told you,' Shannon tells her, simply. 'In the trees that afternoon. And then there was some part of me that couldn't bring myself to say the words. So I told you the story, but I substituted someone else.' Her voice splinters. 'But then, when you talked about how it wasn't really rape, how that girl changed her mind afterwards, how she was just trying to cover her own mistakes ... it made me feel so ashamed. Dirty. Like I couldn't ever wash it off.'

'Hence the leeches?' Hayley is nodding, understanding slowly. 'To make Jessa feel dirty as well.' Shannon nods.

'And I guess you put them on all of us to deflect suspicion?'

'It would have been too obvious not to. Sorry.' She shrugs. 'Part of me quite liked the idea of it, anyway. Cleaning the blood. Removing toxins. Or something.'

'Wait,' Jason says, 'wait, back up. What did you say? About changing your mind?'

'Is *that* what this is about?' Brian is catching on, his eyes widening as he starts to join the dots. 'That guy you were all over on the dancefloor?'

'All over?' Jason's voice is deepening dangerously.

'Are you telling me,' Brian whispers, his voice menacing, 'that this whole nightmare has been about you regretting a one-night stand with a Duke stud?'

'You put out for him?' Jason roars, turning furiously on Shannon. 'How many fucking years have I waited for you, Shannon? Jesus Christ, what a cuck.' He's looking at her in disgust, as if he's never seen her before. 'What do you think you're playing at? You're sick, you know that? I think there's something seriously wrong with you.'

'Yes,' Shannon whispers. 'Something wrong.'

'Guys.' Hayley is horrified, watching them, their anger circling Shannon like a tightening fist. 'We're talking about a rape.'

Jason gives a bitter, barking laugh.

Shannon just stands there, looking out at the waves, letting it wash over her. It's almost like they can't reach her. In and out. In and out.

And Hayley is thinking that it is Shannon's life, Shannon's injuries, Shannon's pain they should be talking about, but they're focusing on themselves. She doesn't know how to make them realise that they're looking at this all wrong.

Quietly, before Hayley can find the words to say anything, Shannon stands up. She brushes the sand delicately from her fingertips. And she walks away.

'So we know what to do now,' Brian says, his voice flat and hard. 'We watch Shannon 24-7. Or we lock her up. And if we ever get off this goddamn island, we turn her in to the police.'

'Excuse me?' May is standing now too, materialising next to Hayley. 'Turn her in? Are you kidding me?'

'No.' Brian glares up at her defiantly. 'She tried to kill me, May. I literally went swimming in shark-infested waters with shark bait in my pockets.'

'It's a deep cut, Brian, I know. But someone's going to find us. You'll live. If we're talking about going to the police, it should be to report that Duke bastard, not Shannon. She's the victim here.'

'She's not the only victim,' Elliot chips in, quietly, rubbing the spot on his head where an egg-like bump had protruded for several days after his fall.

'Right, because a bump on the head is the same as being assaulted,' May retorts, sarcastically.

'Okay. Maybe this is what we have to decide.' Hayley says, slowly. 'This was never only about protecting ourselves. It was about justice. So we sit here and we talk this through and we make a decision. What we'll do if we ever get off this island. Whether we go to the police. And who we report.'

'What's the point?' Jessa looks sullen, tired. 'If we might never be found.'

'All the more reason to decide,' Hayley says, firmly. 'If we're going to survive here any longer, we need to know where we stand. We need to decide for ourselves, to give ourselves a moral code. Who's to say something like this doesn't happen again, here on the island? We decide this once and for all, for all of us, separate from home, separate from the law. We make our own decision.'

'Like a legal judgement?' Elliot looks doubtful.

'Well, sort of. Majority rules. We all have to commit to that.'

'What the hell happened to innocent until proven guilty?' Brian splutters, angrily. 'We all know Shannon attacked us but we can't just decide this other thing, ruin some guy's life, his reputation, without any proof, just take her word for it.'

'Why is it innocent until proven guilty for him but disbelieved until proven true for her?' May snaps.

'It doesn't have to be innocent or guilty,' Hayley cuts in, holding up her hands for calm. 'We're not convicting him, we're just deciding, as a group, whether to support Shannon by reporting him to the police. Okay?'

'What are you, her lawyer?' Jason's voice is heavy with sarcasm.

'Yeah, maybe I am,' Hayley shoots back, defiantly.

'You're talking as if Shannon was ambushed,' Brian complains. 'That's ridiculous. Why didn't any of us hear her scream? She was only upstairs. If she was being raped up there, we would have known about it.'

For a long moment, they all seem to be digesting this,

and there is no sound but the white noise of the sea and the swishing of the breeze in the palm leaves.

'She knew exactly what she was doing!' It bursts out of Brian, as if he knows he shouldn't say it but can't help himself.

'Well, she did. She did,' he croaks at Hayley, and it's almost like he is pleading with her, like he needs this to be true for everything to stay the same. All the moments of his own past that will suddenly look different. The future that he will need a new map to navigate. It would be so much easier if Shannon would just say 'Yes, I knew what I was doing.' And the world he has always known could stay the same.

'How did you feel, when the shark was closing in on you in the water?' Hayley's voice is trembling slightly.

'What has that got to do with anything?'

'Just answer the question.'

'I was scared, obviously.'

'Scared?'

'Okay, I was really scared.'

'Why didn't you punch it?'

'Oh, come on, Hayley.'

'You were scared, right? It was bigger and more dangerous than you and the last thing you wanted to do was go on the offensive and risk provoking it.'

'I—'

'You didn't swim away.'

'What?'

'I noticed you were frozen there, in the waves, sort of waving, for over a minute. Why didn't you start swimming for the shore straight away?'

'I don't know, I was— it all happened so fast.'

'You were shocked, right? It was terrifying. You froze. Panic set in. You didn't know what to do. Your body took over . . .'

'That's not the same.'

'Why? What's the difference?'

'Brian didn't dance with the shark before it attacked him,' Elliot says, quietly. 'I mean, Hayley, we all saw her draped around the guy's neck, rubbing up against him, nobody had a gun to her head, did they?'

Hayley watches a muscle tighten and twitch in Jason's cheek.

'Does it even matter?' May has leapt to Hayley's side. 'It wouldn't matter if she'd ripped her top off and started grinding on him, the point is what happened afterwards, isn't it? When he raped her.'

'It matters to me,' Jason mutters, through gritted teeth.

'Of course it matters!' Brian splutters. 'You're asking us to make a judgement about what happened that night. I'm sorry, but I'm less likely to believe that someone was raped if I saw her all over the guy like melted butter on pancakes an hour before she claims he forced her to have sex with him.'

'Raped her,' May repeats, mulishly. 'And it doesn't matter how enthusiastic she might have been earlier on, if she changed her mind once they were in the bedroom and didn't want to go through with it then it was rape.'

'But she seemed . . .' Jessa swallows. 'I mean, wouldn't we have known? She seemed okay, the next morning.' Jessa studiously avoids May's eyes. 'Look, I want to support Shannon in whatever she's going through, I really do, but I'm finding it hard to understand why she would've gone upstairs with that guy in the first place if she wasn't, you know, up for it.' She shakes her head nervously. 'I'm sorry, but it doesn't totally add up.'

'Yes! Thank you!' Brian applauds, and Jessa looks away uncomfortably.

'I'm sorry to be the one who has to say this, but we're also talking about someone making an active choice to put herself in a dangerous situation. What did she think was going to happen?' Jessa can't meet anyone's eyes.

'Maybe she thought she was going to fool around, maybe she thought she'd have a little bit of fun, maybe she never planned to have sex, but she wanted to do other stuff,' May says, 'Some of us like to have fun, you know, not all of us are married to our own fathers in weird, fucked-up ceremonies.'

Jessa draws in a sharp breath. 'That was a purity ball, and you know it meant something important to me. I can't believe you'd throw that in my face.'

May looks guilty, like she knows she's gone too far. 'I'm sorry, Jessa. I didn't mean that.' Jessa turns away from her, eyes filled with tears. May twists her fingers in frustration. 'I just hate this idea that any girl who wants to experience some pleasure on her own terms is somehow asking for trouble and deserves all she gets,' she bursts out. 'You know? In this group of – what – four girls? You're looking at one rape. And how many sexual assaults? Who here has been grabbed, or groped, or had a guy expose himself in front of you in the street?'

Jessa sniffs, and raises her hand. May puts her own up as well. So does Hayley. 'Four for four,' she says, grimly. 'Virgins included.'

'Any of that happened to any of you?' May looks at the boys, her glare like a laser. They all sit motionless.

'It's officially one in three for women,' Hayley adds. 'I looked it up for that article. It's one in three in the records because those are the ones that have been reported. One in three women are physically or sexually assaulted.'

'See?' May says, angrily. 'It's not that you're all just far more cautious than us. This isn't some awful, rare accident that happens to careless girls who go to the wrong place on the wrong night or wear the wrong skirt or drink the wrong thing. It's literally our day-to-day – you just don't know anything about it because you're not living it.'

'Oh, come on, you're not "living it", May. I'm sorry that happened to you but stop exaggerating.' Jason sounds like a patronising dad reining in an overdramatic kid.

'I hold my keys between my fingers every time I walk home after dark,' Hayley says, quietly.

'Have any of you guys ever done that?' The boys look back at her, blinking.

'I call my mom so she'll hear if anything happens when I'm walking at night.' Jessa says, quietly. 'I send her a tracker of my location so she would know exactly where I was if anything happened.'

'I never come home through the park after dark,' May chips in. 'Even though it adds, like, twenty minutes to my journey. And on Thursdays I wait an hour at school while Jessa has yearbook club so we can walk home together.'

'We go to the bathroom in groups if we're out,' Hayley puts up the five fingers of her right hand and starts ticking them off, one by one. 'I carry pepper spray. I never wear headphones when I jog, so I can hear if someone comes up behind me. I cross the street if I see a group of guys up ahead. I check behind me before I put my key in the lock.' She folds down her thumb, leaving a tight fist. 'Shall I go on?'

The boys are silent.

'Like I said,' May says, quieter now, 'it's our whole lives.'

May puts her hands to her face, as if her head is too heavy for her neck to hold up. 'And I made it worse. I did this to her. I put Shannon in that situation and took away her control.' She shakes her head miserably.

'I never said a word about those jokes. I just ignored them.' Elliot is looking down at the palms of his hands, his forehead creased with guilt. 'I didn't know it could mean anything. And everything you've just described, it's like … it's like there's a completely different world you're all living in, and I've literally never seen it or heard of it before today. Even though it's the world I live in too.

'And I didn't stop them. I saw him taking her upstairs, he was half dragging her, she was so out of it. But I was so caught up in my own thing …' He looks at Hayley, cringing, as if she can somehow forgive him. 'I was so busy trying to get into the bathroom to hide how sick I felt, so preoccupied with the fact I'd just kissed Jessa … I just gave the guy a grin as he went past. Jesus, I might even have fist-bumped him or something, I can't remember.'

'That's just great, dude. Good to know you had my back.' Jason mutters.

'*Your* back?' Even Jessa is looking indignant now.

241

'Uh, yeah, Jessa. Mine. She went into the bedroom with this guy. She was laughing and joking with him. Everyone's acting like this is all about Shannon and some guy and Brian's leg, but what about me? I'm the one who had something taken from him that night.'

Hayley and May exchange an incredulous glance.

'So what exactly are we supposed to decide here?' Brian demands. 'That we condone revenge? That it's totally okay what Shannon has put us all through? It's okay that I can't even walk? We all agree that it's totally fine for girls to go psycho on everyone if they get "raped".' He does the air quote thing and Hayley feels a hot flash of anger. 'That guys have to be mind-readers, and if they're not, they're automatically condemned as rapists?'

'No, Brian. That's not what Shannon wants. She doesn't want other girls to go out wreaking revenge on people. She didn't want to do that herself. She wanted justice. But she knew that wasn't an option for her. Because we all know the story of Chad Maxwell. And we know a dozen other stories like it. We know what happens to the girl who accuses the star athlete. Or the supreme court judge. Or the President. We all know how that story goes.'

'We're supposed to decide that girls' lives mean more than boys' sports,' May says, simply. 'We're supposed to decide there's something wrong if we're at a point where guys need to be mind-readers during sex because we've normalised sex where guys are so busy doing what they want to us that they don't even notice what we're feeling, or whether we're into it or not. That it matters if a girl is raped at a party where her so-called friends spent the night joking and laughing about rape and she doesn't think anyone will take her seriously.' She chokes out a half sob.

'What happened to your leg, Brian, it's awful. The idea it might get worse, that it could get infected, that's unbearable. But why is it that we can all see that, but we can't see what's happened to Shannon in the same way? Why are we okay with leaving so many girls so badly injured?

Hayley nods and lets out a breath she feels like she's been holding onto forever. 'We should take the scars we don't see as seriously as the ones we do.'

DAY 15

The next morning, Hayley finds Shannon in the quiet shade of the grove of mango trees, their reddening fruit bulging from the branches, their vivid green leaves moving gently in the morning breeze.

On the way she passes Jason, sitting at the edge of the beach with his back against a tree, staring out at the waves. He looks small and crumpled, like a little boy on a time out. Hayley knows he doesn't understand. He hasn't had some great epiphany, some sudden rush of empathy or gender bias education. She doesn't know if he ever will. But he knows that everything has changed. The ground has slipped from beneath him, whether he changes his mind, or his behaviour, or not. And they did that. They can't make him understand, any more than they can force Brian to change. But they can change the reaction. They can change the response guys get to those behaviours. And Jason looks like he's realising that. Hayley almost feels sorry for him. Everything he knows, everything he's grown up being taught by his friends, his favourite movies, his video games, his online world, even his own parents … it's all falling apart. And that's a scary place to be.

But it will never be as scary as what Shannon has been through, she thinks, as she passes him and makes her way into the cool of the trees.

'You're up early.'

Shannon nods, quietly turning over a waxy-skinned fruit that has fallen to the forest floor with her toe. On one side, it is perfect, the dark red blush slowly transitioning to bright, luscious green. When it rolls over, the other side is rotten and putrefying, its orange flesh darkened and congealed like treacle, ants swarming greedily into the gashes in its skin.

'You didn't murder Rocket, did you?' The thought pops suddenly into Hayley's head. Had Shannon tried to sabotage their water supply as well?

A wry smile flickers around Shannon's lips. 'No, I swear. May he rest in raccoon heaven.'

Hayley nods.

'I never wanted to sabotage our survival, Hayley. I could've, if I'd wanted to. All it would have taken would have been one of those beach apples. Squeeze the sap into that tarpaulin. It would have been so easy.'

Hayley feels suddenly cold. The fact that Shannon has had this thought throws her. Before they got here, she thought she had so much figured out. Standing up for what was right. Fighting for justice. But nothing here is easy, or black and white. Shannon is a survivor, she believes that. Believes she deserves justice and support. But is what she did to the others acceptable? Forgivable?

'You didn't do it, though,' she says, more to herself than to Shannon. And she realises how much that matters. How bad Shannon's pain must have been to even have had that thought in the first place.

'We voted. In your favour.'

Shannon nods again. Hayley feels deflated. She doesn't know what she was hoping for. She suddenly feels very young, and inexperienced. Foolish for thinking that she could somehow fix things. She felt proud that she'd managed to get to the bottom of what had happened. She'd advocated for Shannon, powerfully enough to get the others to agree. But she can't fix it. It's not really justice, for a few of them to realise how fucked up the whole night was, and how much they all had to do with it. It doesn't change what happened.

Will it stop it from happening again? Will it mean one of them is more likely to step in, to stop the downward spiral that becomes a sexual assault before it happens? The part of the spiral that we don't usually see, the bit that consists of all of us, our jokes, and split-second reactions and the moments when we decide whether to say something or to look away? Hayley doesn't know. Maybe.

Perhaps just trying to make those little changes, in the small moments nobody knows are important, perhaps, Hayley thinks, that's as important as the big, triumphant exposé It's not the satisfying ending she's used to tying up with a neat payoff in her articles. It's not the neat perfection Hayley Larkin is used to striving for. But maybe moving forward has to be messy and imperfect, or we'll never move forward at all.

She wishes she were better at this. Wishes she knew what to say. Wishes she had Jessa's easy warmth or May's wit.

She knows enough, at least, to realise that Shannon doesn't need to know how close the vote was. That Jason and Brian both voted against and Jessa only came down on her side at the end.

'We'll report him, if we ever go back. All of us. We agreed to stand with you. We'll tell the police what happened, and back you up. And nobody is going to mention any of what happened here, on the island.' She pauses, wondering how to word this delicately. 'As long as it's over now.'

Shannon takes a slow, deep breath, tilting her pale chin upwards so that the dappled sun plays over her face.

'No. Nobody is telling anybody anything.' She says it with a quiet finality, the tone Hayley recognises from moments in practice when they'd been debating a new move or a change to the sequence and Shannon had held up a hand and ended the discussion, overruling them.

'What do you mean? I got them to understand. I spoke up for you.' Hayley feels stupid, and a slow glow of embarrassment spreads through her stomach as she realises how hurt she is, how much she needs to make this right. 'I don't get it. I thought you wanted justice. That's what you wrote, isn't it?'

Shannon shakes her head. 'Justice isn't available. It doesn't exist, not for me, not for this. Not back home. Not without a cost that's not worth paying.'

She looks at Hayley. 'You know what happens to girls like that. Girls from places like Dillard Park. People will find out where I live. And what my upbringing was. And the story will change. You know it will. You've seen it.'

So she does remember, after all.

Hayley starts to reach out a hand towards her but Shannon twists away, turning her back and reaching a birdlike arm to start plucking plump mangoes from the tree.

'Did you look it up, for that article of yours?' She looks at Hayley, that hollow, haunted look on her face. 'Did you check what percentage of rapists ever spend a day in jail?'

Hayley swallows. 'Two point five percent.'

'Exactly. So it'll be my turn. My turn to be the gold digger, the liar, the slut. My turn to be ripped apart online, to be disbelieved if I didn't scream loud enough, or my injuries aren't considered bad enough to prove it. My turn to be cast as the vindictive bitch ruining an innocent athlete's chance of a shining college career. It'll become who I am. And for what? His shine won't even be tarnished. He'll just shine brighter than ever. I won't let this define me. If his life won't be defined by it, why should mine?'

'So, this was all for nothing?'

'Not for nothing,' Shannon says, quietly. 'The others. What they did? That doesn't even count. There's no punishment, no crime. Even though none of it might have happened without each one of them. What they did that night will affect me for the rest of my life and before this they'd never even have thought twice about it. They wouldn't even *know*.'

'But now they do,' Hayley says.

'Exactly. Now they do.'

And suddenly Hayley realises that the trial hasn't just been the last forty-eight hours. They've all been on trial, the whole time. On the island, at the party; the whole time they've been living in a world where treating one half of the population like disposable objects is so normal you don't even notice it. They'd all been complicit, one way or another. Some just more than others.

'Shannon, can I ask you something? Was I right, about Jason? About the part he played?'

Shannon smiles dreamily. 'Jason Angel. Jason always shines so bright, always has, no matter what he's done.'

She closes her eyes, letting the breeze gently stroke her cheeks. 'A guy from the Duke team came over at lunch, the day of the final, and asked me if he could borrow the salt from our table.'

Hayley frowns, but waits.

'That's what the fight was about, at the party. He only wanted the salt, but Jason thought it might be something else. Jason is always seeing things that aren't there.'

'He was honestly mad at you because someone asked for the salt?'

Shannon smiles. 'That was nothing. When we were fifteen, I wore my hair in a French plait for a varsity match one afternoon. Jason thought I was trying harder than usual with my appearance. He said he suspected me of trying to "catch the eye" of one of the guys on the opposite team. "I thought you'd be wearing your hair in a bun, the way you know I like it," he said, and I knew something was off because his voice was kind of low and flat, but I thought he was just in a weird mood.' She sighs. 'When we were on our way home that night, we stopped to get a burger. Jason went in to pick up the food, and he handed mine to me in the passenger seat. When I bit into it, there was a pebble in the bun. I chipped my tooth.'

She opens her mouth and points to a nick in one of her teeth.

'And Jason just kept his eyes on the road and said "it's not nice to find something different from how you expected it to be, is it?" In that same flat voice.'

She looks up at Hayley, like she's checking to gauge her reaction. Like she's worried she might not believe her.

'He's always liked me being friends with Jessa. Said he thought her chastity would "rub off on me". Not that I'd ever so much as looked at another guy. But last year, I went over to study at May's house and he turned up at the door, all charming and apologetic, telling her mom he was there to drive me home, even though I'd never told him I was going. He'd used an app to track me there. Said he didn't like me hanging out with her alone, thought we might be gossiping about guys, or planning to sneak out to a bar together. May was too "loose" he said. And when I left with him, May's mom was practically swooning over how lucky I was, to have a guy so dedicated and sweet that he'd come all that way to get me home safe.'

Shannon picks up one of the mangoes and uses a fingernail, grown long and sharp since their arrival on the island, to slit its skin from top to bottom, a single, glistening cut.

'It started so, so slowly. When Jason and I first met, I was so new, I didn't know anyone or anything about Oak Ridge, and he sort of took me under his wing, guiding me, introducing me, helping me. And somehow, somewhere along the way, the guiding became more like controlling. But he always made it seem like he was just doing it for me. Helping me. Letting me know what people would think of me if I wore that top to school ... for my own sake. Checking I really wanted to eat that cookie ... because he knew how much I cared about making it onto the cheer squad. And so, for a long time, instead of feeling angry, I felt—' She looks down at the mango, swallowing, forcing her fingernails under the skin and peeling it back.

'I felt grateful. And stupid. I didn't know why I kept making so many mistakes. And I felt lucky Jason was there to help me.'

She lifts the fruit to her lips and takes a small bite.

'There were times when I did stand up for myself, a little. I think. But each time I did, Jason would drop something about Dillard Park, just in passing, just a casual mention. And I'd feel myself freeze. I'd see everything I was working for sort of hanging in the air above his head, like it was suspended in a bubble, and it would have been so very easy for him just to reach up and pop it. Just like that. So, I learned how to please him, most of the time at least.

'I love my mom, I love her so much, but I don't want my life to look anything like hers. After my dad left, she had almost nothing. She had me so young. She never went to college, didn't have any qualifications. She moved to a completely different neighbourhood, saved every penny of my dad's alimony for the Oak Ridge fees, worked two jobs to make rent, bought my uniform second hand and sat up at night for a week taking it up to exactly the right length so it looked new. I've spent the last decade making up increasingly elaborate excuses for why my friends can never come round to my house, all the while working to make sure my story will be different. Mom was never going to be able to pay for college, and I'm not academic enough for a scholarship, but I knew I could get a free ride with cheerleading, if I was good enough. And you know as well as I do, being good enough isn't the only thing that matters.'

'Jason,' Hayley says, finally beginning to understand.

'Yes. Jason. He was my ticket to freedom. But he was also dismantling my freedom, he just did it so slowly and so lovingly that I didn't really realise what was happening until it was too late.' She shrugs, licking the juice off her fingers. 'It just became a habit, like second nature. I didn't even think twice about it. I'd dress the way I knew he'd want me to. Never send a message I wouldn't want him to see if he checked through my phone. Be where I knew he would want me to be and when.'

She looks up at Hayley. 'I think, that night, I just wanted to be free, for a little while. After I had that drink, I started to feel out of control, and at first, it scared me. But then I realised it was the first time I hadn't been in control – tight, tight control – for as long as I could remember. It wasn't about the guy. It was about being me, about making my own decisions, the intoxication of being unshackled, just for one night. And I didn't want it to stop. Until I did.'

She takes a long, deep breath and lets it out slowly. Hayley knows, instinctively, that this is the only time she has ever talked about this to anybody.

'What are you going to do now?'

'Ask the others to keep their mouths shut. If they could decide to go to the police for me, they can decide to do that instead.'

'I mean about Jason.'

'I don't know. I thought about trying to end it a few times, especially recently. But you don't know what he's like, Hayley. What he might do. I'm so scared he'll come to my house, or he'll undermine me with the squad, somehow. After everything that's happened, I just want it to be over. I don't want this to define my life and I don't want to let Jason control it either. But I don't know how to get out. I don't think he's ever going to let me go. Even after this. There were times before, when he was so angry, like he was disgusted by me, and I thought maybe it was over. But then he'd change, after a few days. He'd need to have me again. And he'd flood my locker with flowers or bombard me with love songs and gifts. Everyone else always thought it was so romantic. He always finds a way to trap me.'

'We'll do it together,' Hayley says, immediately. 'You can stay at mine, for as long as you want – Jason doesn't know my address and nor does anyone else on the squad ... or in the school, for that matter,' she realises, slightly embarrassed. 'My mom will be thrilled to think I've got a good enough friend to stay over.'

She falters for a moment, over the word friend. And looks up, half expecting that dreaded eyebrow, a shriek of laughter, a scathing putdown. But it doesn't come. Shannon has set the mango gently on the ground, her hands in her lap, her face softer, somehow. She's crying.

'And if Jason tries anything, we'll fight back. We'll expose him for who he is, we'll tarnish his perfect image: we'll put it on the front page if we have to. He's not taking you down, Shannon. I won't let him.'

That's when the shouting begins. They look at each other in alarm, and Shannon shakes her head slightly to answer the unasked question in Hayley's eyes. 'I haven't done anything else. I swear.'

They move through the trees towards the noise, half expecting another disaster, an emergency with Brian's leg, but instead there's a plane. A seaplane floating gently just off the beach.

There is no dramatic screaming from a helicopter, no rescuers hanging out and urging them forward. No billowing storm of whipped-up sand. There's barely even a ripple.

And Hayley feels none of the huge relief, the dramatic joy, the hysteria she had imagined when she pictured this moment.

She watches, as the others stream across the sand towards the plane, splashing through the shallows, Elliot and Jason supporting Brian between them.

Inside the plane, she can see Jessa talking rapidly as she gestures towards her arm, a medic hunched over her. May stroking her hair, sobbing with relief.

And as she and Shannon walk across the beach, side by side, Hayley looks back over her shoulder. The island is watching them go. Their footprints shimmer for a moment and then disappear.

AUTHOR'S NOTE

In the past 10 years, I have visited over 500 schools and universities, working with tens of thousands of young people in mixed sex and single sex, private and state, rural and inner-city settings. I have never visited a school where sexism, sexual harassment and sexual assault aren't problems. In the same period, I have received around 50,000 testimonies from young people describing their experiences of being harassed by adult men on their way to school, being groped and spanked by peers in school corridors and playgrounds, being abused both on and offline.

The young people I work with feel that sexual harassment and assault is so commonplace it has become a 'normal' part of childhood. They feel that coercive control and other forms of abuse are hallmarks of any relationship. They feel abandoned by adults who tell them that 'boys will be boys', or send them home for 'distracting' their male peers with short skirts. They feel forgotten and failed by a legal system where rates of charging and summons are so low (1.5%) that rape has effectively been decriminalised. And they are furious at a world where men accused of sexual harassment and violence go on to receive sporting awards and cultural accolades, to be elected to government office and seats of 'justice'.

This is a generation of girls who are courageous, powerful, resilient and bold. They are finding their own ways of fighting back, speaking out and refusing to be silenced. They are keen to redefine our societal understanding of consent and our idea of what relationships look like. And above all, in the face of a world where they feel that justice isn't available to them, they are absolutely determined to create change. This book is my way of standing with them.

Laura Bates
July 2021

ACKNOWLEDGEMENTS

I am hugely grateful to the whole wonderful publishing team at Simon & Schuster. Special thanks to Lucy Pearse, my brilliant editor, for her enthusiasm, support and eagle-eyed attention to coconut-related specifics. Thank you to the fabulous design team for their evocative cover, and to Eve Wersocki-Morris and the marketing and publicity teams for being the real-life kick-ass cheerleading team making sure this book reached its readers! And to Lizzie Clifford for her fantastically forensic editing skills (including my first ever editing query about the direction of a stream of urine), and Anna Bowles for her meticulous proofreading.

A huge thank you to Steve Geck, Beth Oleniczak and the fantastic Sourcebooks dream team who bring my books to a US audience. And a special mention to Lucy Rogers, to Megan Staunton and everyone at Gleam Titles for helping to launch this book on its journey.

I'm so lucky to work with the incomparable Abi Bergstrom at Bergstrom Studios, the most hardworking, compassionate and supportive agent a writer could have, and Sarah Williams and Stevie Grace at Independent, who work so skilfully to help my ideas come to life beyond the pages of my books.

I am indebted to a number of experts who helped me with questions about the climate, flora and fauna of the Gulf of Mexico. They include David Williams and Duncan Allen, who furnished me with fascinating facts on everything from birdsong to pygmy raccoons. And the compulsively watchable Emmy Cho of Emmymade for her very detailed description of the flavour and texture of obscure tropical fruits. Special thanks to Harry Kiely for his encyclopaedic knowledge of all things related to aviation and plane crashes.

Thank you to Aileen, Emma, Lucy, Eily and Hayley for being such kind and enthusiastic early readers, and to Nick and my family for your incredible ongoing support.

Most of all, I am very grateful to every single young person I have worked with in the past decade at schools and universities across the UK, and the tens of thousands who have shared their stories with me via my Everyday Sexism Project. Your voices and stories matter enormously, and I feel very privileged that you have entrusted me with them. Your courage, your hope and your spirit of resistance inspires me every day. I promise you that you are not alone, no matter how much it might sometimes feel that way. And I promise you that we will keep fighting, together, to make things better.

HELPLINE ADVICE

If you have been affected by any of the issues in this book, you are not alone. A 2021 Ofsted report found that 80% of girls had experienced some form of sexual harassment at school and 79% had been sexually assaulted. A YouGov survey found that 71% of young people hear girls being called 'slut' or 'slag' at school more than once a week. On average, one rape per school day is reported to UK police from a UK school. And young women aged 16-24 are the single largest category of victims of domestic abuse.

I want you to know that change is coming. Every week I meet young people across the country who are taking action, determined to make things better. From launching a campaign, to starting their own feminist societies, a generation of girls is taking matters into their own hands and fighting back.

And for the days when you might not feel able to fight back (we all have days like those), help is out there. The following organisations provide information, confidential support and a listening ear when you might need it the most. Don't be afraid to reach out for help. You are not alone, you are not to blame, and you deserve to feel better.

Rape Crisis (rapecrisis.org.uk) 0808 802 9999
Free, confidential support for women and girls who have experienced sexual assault, recent or historic

Refuge (refuge.org.uk) 0808 2000 247
National domestic abuse helpline

Women's Aid (womensaid.org.uk)
For women and girls experiencing any form of relationship abuse. Live chat and email support available

Survivors UK (survivorsuk.org) 0203 598 3898
Support for men and boys who have experienced rape or sexual abuse

BullyingUK (bullying.co.uk) 0808 800 2222
Help for issues including sexting, online bullying and more

Revenge Porn Helpline (revengepornhelpline.org.uk) 0345 6000 459
Support for anyone who has had intimate images posted online without their consent

The Mix (themix.org.uk) 0808 808 4994
Free confidential support for young people on abuse, bullying, sex, relationships and pregnancy

Disrespect NoBody (disrespectnobody.co.uk)
Information and support on relationship abuse for young people

Papyrus Prevention of Young Suicide (papyrus-uk.org)
0800 068 4141
Help for young people experiencing depression or suicidal thoughts

Galop (http://www.galop.org.uk) 020 7704 2040
Advice and support for people who have experienced biphobia, homophobia, transphobia, sexual violence or domestic abuse.

ABOUT THE AUTHOR

Laura Bates is the Founder of the Everyday Sexism Project and writes regularly for the *New York Times*, *Guardian*, *Telegraph* and many others. She is a regular contributor to the *Today Programme*, *Woman's Hour*, *Channel 4 News*, *Newsnight* and more, as well as working closely with politicians, businesses, schools, police forces and organisations from the Council of Europe to the United Nations. She has been awarded a British Empire Medal in the Queen's Honours List for services to gender equality.

Her critically-acclaimed and award-winning non-fiction for adults includes *Everyday Sexism*, *Misogynation*, *Girl, Up* and *Men Who Hate Women*. Her first YA novel for teens, *The Burning*, was declared 'essential reading' by the *Guardian* and her second, *The Trial* is out now.

A RUMOUR IS LIKE A FIRE . . .

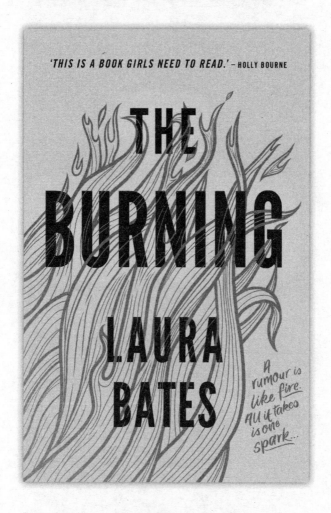

'THIS IS A BOOK GIRLS NEED TO READ.' – HOLLY BOURNE

THE BURNING

LAURA BATES

A rumour is like fire. All it takes is one spark...

'A book teen girls NEED to read' Holly Bourne
'Essential reading' *Observer*
'Brilliant' *Stylist*